I0564448

AN ENIGMATIC
WITCH

WITCH KIN CHRONICLES, BOOK 5

E M GRAHAM

An Enigmatic Witch

Copyright © 2022 by E M Graham

All rights reserved. No part of this book may be used
or reproduced in any manner whatsoever without written permission except in the
case of brief quotations embodied in critical articles or reviews.

This book is a work of fiction. Names, characters,
businesses, organizations, places, events and incidents either are the product
of the author's imagination or are used fictitiously. Any resemblance to actual
persons, living or dead, events, or locales is entirely coincidental.

Ebook ISBN: 978-1-990667-00-8

Print   ISBN: 978-1-990667-06-0

Mom, this one's for you.

CHAPTER 1

After Tomnahurich and my non-sanctioned journey to the Ice Kingdom, my Kin-issued credit card was revoked. Technical difficulties, they said, and I believed them. But then the Kin sent me home for 'rest and relaxation' after that intense spring, and that's when I knew, in that place deep inside my gut, there was something more to this story.

Turns out I was right.

'You want to go back and reconnect with your mother, don't you?' Hugh asked, reasonably enough. He sat on the low stone wall next to me, looking off into the distance over the darkening horizon.

'Yeah, I do,' I admitted. Despite my words, my voice was slow with reluctance.

'And Alice?' His eyes slid down to me.

'Of course! And Aunt Edna, and Brin, but...' I stared across the valley of Edinburgh, my back to the setting sun, and I thought about leaving this city. The Old Town was wreathed in wisps of mist rising from deep alleys, caught golden by the angle of the light. This place was magical, and it was the place I had really come into my power, and for that I would always remember Edinburgh fondly.

But this wasn't the reason I was reluctant to return back to Canada. And it wasn't that I didn't want to see my loved ones. It was just...

'You're going to China!' This ripped out of my mouth before I could stop it, then I figured, why bother holding back? 'I thought we would be working as partners, but you're going off traveling to do all kinds of exciting stuff, while I am having a period of enforced relaxation. It's not fair.'

'After all you've been through,' Hugh began.

'I'm fine, I already told you,' I cut in as I jumped off the stone wall and turned to him. 'I've had plenty of time to recover from Tomnahurich and the whole Ice Kingdom thing, haven't I just spent the last two months in Nachtan's classroom? I don't want to sit still anymore! I want to be using my power, pushing myself, learning the... the practicalities of it all.'

Yes, I'd spent all those dreary hours with the Venerable Nachtan in his ivory tower as he drilled me with theory and he droned on about historical precedents and stuffed my head with all this useless information till it felt like bursting. 'I want to be doing!' I ended as I crossed my arms and stared at Hugh.

He calmly gazed back at me, the wind ruffling the waves of his hair, his green eyes level with mine, then he crossed his own arms to mirror me. His white t-shirt glowed against the tan already beginning on those muscled arms. I didn't allow myself to be distracted by his finely defined wrists and strong fingers – which were absolutely beautiful by the way. Before meeting Hugh, I'd never realized how sexy a man's hands could be. I wrenched my eyes back to his.

'You're pouting,' he remarked with the slightest hint of teasing in his voice.

'It's not funny.' I could feel a full-on scowl spreading over my face. 'Why can't I go to China with you?'

He sighed then held out his arms and pulled me inside his hug, his bare arms warm through the thin cotton of my blouse. 'You will,' he murmured into my hair. 'This is just the preliminary talks. It's dead boring, I promise you. There's no action happening there, just bla-bla-bla between the political sides. You won't be missing any action. Just go on home and relax.'

I leaned my head against his chest.

'You'll come over after the end of the summer,' he whispered. 'And China is much lovelier in the autumn, when the August heat is finished. We'll take a week for sightseeing, or two, as the place is huge and there's so much to see. We'll hike the Great Wall, tour the Emperor's Palace...'

He took a deep breath. 'And also, it's very important for you to go home and spend time with your loved ones whenever you get the chance,' he said, slowly. 'Y'know, in our line of work, we're away so much travelling everywhere, working under very stressful conditions. It is vitally important that we maintain strong links with our family and friends so that we have a place to go and destress. We need this for our mental health.'

'I suppose so,' I agreed. 'Still...'

Still, I felt I hadn't had a true education in using my power. I knew my potential far outstripped my knowledge base, and I wanted to know so much more. But it wasn't like I had any choice no matter hard I complained, for the Kin Elders had made this decision and nothing was going to change it. As an official employee of their Special Operations branch, I had to do what I was told, go where I was sent, and I was proud of my new position.

I lifted my head and looked off to the distance, to the soft raggedy clouds shining golden in the sunset, and I thought of the places I would go in my life, beginning with China. The land of mystery, of elegance, of soft draping greenery and silk, of mists and mountains, of dragons and their magic. As I looked upon the clouds, I saw them changing form, coming together, then elongating. Almost imperceptibly, a dragon's snout grew out of one end, and then the main body of the cloud morphed into a thrashing tail and four legs and even wings, the diaphanous mist solidifying before my very eyes. It lifted its head and blew steam out into the deep blue sky over the east.

I laughed with delight, I couldn't help it. I'd done that. Without even trying, I'd created the dragon from the watery clouds, and it flashed golden and red and solid in the light.

Hugh glanced over his shoulder to see what I was laughing at and I felt him start. My dragon turned its face towards us and let loose a bellow of ethereal fire.

'Are you doing that? Stop it, stop it right now!' He stared from me to the dragon.

I loosened my hold on the clouds and they dissipated, slowly yet thoroughly, as if the beast had never been. Within moments, the clouds floated back to their innocuous path along the sky, the reds becoming purple and peach, and the gold of the dragon's scales became the underside of the stratus clouds, now orange in this spectacular sunset.

'You can't do that!'

'But I did. You saw it.'

'Yes, I know you *did*, but you shouldn't. You can't simply spread your magic around like that.' He looked shocked, horrified even. 'Haven't you learned anything about professionalism yet?'

His sharp tone cut. 'Jesus. It was just a bit of fun,' I said as I turned away, and felt my cheeks burning. Yes, Nachtan had added that particular subject, about why we as witches used ours powers judiciously and not just for amusement but only to effect change in our favor. I kicked an empty chip bag out of my way with more force than it required.

'Why the hell are we given power if we can't use it?' I turned back and yelled at him. 'What's the point of it all?'

'The point is... Oh, for God's sake.' Now he shoved his hands in his jeans pockets and began walking away from me towards the exit of this private stone courtyard high above the city of Edinburgh.

Oh, no, he didn't get to do that. We'd already had that discussion. I ran after him and grabbed his shoulder, pulling him back to me.

'We agreed that arguments would be settled right in the moment. No turning your back or pulling that sort of bullshit. Look me in the face and tell me how you're feeling.'

I watched as a play of emotions ran over his face.

'Look, I'm sorry.' I took pity on him. 'Yes, it was a really stupid thing to do, and honestly? I wasn't even trying, it just happened.'

He glanced back at the innocuous clouds now drifting in the darkening sky.

'That's what I'm concerned about,' he said, finally. 'You have to keep it reined in, you can't just let loose whenever the fancy takes you. You need to be conscious of everything you do.'

We stared at each other a moment longer, then I nodded because he was right. It wasn't just that I shouldn't go putting off displays of magic and upsetting the Normals, but as Nachtan had drilled into my head, every single time magic was used, it had an effect, somewhere. It might just be that a single pebble on a beach rolled, or perhaps just a slight change in a gust of wind somewhere in the desert where no one could feel it, but there was always a counter-reaction, somewhere, somehow.

'Yeah,' I said. 'Got it.'

We walked downhill toward the exit of Edinburgh Castle, the one the tourists used, and pushed past the lingering crowds outside the walls. Those who had spotted my momentary cloud dragon were still talking about it, trying to express their amazement to their disbelieving fellow travellers.

I couldn't stay contrite for long. A secret smile formed on my lips.

'It was really good, though, wasn't it? Like, that dragon was pretty solid, not like an illusion at all.'

He said nothing in reply, just kept walking. I drew closer to him and nudged him with my shoulder. 'You have to admit, it was pretty fantastic.'

Hugh stopped and put his arm around me, and drew me tight again. My transgressions had been forgiven, and we were good again. I smiled up at him.

He nodded back at me and admitted the truth. 'It *was* good.'

'And real.'

He nodded. 'Yes,' he said, then paused as if searching for the words. 'But... how exactly did you do it?'

I shrugged as I thought back to the creation of the sky dragon. 'China was on my mind, about all the fabulous things there, and dragon magic. It just started forming. I didn't intend to create a dragon in the sky, but it's pretty cool that I can do it, don't you think?'

'Hmmm. Cool. I guess it is.'

We continued walking down the path nestled close together, but I could feel a tenseness in his body that hadn't been there before. I glanced up at him at the exact moment he looked down at me, and it was then I saw something new in his eyes.

There was apprehension there, and - was that the slightest tinge of jealousy? I laughed to myself. Finally, I'd found a chink in Hugh Sabiston's perfect armor.

Imagine that. I was turning out to be a more powerful witch than him. Ignoring the tourists on either side of us, I stopped him and reached my mouth up to his, and kissed him with even more passion than normal. Being powerful was a turn on like nothing I'd ever felt before, and I intended to make the most of it.

CHAPTER 2

Once the Kin's bureaucracy finally got around to making a decision, they acted fast. I was soon on a plane out of Edinburgh and headed back home, compliments of my new employer. I was not, I might point out, given the use of one of the fleet of private Kin jets. As a lowly and fresh subaltern in the ranks, I didn't even merit a First Class ticket on a commercial flight. I was stuck in the rows of Economy, squished in between a family from Toronto returning from their visit to relatives, and a very quiet student headed out to Vancouver.

It was uncomfortable but I sucked it up for the duration of the six hour flight. As Hugh had explained, I would have to earn any privilege that came my way within the structure of the Kin, and I had every intention of doing so. Right now I was known as Ensign Martin, but everyone knew I had de Teilhard blood, and one day my name was going to be right up there with the best of them. I was going to be famous amongst the Kin all over the world.

I sat back in my seat, closed my eyes, and dreamed about all the wondrous achievements in my future, only waking when the pilot announced our approach to St. John's.

The trees down below, the deciduous ones, were all wreathed in their brightest spring green garb, and the streets were sparkling in the early morning sunlight. It was the first time I'd ever seen my home city from the air, and I was entranced. I could see our house from up in the plane! And the boulders which marked the fairy den on the Southside Hills, and Alice's house tucked away by the overpass at Riverhead. Then there was Dad's mansion on the hill in the east end of the city, surrounded by the green of his estate, and finally we were coming in to land.

As I walked down the steps to the baggage claim area, my heart caught in my throat at the sight of the welcome party waiting for me. It was small, yes, but I'd never had a lot of friends or family. First of all I spied Brin, the refugee elf from Alt, he stood out from the crowd with his height and that silly top hat he still wore with his straw like hair stuck out in all directions under it. Other than that, he could pass as a fairly normal person.

His long gangly arm rested on Alice's shoulder. What a couple they made, both so tall and slim. I wondered if Alice had accepted the fact of her elf-blood yet, a gift passed down from old Nan Hoskins which had skipped generations of their clan.

And next to them stood Mom. Would I ever get enough of looking at her? She'd been ripped away from me for half my life, yet she looked exactly like she had ten years ago, and then those months ago when we'd snatched her from the Ice King's grasp. We looked alike, me and her, the same thick brown hair and blue eyes, we matched exactly in height, even, and the same dress size. I still wore her old jean jacket and long blue scarf. I hoped she wasn't expecting to get them back.

My eyes wandered to the person standing close by, a little apart from her as if reluctant to join this welcome party, and I stopped my descent. I couldn't force my legs to take the next stair, for my head was pounding and I had to blink a couple of times, to make sure I was seeing him.

It was Dad. Jonathan de Teilhard, waiting to greet me on my return just as if the past ten years hadn't happened, as if all of the hurts and the hard words between us had never been said. As if he cared about me.

What the hell was he doing there? He of all people had no right to make himself a part of my family group. I was tempted to just turn back up those stairs, keep on walking till I found the next plane out of there and not return until I'd gotten a promise from Mom that I would never have to see him again.

He must have noticed my hesitation, for I saw him whisper in Mom's ear then turn as if he was going to make himself scarce. She was having none of it, I could almost hear her scolding tone as she took a firm grasp on his arm and planted herself solidly, not letting him move from her side.

What did this mean?

I ignored him for now and jumped down the last few steps to land in the middle of my three loved ones. We babbled and cried and laughed for a full two minutes. Dad had disappeared by the time I lifted my head.

'Where's Edna?' I finally had to ask. It burst from me like an accusation, as if to suggest my father had now banished my aunt to some inhospitable land, for surely she should have been the part of this group, not Dad.

'She had a chance to go the south of France, a Writer-in-Residence year,' Mom said, still squishing me in her arms. 'Mark retired from the RCMP, and they're gone off together. She sends her love, and she knew you'd understand.'

And I did. There'd be plenty of time to travel and see her, perhaps before I started my new job.

We collected my luggage and went out into the brilliant sunny day, and there was his big dark blue SUV, parked blatantly right in the 'No Parking' zone, waiting for us.

'You sit up front, Dara,' Mom urged. 'It's been so long since you've been home. Go on, sit in the front so you can see everything as we pass.'

And be forced to make polite, uncomfortable conversation with Jon? Not a chance in hell. I slipped into the back between my favorite elves before anyone could stop me. 'S'okay Mom, I'm good here, right between my two besties.'

It was a weird ride home, to say the least, but maybe I was the only one who felt it. Mom and Alice kept the patter of conversation going in a bright, almost forced way, while Dad was in a pleasant mood and contributed when required. Brin chattered in his way, outwardly very comfortable with everyone, I even saw Dad crook a grin at him through the rear view mirror. Yet beneath his light tone, I could feel the tenseness in Brin's body, the way his long legs flinched back when they brushed mine as the SUV took the sharp turn onto Higgin's Line, as if afraid that our touch might reveal something hidden inside him. Mired in my crookedness at having Dad present for my homecoming, I didn't really think about it, just put it down to his elfish dislike of physical contact.

'Is that my old jean jacket?' Mom turned around in her seat and asked me at one point. She didn't seem annoyed that I had been into her closet. 'It looks good on you. And that brooch – I love it. Where'd you get it?'

The dragonfly brooch, the one that had appeared out of nowhere one day. I smiled as I fingered the delicate gold wings and the bumps of the jewels in their settings. It was probably worth a lot of money, but more important to me, it was a present from Margaret Forsythe.

'A gift from a friend,' I told her. I wore it almost every day, touching it like a talisman, a reminder of the one witch in the world who, like me, carried the effects of the Crystal Charm Stone.

Margaret was my hero. I wanted to be like her. She moved through the world carefree and powerful, unmindful of society's and the Kin's strictures, and she'd promised that she would teach me everything she knew. I fully intended to take her up on her offer, later, after I'd established myself with the Kin. I had so many plans for my life then, and believed there would be time for everything in my shiny bright future.

We dropped Alice and Brin off in front of a funny little crooked two and a half story townhouse on a tiny lane off Casey Street. The dwelling had seen better days, many years ago perhaps. It slumped a little to the left like a drunk meandering home, and what was left of its vinyl siding was faded and dirty. The original clapboard was visible in spots where the siding had fallen off, the dark green marine paint of fifty years ago curled and peeling, and the top story had a definite sag between the two dormer windows.

'This is Brin's house,' Alice said proudly as she got out of the SUV. 'He's renting it. It's a little tired on the exterior, but really cozy inside. You need to come see it, later.'

Last Christmas, the elf had been a refugee from Alt with an uncertain future here, but now he had somehow found the means and credit rating to rent a whole house for himself? I looked over to him where he stood outside Dad's vehicle, the obvious question in my eyes, but he avoided me.

'Thanks, Mr. de Teilhard,' he said cheerily enough. 'See you soon, Dara.'

Yet he still didn't look at me, just glanced over in my direction, not quite meeting my eyes.

What was happening here? Before I'd left town, Brin had been a happy-go-lucky elf, ecstatic to be freed of the terrors of Alt, an open soul without the means to be devious. This inability to be false and calculating had been the reason the other elves had shunned him, and why he looked to escape. Everything was going well for him. Dad had even paved the way for his new citizenship and gotten him employment, perhaps he did all that as a favor to me. But right now my friend was hiding something, and he wasn't schooled in the ways of deceit. Not like me.

I would hound him this evening, make him tell me whatever was going on in his life. It couldn't be that serious, not with Brin, for he was the gentlest, most unharmful creature I'd ever known.

When we arrived back to Richmond Cottage, Mom's family mansion on the hill, I could hardly believe my eyes at the changes which had occurred to the outside. Someone was spending a whack of cash to restore the old girl up to her former glory with fresh paint, and all the rotten clapboards and window frames had been replaced. The shrubberies were trimmed and the lawns mowed. The driveway had a layer of fresh asphalt, gleaming blackly in the morning sun.

'Do you love it?' Mom asked as she hugged me from behind.

I took her hands and nodded. 'Yeah, it's fantastic,' I said as I turned to her. 'You've done all this since you got back?'

She stepped aside a little to include Dad. I hadn't realized he'd gotten out of the vehicle too. I shot daggers at him with my eyes, trying to get him to take the hint that he could go now, get back into his luxury vehicle and drive away back to his wife Cate and his estate and his rotten kids, my half-siblings.

'This is Jon's project,' she said, beaming up at him. She took his hand, making us a circle with only the one broken link between me and my father. 'He's living with us now.'

CHAPTER 3

W e stared at each other in the warmth of the morning sun, me and Dad, across the divide of the years. Oh no, this was not happening. In my mind, he'd been half responsible for having her exiled to the Ice Kingdom in the first place. If not directly, then at least the evil Cate had certainly a hand in it and thus he was also guilty by default.

This was supposed to be my home coming, my precious time of rest and relaxation to spend with Mom. I could not, would not have him around. But before I could even summon up the words to express my anger, he spoke out.

'I told you Marian, it's too soon.' His tone was gentle. 'You two need to reconnect, and it's better if I'm not around.' He turned to go.

'Wait just a moment, Mister,' Mom said, her hands on her hips and feet firmly planted on the ground. She glared at both of us in turn. 'You're not going anywhere, Jon. And Dara, this is your father, in case you don't remember. We are a family unit, and now that he's finally summoned the guts up to leave that wife of his, he lives here, with me and you. It's my house, and my rules.'

He left Cate? What was this? The arranged Kin marriages never, never publicly broke down. To do so would be to admit weakness to the outside world, that they were capable of making mistakes, and that wasn't the Kin way at all.

Before I could demand details, he walked over to Mom and laid his hands softly on her shoulders, caressing the cotton of her short sleeved sweater. They made a beautiful couple, no, a handsome couple, and it cut my heart to see how they fit together. 'I'm going into the office for a few hours, you two need some time to yourselves.' He turned to his SUV, then looked at me. 'I'll be back,' he said pointedly.

'What's going on, Mom?' I demanded of her before his vehicle had even left the driveway. 'Why? How could you? Do you even know...'

'What do *you* know of anything?' She cut me off. We stared off, equally matched in height and looks, the only difference between us were the years and our life experiences.

'He was responsible for you being taken to the Ice Kingdom, I know that,' I finally spit at her.

I had her there. She gaped at me like I'd slapped her in the face. 'What utter nonsense.' She took a deep breath and closed her eyes. 'Sweetheart, you know nothing about that... that whole thing.'

'So why don't you tell me?' I was not going to let this go. 'I have a right to know what happened, who did it, and why. Mom, I'm working for the Kin now. I can get back at them, get revenge for you.'

And whupping Cate's ass would be a great and very satisfying start.

'I'm powerful now, Mom,' I said, as if she hadn't heard the news. 'I'm going places. I can...'

She held her hand up. 'Yes, Missy, I've heard all about what you got up to in Scarp and Edinburgh,' she said, then her face melted and she slowly shook her head.

'You are *so* your father's daughter. My little idealist, my dreamer.' She took me in her arms and almost smothered me with the strength of her hug.

'I can't tell you the whole ins and outs of what happened,' she murmured into my hair. 'I simply can't, not yet. Come with me, let's just have a day for us, in peace, no quarreling. Trust me that you will hear the story. Sometime soon.'

I had to let it go, for now anyway. But there was still the matter of Jon to be discussed, and no way was I going to let that drop.

I waited till she had the tea steeping in the pot and everything set out for a late breakfast. Croissants and my favorite bagel sandwiches, and we were drinking from the fancy china teacups that used to belong to my great-grandmother – it was as if Martha Stewart had taken over the house. I'd forgotten how Mom loved the fancy little touches, and I smiled despite myself. In the ten years that it had just been me and Edna here, we'd been a lot less formal. Tea had been made in the mug with the bag left in, the bread sat in its plastic bag on the cutting board next to the peanut butter, and every flat surface had been taken over by clutter.

Today, the kitchen shone in the early morning light, the fridge handle gleamed and even the old farm sink was spotless with no sign of the two-year old blue dye stains I'd grown used to.

'Freshly squeezed orange juice?' She brandished the glass jug as the smell of sunshine and childhood permeated the room.

'That would be nice. Really nice.' I hadn't realized just how starving I was. I ate in silence for the first few minutes, the only sounds were the birds chirruping around the feeder outside the open window. She looked at me the whole while, a smile on her face as if she was bursting with pride at the woman I'd become. It was a good feeling to sit in that gaze.

'So,' I said after I'd swallowed the last of the orange juice in my glass and let her top up my tea from the pot. 'Jon. What gives?'

'We'd always dreamed of this,' she said after a pause. 'Then, things... happened.' She brushed her hair from her face.

'But leaving his marriage? I thought Witch Kin marriages were forever.'

She nodded and sighed, and folded her hands together on the tabletop. 'Yes. I know, right? Unthinkable for the Kin. But times have changed, and now Cate's kids are just about grown, and I'd returned, so we thought – why live our lives according to someone else's rules? Why not be happy?'

I kept my lips firmly shut as thoughts and feelings ran amok through me, and my face was blank of emotion, just like Hugh had taught me. But how about me? I longed to ask. What's my place in this new order?

She smiled, taking my silence for acceptance. 'We can be a family again, a real family, like we always should have been.' She spread her arms all around. 'And the house, Jon is doing it all up for us, bit by bit. It's going to be restored to the grandeur it should have.'

And why couldn't he have done this over the past ten years, for me? I swallowed the words, not allowing them to escape my lips.

'Dad...' I began. How to start? I hated to burst her Happy-Families bubble, but it just wasn't going to happen. 'Dad and I don't get along real well.'

How could I begin to tell her the hurts I'd suffered at his words and treatment of me over the years?

She nodded. 'He told me all about the difficult times during your adolescence,' she said. 'But...'

'My adolescence?' I cut her off. 'It wasn't me. It was him and Sasha and Cate and they were all so horrible to me!' I slammed my hands down on the table, causing the fine china cups to rattle in their saucers. 'Do you know the hell I went through for the past ten years? The poverty we suffered?'

At this, her mouth drew into a thin line, and she sat back in her chair. 'Jon supported this household the whole time, despite Cate's insistence that he cut you off. He loves you Dara Martin, you may not realize this, but he loves you like you are a part of his very soul.'

'You don't know anything about it!' I was shouting now, I couldn't hold back any longer. 'How could you? You're just listening to him and his side of the story, he's got you so blinded that you can't see anything. And how can you let him move in here? This is my house too, not his. He doesn't belong here!'

She got up from the table and stiffly gathered the china to hand wash in the sink, her actions speaking the words she didn't have to say.

I sat with my head in my hands, feeling like absolute shit with the sinking feeling I'd just ruined my home-coming, the special time for me and Mom, and I wished with all my heart I could unsay those words, stuff those emotions deep inside me. Some Kin worker I would make. Ensign Martin couldn't even get past the 'Stiff Upper Lip' rule that was requisite for a witch, the one that said strength was measured in unemotionality. I could almost cry, but I felt utterly spent.

Then her hands were on my shoulders, rubbing them softly. 'Come with me, sweetie,' she whispered. 'I want to show you the garden.'

She led me through the house, into the parlor with the high French windows. They were no longer nailed shut against the elements, and the shutters were wide open. The summer sun streamed through the spotless, polished glass of the doors.

'We're doing the courtyard garden up for you,' she said. 'It was always your favorite spot.' She stood back to watch my reaction.

Now the tears came streaming down my cheeks. The tall cedar hedge which shielded the space from wind and onlookers had been neatly trimmed, and the new growth was already glowing greenly. This must have been one of the first jobs she'd tackled on her return. About half of the courtyard was free from weeds, show-ing the beautiful paving as I remembered it, no yellow dandelions or grass, just the creeping lemon thyme be-tween the flat blue, red and green slates.

And the fish fountain – oh, my sweet fish fountain! The green verdigris had almost all been scrubbed off him, and he glowed bright copper in the sunlight, the water cascading like a shower of diamonds from his mouth. We stood in the open doorway, me in her arms. Despite all the care the rest of the house required to bring it back to glory – the dusting and polishing and plastering and painting, she'd begun in my garden. She'd done this for me, knowing I would return, even if just for a visit.

I turned and hugged Mom, relaxing, feeling the love flow between us, and I knew, for her, I had to swallow my pride and shut up about Jon. His presence made her happy, and he was going to be a fixture in our house. I had my own life now, I'd flown the nest and I was now the visitor in her home.

But that didn't mean I had to like it. Or him.

The one positive aspect of this whole situation was that Cate must be pissing mad by now, and that was consolation of a kind.

··········

We hung out for the rest of the day just the two of us, she was cooking and baking the whole time while I drank endless cups of tea and helped myself to whatever came out of the oven. I missed Edna in this hang-out, it used to be the three of us around the kitchen table. Mom went into a further explanation of how Mark had taken early retirement from the RCMP, and the writer-in-residence program had opened up in the south of France, and it had been such perfect timing for them they couldn't say no.

'So how is Mark filling his days in France, of all places? I suppose he can speak the lingo, the RCMP are all bilingual these days.' I paused and let the smell of brownies baking fill my nostrils. There was never a more homely and comforting aroma than the glorious combination of chocolate, brown sugar and vanilla, steaming fresh from the oven.

'He's discovered a love of cooking, so he's taking some kind of Cordon Bleu course.'

I smiled to think of big Mark in an apron and chef's hat. It would suit him.

The long afternoon morphed into the evening. The smell of macaroni and cheese now filled the kitchen, the extra layer of shredded cheddar on top getting all crispy and brown just as we loved it. The chat was idle now, the catch up of funny stories of what had gone on in my life, well, things I could laugh about now that the danger was past.

'Jane has three babies of her own,' Mom echoed with a smile. 'Little Jane who used to walk you to school.' She shook her head in wonder.

'She started having youngsters early,' I said. Mom could even make salad taste good, she added all sorts of things that weren't vegetables, like goat cheese and cranberries. I swallowed the last mouthful down. 'But she continued on at high school after she had the first.'

'And a changeling? You really think the fae got the baby and switched her out?'

I shrugged. 'It's hard to tell. The kid gave me the stink-eye whenever it saw me after that, so yeah, I think so. Babies usually like me.'

Dad didn't reappear that whole time, allowing me to pretend that he hadn't moved in, hadn't usurped my place in the household. I finally shoved myself away from the table and prepared to make my way to go down and catch up with Alice. We were going to meet by the river, walk a bit along the trail, or maybe in the other direction down to the lighthouse at Fort Amherst right at the mouth of the harbor. Didn't matter much where we went as long as we generally just hung out, like in the old days. And I really needed the exercise.

She was waiting for me on the footbridge with a big smile on her face at my approach. She didn't let me hug her this time, but that was just Alice.

'So what's been happening over the past months?' I asked as we turned to walk down Southside Road, heading east.

We talked back and forth. She told me about the Master's program she was accepted into come the fall, and I gave her an edited version of the happenings in my life. I say edited because although Alice had come a long way from when she had denied that the whole super natural and magic thing existed, she still had a hard time acknowledging that it was real.

Even though her boyfriend was an elf. Even though she had a strain of elf blood in her. And even though the ghost of her dead nan saved the day last year, showing us the path through her secret berry patch.

But I didn't push it.

'And how about Brin? He seems to be doing well, he seemed pretty happy this morning.' I didn't touch on the strange tenseness I'd felt emanating from him.

'Yeah, he's thriving,' she laughed, and flicked her long colorless hair from her face. Once I'd realized that she was part elf, it wasn't hard to see it – tall and slim, smart as a whip, and she had the general look of elfness in her hair and ears. 'I know you and your dad don't get along, but I have to say, Jon has done so much for Brin. He is such a nice guy!'

'Hmm,' I said. 'I guess, if you say so.' I kicked a pebble out of my path, then noticed that we were outside the entrance to the Dwarf Hall now. The heavy oak door was firmly closed and there no signs of life in the vicinity, for we weren't in Alt, but I picked up my pace and hurried Alice along too. Just in case. I'd annoyed the dwarves last fall, and that species liked to hold on to their grudges long past the sell-by date.

Once we were safely past the caves and almost at the breakwater, I resumed the conversation about Brin. 'So he's working at Dad's company, has his own house – what else is he doing with himself?'

She smiled again, fondly. 'You'd never guess in a million years. He's turning political.'

I laughed, because it was hard to picture my elf friend getting involved with the mainstream parties, either Liberal or Conservative. 'He must be a socialist, is he?' I surprised myself with a yawn, and only then realized what a long day it had been, getting up so early on the other side of the ocean and following the dawn home. What with that and eating all day, I was ready to sleep right where I was. I had to get home to my bed real soon.

She nodded. 'Sort of. He wants to work on getting rid of the Veil.'

I blinked and stared at her. 'That's pretty ambitious,' I said, then couldn't help as another yawn escaped. 'It'll keep him occupied for years. The Kin aren't going to let go of that.'

Not long after that we turned and made our way back up the road and I went on home up the hill, not giving this news another thought. I should have enquired into this more thoroughly, but I could never have suspected what Brin was really up to, not in a million years.

CHAPTER 4

M y old lumpy mattress enfolded me in a hug, remembering my body's every curve and how I
loved to sleep on my side, my face toward the window
so I would be woken by the first tendrils of light.

I didn't see the next day's dawn, though. I remained
oblivious in my sleep until the morning was almost gone
and over with. I stumbled downstairs to the kitchen
where Mom was placing the kettle on the burner.

'Just in time for tea,' she said. 'Come here and let
me squeeze the sleep right out of you.' We stood for a
moment in that tight embrace.

'Coffee,' I said when we finally let go of each other.

She opened her mouth to object.

'I'm an adult now. And you can blame Edna.'

'A decade is a long time,' she said sadly and looked at
me some more before she busied herself with the coffee
percolator.

I was looking forward to another long lazy day with
her, catching up, and generally just being. I followed
her into the back yard, coffee in hand and we sat in the
refurbished Adirondack chairs, soaking up the sun.

I'd almost nodded off again when I felt her staring at me. 'What?' I asked lazily, opening one eye.

'We have to get this out of the way, and the sooner the better.' Her tone was brisk, and she meant business.

'Do we really have to? Can't we just have another day, twenty-four hours of you and me?'

She shook her head, then leaned over toward me. I sat up, reluctantly, and faced her full on. No more avoiding it, I could tell from the look in her eye that we were going to have the 'Jon' conversation. My formerly-absent father who was now too much in evidence in our lives. I groaned.

'Your Dad. He's living here now. Moved in. This is his home.' Her voice held a warning, and it brooked no dissent.

I played with my half-empty mug and nodded, all the anger of yesterday quiet now as doomed acceptance threatened to fill the void. A chill settled over me. I may not have liked it, but I'd gotten the message. I was grown, had moved on with my life, and Richmond Cottage was no longer the place I could call home. A visitor in my mother's house, and I was expected to accept the status quo without a murmur.

Like that would ever happen. My father was a shit, and she had to know that, or at least she had to hear my side of the story. I allowed my righteous anger to bloom.

'For ten years,' I began, my voice low as a growl. 'For the whole ten years you were gone, he ignored me. He didn't act as a father should to a child who had lost her mother with no explanation. One day you were here, and then poof! You were both gone from my life. He acted as though I was some kind of pariah.'

I looked up at her. Her shoulders were stiff and pain was written through the lines of her face. Good. She needed to know how it had hurt.

'He abandoned me.' My voice was louder now, more confident of my ground. 'But the minute you return from the dead, he moves back into this house and it's no longer my home. He's making it a little too obvious, don't you think, that he never did love me, only you. I was nothing but a nuisance, an unwelcome by-product!'

'No,' she said, tears sprang to her eyes as she shook her head from side to side. 'No, Dara, that's not the way it is.'

'Really? Sure looks like that from where I'm sitting.' All this pain had been boiling away for a decade, and now the mess was spewing over, unable to be contained.

'But Tomnahurich! He was there, doesn't that say anything at all to you?'

'Scotland! He only went there because he was embarrassed about me! He had to show up in order to let the Kin know he didn't approve of me and my actions.'

'No,' she said again. The tears were spilling down her cheeks. 'He was prepared to go after you, yes, through the Land of the Fae and on to the Ice Kingdom to save you! Even though...'

It hurt me to see her so upset, but the anger in me wouldn't let it go. 'Even though what?'

'It's complicated.'

I gave a snort of disgust. 'Complicated? That word is nothing but an excuse for bad behavior, and you know it!'

'But Cate...' She gave a deep sigh and looked at me through the wetness, then her head drooped like she didn't have the strength to hold it up. 'He has to explain it all himself. I can't do it for him.'

'It's too late for his explanations! I don't want to hear his false excuses, I don't want to hear anything about that bitch of a wife of his, and I bet you they're still married, aren't they? There's no way he would get a divorce and marry you, it wouldn't look good for his standing in the Kin, would it?'

Now I'd gone and done it. I'd pierced her through the heart with my accusations, true though they might be. I was hardly back twenty-four hours, and look at the mess I'd already created. And yet I didn't stop. Couldn't stop.

But she didn't back down, she didn't run away or even get angry. She just sat there, accepting all my pent-up hurt and pain from the years and let the tide run over her until at last I was spent and there was nothing left to say.

We ended up in each other's arms again, both of us crying and sobbing, clinging to the wreckage of the years as if our lives depended on it. When that flood too had passed, we drew apart a little but were still sitting close together. At last she looked at the gold watch on her wrist. It was new.

'I'm going to get supper ready,' she said, then she looked back at me. She wiped the wetness from her face. Her eyes were all swollen and damp still, with her mascara smudged and streaked, but her mouth was set in a firm line. She drew up her shoulders and sat straight and determined. 'We are going to sit down and eat as a family. Jon will be here. And you will be here. And we will all be civil.'

I opened my mouth, but she cut me off before I could utter a word.

'What's between you and your father, well, you both need to talk, and in depth,' she continued. 'There's so much you don't know, and so much he needs to tell you. But this will take time, and the healing of your relationship will not happen overnight, and it will not happen over my dinner table.'

With that, she got up, went back into the kitchen and began preparations. It was to be a stir-fry with lots of colorful veggies being chopped up, served with rice and crispy tofu, and it was without a doubt the healthiest meal that I'd seen cooked in that kitchen for a decade.

Yes, things had changed at Richmond Cottage. I'd gained my mother, but along with her had inevitably come my father too, and I had no choice but to try to make the adjustment.

·····•••····

It was a civil meal, as she had demanded, although the tension in the room was strained. When Dad first got back to the house, he hesitated in the doorway as if uncertain of his welcome, but by this time Mom had recovered her equilibrium and was acting like it were the most normal thing for the three of us to be sitting together in celebration of my return.

She was determined to make this work, despite the reluctance so evident in me and Dad. The conversation was almost wholly carried by her, while we remained, well, civil.

I excused myself shortly after the chocolate cake was served, saying I really wanted to catch up with Alice and Brin, and I could have sworn I saw Dad's face relax a notch at my words. That must have made two of us who hadn't been looking forward to a stretched-out continuation of this civility.

My bike was where it had been left, stored in the garage, but I noticed everything had been sorted and organized there now. It was no longer the higgledy-piggledy storehouse of undealt-with detritus from the past century. Dad had set up a workshop here, with fresh clapboard laying on top of saw horses in different stages of being painted, and one corner was taken over by various machinery and other 'guy' stuff. On one wall hung a large piece of pressboard with holes in it, where a lot of unfamiliar tools hung in an orderly fashion. I paused to take it all in. I'd never known that Dad had a handy streak in him, never suspected that even an ounce of creativity lurked under that uptight suit and tie.

The bike was hanging from a new pulley system designed to keep it safe and out of harm's way, and the brakes had been recently oiled, the old squeak not in evidence as I made my way across the streets to Brin's new home.

I hadn't texted either him or Alice to warn of my imminent visit, for where else would the elf be but at home? And Alice, even if they weren't living together, she'd always been a homebody. If she could find an excuse not to go out, she would, and I was pretty sure she wouldn't have changed. Besides, she'd mentioned that she was beginning to consider Brin's home her own. I took the precaution of locking my bike to the stoop, because theirs was a sketchy neighborhood, a bit of real estate that appealed to drug dealers and their customers, prostitutes and other folks living on the margins of society.

As I stood and cast my eyes over the adjacent houses, I wondered that this little piece of downtown St. John's had not yet been gentrified. Most of these houses had a view of the harbor and the Narrows and the ocean beyond, much prized by the new generation desperate for a foothold on the property ladder. Yet this crooked little street still had an air of dilapidation, with weeds growing through the cracks of the house foundations, faded and dirty vinyl siding on every home, and full garbage bags littering the sidewalks. In front of the house across the street sat a beat-up old sofa missing its legs and one cushion.

Perhaps it was the poverty evident in the present day aspect of this street which did it, the desolation and the hopelessness seen in the broken and cracked plastic miniblinds in the windows of the houses, but whatever kicked it off, I felt my vision wavering and the outlines blurring. It was a familiar feeling but one I hadn't felt in a long while.

Yet I wasn't trying it this time. I was being pulled into Alt against my will, sucked past the separating curtain and although I fought this transition, there wasn't a thing I could do about it. I blinked, and there I was in Alt again, and this formerly empty street was alive.

CHAPTER 5

I was in full-on Alt, and what a shock to the senses it was to return behind this grim curtain after so many months away. The Alternate St. John's, the one behind the Veil put in place by the Kin all those years ago to keep the super naturals contained and imprisoned in this timeless place of poverty, terror and other hells. It was like stepping back into a sepia toned photograph of the late Victorian or Edwardian age, into a land neglected by time.

The houses surrounding me were the same houses as in real time where I'd just come from, and they were still ancient and leaning too close to each other as if fighting for space and air to breathe. No vinyl siding here. The wood cladding these buildings was painted in dark colors. Oxblood, gray, ochre. Some weren't painted at all, just silvered wood, rotted and damp stained. All overlain with years of smut from the coal fires pumping out of every chimney.

Through a vacant lot that still held the remnants of a burned out house I could look down to the harbor from here, way down the hill to the forest of masts afloat in the water, and the finger piers stretching out from the backs of the merchants buildings. Tiny figures labored back and forth, bringing in the trade goods and lading up the boats with products intended for overseas.

Alt was alive and thriving, in its fashion. All the super natural creatures went about their daily business, for everyone had to eat and scrabble a living as best they could. There were humans here too, I knew, poor tired beings dwelling below the poverty line in their hopeless lives trapped behind the Veil with no way out. Jon had told me it had been their choice to remain behind, or at least the ancestors of the present human population had made the choice. They hadn't wanted to live in a world divorced from magic, they had said it was an unnatural state of affairs and had thrown their lot in with the super naturals.

Only the Witch Kin had the ability to move through the Veil they had erected.

As I stared all around me at the poverty and filth, I was seeing the results of that separation with new eyes. An anger began deep within me, for I knew it didn't have to be this way. My recent time in Edinburgh and Scarp had shown me another way of being, one in which there was no artificial Veil separating the two populations of magical and Normal. And as I stood there in the Alt of this tiny lane looking down on the hustle and bustle of daily business, I realized I had many unanswered questions because I'd never thought to ask them before, questions that emerged through my exposure to the larger world outside this insular port town.

For example, if the Veil was unique to St. John's and my home province, then with whom were these sailing ships plying their trade? Where were they going, all laden with salt fish and lumber? And the incoming rum, the silks, the fruits and wines – where were all these coming from?

The answer must be, of course, that the Veil was not solely placed over my island. That it was endemic in other parts of the world, possibly the whole of the New World, the Americas, with their underlying puritanical structure of philosophy. The Caribbean? Probably, that's where the rum and molasses were created. Africa? Undoubtedly, given the history of European conquest there, conquest led by the Kin. The whole of Asia? I gasped at the extent of this possible world-wide web of intrigue, of the domination of the witches over the world. Could it be?

And what did this mean for my future work within the Kin? I shook my head, couldn't think about it right then. I needed to find out why I had been thrust behind the Veil in this particular spot. Brin had escaped Alt last Christmas, tagging along with me as I switched back to my own reality. My elf friend had been an outcast from Elven society, he'd run away from their strict and cold ways, and also, he didn't fit into the roughness of Alt. He'd been desperate when he jumped ship, grabbing me at the last moment so I had no choice but to carry him back with me across the Veil. So desperate that he was willing to brave the totally unknown instead of returning to the familiar which he hated.

I turned toward his house. I'd said before that this home had seen better days, but these weren't them. It still slumped between its neighbors, a sad ramshackle building hastily erected on the crumbling stone foundation left after the last great fire which had ravaged the town. The original paint was half peeled off and the window frames sagged.

But it was glowing from within, as if a pulse beat deep inside the structure with a magnetic pull, and it was this that had caused my shift. My nose detected magic emanating from whatever was inside the house, but not any kind I'd ever come across before. Or had I? It smelled like the mist on the highlands, the almost salty, almost sweet air of untouched nature. It was foreign, from another species, certainly not Kin related, or sorcery or wizardry. My blood ran chill in my veins, my body instinctively kick-started into fight or flight mode at this unknown threat, and I had to force myself to take deep breaths to calm my nervous system. I needed my wits about me, for something was very wrong here.

That power emanating from Brin's home had pulled me into the Alt, and I'd lay good odds that Brin also was stuck in that dimension right now. Last year when he'd leapt between the worlds and refused to return, he'd sworn this move was irrevocable, that nothing would ever make him return to that dimension, that he wanted nothing to do with super naturals and other elves ever again.

Elf magic. Could it be? Yes, that was the smell. I caught my breath. With a sinking heart I suddenly knew why I had been pulled into Alt so abruptly. My friend's home was infested with elves.

His Kith in Alt must have found him. Were they even right now forcing him back to the confines of their world, intent on punishing him for having the temerity to be different? I knew little of these creatures or their culture, for they were a closed society and preferred no contact with the outside world if they could help it, either in Alt or Normal time.

But I had to go in and rescue him, this wasn't optional, even though I was unarmed. When I'd left Mom's home to bike across the roads for a visit to my friend on this spring evening in sleepy St. John's there'd been no suspicion that I would have any need of weaponry. But I had magic power, and lots of it, even if my strongest point was the theory behind it all and not its practical usage. Yet my adversaries weren't to know that. I pulled together my own protective cloak of magic, a shield of sorts and prepared myself for battle.

I screamed my best warrior cry as I stormed the rickety steps leading to Brin's front door. I had no trouble breaking through the old latch and so I burst directly into the front room of the narrow house.

The only sound to greet me was the rasping of steel swords unsheathed from scabbards.

With my arms high above my head, prepared to launch ice balls at those who threatened Brin, I froze as I took in the scene before me.

Five perfect silver sword tips pointed directly at me. Each was etched with strange and wondrous scrollings, each gleamed with an unnatural brightness far greater than the reflection taken from the single oil lamp burning in the room. And holding these swords were the most beautiful beings I'd ever seen in my life. Their skin tones were perfect and unblemished, glowing pearly bright in the reflection of their swords. Everything about them shone unnaturally, even their defined yet loosely fitting clothing of a style I'd never seen before, their fine uncolored hair, each with his own intricately braided fashion. They towered over me, these five, slim and tall and... perfectly elven.

Their drawn swords meant business, and their cold, ruthless faces looked prepared to dispatch of me as soon as they were given the word.

This is precisely why I'd always avoided elves when possible, the rare times I sighted them in my former forays into Alt. They were totally without heart, at least in the human definition of the emotional compass. Elves were so foreign in their genetic makeup – they looked like us, yes, but they were a breed apart, beautiful and untouchable, emotionless, haughty.

Brin could never have fit in with his brethren, for he'd been born with a defective elven heart.

I tore my eyes away from their cold perfection to find my friend. He sat at a small table before the fireplace, the grate cold and empty now it was almost summer. The curtains were drawn against outside eyes, with only the lamp to cast a soft glow in the room. He'd been writing on thick paper, parchment perhaps, a feather quill caught midair, arrested by the noise of my rude entrance.

Then I saw his companion at the table, and all breath left my body. I'd thought the five warrior elves beautiful, but they were mere shadows of the personage who sat across from Brin. He was a magnificent being, tall and slim, an asexual creature dressed in a silvery irides-cent material with hints of royal purple deep within the weave. Surely he was male, if it mattered, and his visage was terrible and cold and haughty, his skin tinged a pale lavender. My hands faltered.

That skin color. Only one kind of creature ever had that natural skin tone, and many people didn't believe his ilk really existed. This was one of the Dark Elves, rumored to dwell in the depths of the Avalon Wilderness and in the northernmost reaches of lands where few dared to go. I'd heard of this breed of elf, but never yet seen one in the flesh.

What had I stumbled into? Had they come for Brin to punish his transgression of leaving Elfdom? I had to save Brin from their clutches. I lifted my hands further up as if to make myself look bigger and more threatening.

But my friend spoke first, his voice a little put out.

'Dara, you really should have called first.'

CHAPTER 6

B rin laid down his quill, looked apologetically at the magnificent creature sitting across from him, and he sighed, a deep one coming from the heart of his narrow chest. His appearance was a marked contrast to the others with his fine hair stuck off any which way, and his shabby clothes were ill-fitted and made for human proportions. His face was lively with little filter for his emotions, those un-elflike flaws in his genes.

'What...?' I could see he wasn't afraid of his companions, therefore the danger I'd feared was nonexistent, so I tried to relax my body's response. I forced my hands back to my sides. 'What's going on here?'

Everyone in the room, me included, looked at the Dark Elf sitting in this humble room. He in turn raised a finely etched eyebrow at Brin.

'Oh, this is a little awkward, isn't it?' My elf friend pursed his lips together. 'What now?' This to the king, for he was undoubtedly royal.

'She's a Witch.' His voice was like the smoothest iced silk as he damned me.

'But she's not one of *them*...' Brin hurried to interject. After the slightest beat, he added, 'Or she didn't use to be, anyway. Eldric, I must introduce you to Dara.'

'Dara de Teilhard, I presume.' Eldric rolled the syllables around his mouth as if testing them out, then he stared at me, his piercing deep lavender eyes pinning me, silver glints in the irises like knives. I couldn't look away. 'What now? What do you know, Dara de Teilhard? Where do your sympathies lie?'

The elf on my left shifted his stance, ever so slightly, as his sword arm tensed on a hair trigger ready to attack given the slightest nod from Eldric.

'I don't know what you're talking about,' I said. A bead of sweat formed under my hair at the nape of my neck and began its slow trickle down my spine, but I couldn't allow myself to show fear. Reminding myself that I'd been kissed by the Crystal Charm Stone and that I was one of the most powerful witches of my generation, I did my best to put a sneer on my face, one that could out-haughty Cate. 'I don't mess with Elven business or Alt. It's not my concern.'

His eyes remained on me, losing the tiniest amount of threat as he felt me out and took in all the unspoken hints of my body language. 'I believe you may even mean that,' he said slowly. 'Never the less, you are of the Kin ilk, and now you are aware of my presence here in this elf's hovel. What will you do with this knowledge?'

What I most wanted to do was bike quickly back to Richmond Cottage and bury myself under my bedclothes and pretend this meeting had never happened. It would be easy enough to disbelieve the fact of it, for this was the Dark Elf King himself, no longer cloistered in his fabled wilderness mountaintop but sitting in the rude surroundings of Brin's home in the city. Only something huge would have drawn him here, something far larger than could be in my comprehension, and if it was that bad, I simply didn't want to know about it. Whatever the reason he was here, I really didn't want to get involved. The King of the Dark Elves? No way.

I shook my head. 'Like I said, not my business what you're doing here.' My gaze flitted to Brin as I silently beseeched him to help me out. Did he realize the seriousness of this event? I'd stumbled into something the Dark Elf king didn't want me to see, and elves being elves, well, it was possible I might not leave the house with my life intact. They were a very practical breed.

On the other hand, I was a de Teilhard by blood, and thereby untouchable by the Convention. If I disappeared, there would be outright war, Dad would be forced to act against them if only to show them they couldn't disrespect the Kin. I held my breath, waiting to see which way the wind would turn.

Brin still looked a little cross at the interruption to the evening's proceedings and gave a little huff. 'I'll fix it,' he told his companion. 'You needn't worry.'

'See that you do,' Eldric replied, his voice low and silken and scary as hell. He stood up, glanced at his retinue and nodded. They all six disappeared, hardly stirring up the dust in the room as they did so.

The room echoed with emptiness after they'd left. I also felt the shift – they'd taken the magnetic force that had forced me to flip with them, and things gently slipped back into real time. The lantern on the table was now a goose neck lamp, the table itself was plastic and white, a reject from someone's outside patio.

'Holy shit,' I breathed when we were alone. I wanted to know how they did that, simply left the room and thrust us back into Normal time as they did it. This must be the act called 'winnowing', which I'd read of but never witnessed. It wasn't a talent of witches. But my curiosity would have to wait. 'What the hell have you gotten yourself into now, Brin?'

I took the chair Eldric had just vacated and placed my hands on the table. Despite my denial of interest not two minutes before this, I had to know what was going on. It concerned my friend after all, and the Dark Elf king would hardly have just dropped in for a friendly chat over tea.

Brin sat back in his chair and sighed. I glanced down at the paper before him. It was in Elven script, all graceful thin lines and strange curlicues, like the etchings on the swords. I couldn't read it. Never the less he removed it from the surface and placed it securely into a satchel at his feet before looking back at me.

'The Elves are... they're looking to begin negotiations to remove the Veil.'

'Oh,' I replied, and let that sink in. 'Okay. Alice mentioned you were getting political, and it's about time some action was taken on this.'

He looked relieved and he leaned over the table to me. 'It is! It is time to get rid of it!' His large gray eyes were afire. 'I'm so glad you agree.'

He stood up as if unable to contain his fervor. 'It's just not right, is it?' he began. 'All this time, the super naturals have been stuck in this... this time warp, unable to move freely. We must take action and change this. We all have rights and basic freedoms.'

Brin paused, then bent to my level, folding his long length almost in half. 'You've been to Britain, you understand don't you? There's no Veil there, right? That's what I've heard. And everything works fine?'

I nodded. 'Yeah, absolutely.' I pictured in my mind's eye the sight of Trevor the goblin, tip-tapping down the cobbled streets in his red heeled boots in the bright light of day, openly walking past the tourists who did not recognize him for what he was. 'Yet, it's different, I mean there's no Veil, but somehow Normals don't *see* the super naturals.'

'Exactly, it's perfectly fine,' Brin answered confidently as he sat down again. 'Normals will only see what is in their ken. Not having a Veil separating the two doesn't cause an imbalance, no great terror or upset.'

'That's right, there don't appear to be issues.'

'Then why not here?' He spread his gangly arms wide, his shirt sleeves halfway to his elbows. 'And all of North America? There is no harm, nothing for the Kin to be afraid of. We, the trolls, the vampires, the dwarves, even the fae – we can all live peacefully side by side with the Normals and the Kin. Europe has shown that.'

'Yes, you're right.' I felt a tinge of excitement growing inside me at the new world vision he was painting. 'Everyone can take on their own responsibility to live peacefully, and there's no need to have a forceful separation.'

He beamed at me. 'And that's what we're working to achieve. I knew you'd understand!' He swung me out of my seat and around the small room in a dance fired with joy. Brin was beautiful with this new glow in his eyes and his body alive with purpose.

I laughed as he spun me out. 'And you've reconnected with your roots, your elven kin! There's no need for you to not be a part of your family anymore. This is wonderful.'

With that he let go and I fell back with a thump into the sofa. He stood stock still, his arm still reached out to me, but the smile had left his face. 'Well, I wouldn't go that far with it,' he said, a frown now marring his countenance. 'Just because I'm working with Eldric, doesn't mean I've forgiven my own clan for their treatment of me.'

'They didn't reach out to you?'

He resolutely shook his head. After a pause, he continued. 'But I do have them to thank for this, you know.'

I waited as he gathered his thoughts.

'You see, they - my family and Kith - they're the reason I'm here in the first place. If they hadn't shunned me for being different from them, if they'd accepted me for what I am, I would never have left. I would never have leapt the Veil with you if I hadn't hungered for more, a better life.'

His eyes came alive again in a blaze. 'But Eldric understands,' he continued. 'And he's showing me how we can work together. It's *because* I managed to leap the Veil and thrive. *Because* of my connections. That's why he approached me.'

A spasm of unquiet rolled through my gut. I didn't know why or what caused it. 'How does Dad feel about this?'

Brin took a step back, the fervency snuffed out, and he became his old carefree self again in a flash. 'Well, we're just talking right now, me and Eldric,' he confided. 'But when it's time, I'm sure Jon will be on our side. I've had discussions with him already, you know. To sort of sound him out. He's actually a pretty liberal minded guy.'

This stung a little, I wasn't sure why. 'You speak with my Dad?'

He nodded. 'Oh, yes. He's a very interesting man, isn't he, and he's helped me so much.' Brin's face was guileless, and I tried to stuff the pang of jealousy down deep inside me. 'I think he might lean with us. Time will tell.'

Dad? Jonathan de Teilhard, Head of the Avalon Kin be on board with dropping the Veil? I was already shaking my head in doubt. The separation between Alt and Normal was put into place to benefit the Kin, to help them keep absolute power in both worlds and they would surely never agree to loosen that grip. There was something not quite right about all this, about Brin's logic and ideals and expectations.

'Does he know you're in talks with Eldric, that Eldric has actually come here to town?'

He shook his head. 'Oh no, nothing public yet,' he said. 'That's why I must ask you to keep this quiet. Eldric did seem rather annoyed that you walked in here and saw him. He's a very private kind of creature, you know.'

I stared at Brin to see if he was serious. The Dark Elf had been more than a tad miffed that I'd discovered him here, he'd been prepared to have me dispatched on the spot, even knowing I had de Teilhard blood in my veins. And that meant that he was here on serious business, business I knew I didn't want to get involved in no matter the spin Brin had put on it.

'You know how much elves like their privacy. But he's anxious to get the ball rolling. And...' Brin glanced around the room as if to check we were alone.

'And there's a movement all over the country, the continent,' he whispered. His eyes were luminous again and he could hardly contain himself. 'I shouldn't be telling you this, but I can't help myself. I have to share with someone, and you're my friend. We're at the start of something very big, I can feel it.'

CHAPTER 7

Yeah, whatever Brin was getting involved in was undoubtedly 'big'. Huge. The potential to shatter life as we knew it in St. John's and Alt. And I would not be around to witness it, no matter how much I loved Brin. I was just back for a vacation, to catch my breath before my great adventure as an employee of the Kin.

I managed to push myself off the sofa although I was pretty shaky by then. 'You have my solemn word,' I said. 'That I will not say a word about this. About seeing Eldric here or about your plans. And please, *please*, pass that on to him.'

'I know you're to be trusted Dara,' Brin said fondly.

I swallowed back the bile in my throat and nodded. 'I gotta go,' I mumbled, hoping I could get outside before I threw up the supper which had been so hard to eat with Dad's presence at our table.

I raced home on my bike, wanting nothing more than to hide out in my room, away from threatening elves and their nefarious plans and away from any Kin. There were politics involved in this situation, and I'd never had the necessary social skills to deal with that shit.

But before I could take the back stairs up to my hidey-hole, I was stopped by the presence of Dad sitting at the kitchen table, facing the back door. The room was lit only by the over-counter lights, turned on before the evening set in, so he'd been there a while. Waiting for me. There was no way I'd be able to avoid this. Unless perhaps I legitimately claimed illness by tossing my still unsettled chocolate cake up in front of him, and I was pretty close to that point.

'Dara,' he said genially, a ready smile pasted on his face.

'Dad, I gotta...'

'Sit down.' His friendly look was wavering at the edges, and he nodded firmly at the chair across from him. The head of the Avalon Witch Kin was accustomed to being obeyed.

I slumped onto the padded chair and hung my head, willing my stomach to settle, wishing he hadn't chosen this moment for a heart-to-heart father-daughter chat. Bring it on, the Dad version of Mom's talk this afternoon. *Make it quick*, I thought to myself. I would just agree with everything he said, not argue the finer points of blame and get out of there as soon as I could. I forced myself to meet his eyes.

The geniality had all worn off him by now, and seriousness had set in. His brown eyes stared at me, the usual gold glints not visible in the dim kitchen light which didn't quite reach the shadows. Yet even in this darkened room I could see new strands of silver in his hair, they hadn't been there before I left for Scotland. The furrows in his brow had deepened during my time away, and the brackets around his mouth were more noticeable. Was that a slump to his shoulders?

He saw me watching him with a critical eye, and straightened his back, set his mouth into a grim line and was once again the father I'd known for the past decade.

'What I have to say is not easy,' he began. 'This goes against every grain in my being.'

'It's okay,' I interrupted him. 'You don't have to say it, Mom already did. Let's see. It goes something like this.'

I licked my finger and drew a one in the air. 'First, this is your home now, so I have to get over my childish resentment of your treatment of me.'

'Two,' I said as I drew the number. 'Yes, it appears you abandoned me, but it's *complicated* so therefore we have to forget the past and be a happy family again.'

His brows rose in surprise. 'That's not what I was going to say at all,' he said. 'But I'd like to point out that technically, those two points are the same idea, the second being merely a reiteration of the first.'

I could feel my lower lip coming out in a pout. I hated how I always felt like a stupid kid around him. I firmly bit it back. 'And Cate? What's going on there?'

'Ah, well,' he hedged and made a temple of his fingers on the table.

'Kin marriages never break down, at least not publicly,' I continued. 'Of course, I can see why you would choose Mom over that bitch, but seriously? This is a huge move.'

He nodded once. 'Yes.'

'And?' I urged. 'You're not worried about the break-down of ... of power? Of your position as the head of the Avalon Kin?'

'This is a mutual separation between my wife and me, not political at all.' He brushed his hand aside as if waving away all the concerns I'd brought forward. 'But as I said, this is not what I need to speak with you about.'

'So, what?' My stomach had settled somewhat, I could no longer taste the bile in my mouth, but I was exhausted, depleted of energy, and I just wanted to go to bed, to have that space to think over everything that had happened that day. 'Just say it, whatever it is.'

He took a deep breath then began. 'The Kin didn't actually send you home for rest and relaxation.' He watched me closely to see my reaction.

'What?' I couldn't wrap my head around what he was saying. 'But they told me... the Venerable Nachtan himself explained that I needed to reconnect and ground myself after all the theory he'd stuffed into my head, that this time should be spent...'

'Feeling the mantle of your knowledge and seeing how it fit on you?' There was almost a sneer on his face. 'Yes, that was a logical cover.' He shook his head. 'No. The Kin are not that generous an employer, you'll find.'

'Then why? Why have I been sent home?' A thought struck me, one I didn't want to face, but I had no choice, not if I wanted to uncover what was really happening here. It was my life, I needed to be in control, so I had to know the truth. 'They're dropping me, aren't they? They don't want me anymore, and they just haven't got the guts to tell me to my face.'

'No!' He shook his head with incredulity. 'How can you even think that? You are aware of your own power, you know the Kin would never let you go. You're far too useful to them.'

'Oh.' Yes, I guess I knew that I was so powerful, I just didn't really believe it, not right in the depths of my heart. 'That's good, isn't it?'

He smiled and sat back in his chair. My father had the most brilliant smile when he wanted, his gleaming white teeth, the evenness of his features, the piercing directness of his eyes when they beheld you. He was relaxed here, in our kitchen, the top two buttons of his white shirt undone, his necktie long discarded. I could see why the harpies of the Kin were always surrounding him, flirting with him, trying to get attention from him. He was an attractive man.

'You don't change, do you Dara?' He smiled again, and put out his hand to stop me when I opened my mouth in response. 'Don't start, that wasn't a put-down!'

And then I nearly fell off my chair when he actually took my hand across the table. I tried not to flinch. It wasn't that it was bad, he didn't hurt me or anything, the touch was just so unexpected. Physical contact between me and Dad? It had been a long time. Many, many years.

I forced myself to relax and he simply held my hand enfolded in his much larger one and he looked into my eyes. 'You,' he said, his voice serious. 'Are a gem. I want you to know this. Whatever happened out there in Scotland, and I know the story, but whatever, the Kin is counting on you and your talents in the future. And so you, Dara Martin, you have the upper hand in all your negotiations. Remember this.'

He let go of my hand and I was free to withdraw it. His words... they should have been intended as encouragement, to bolster the confidence of a fledgling witch, so why did I feel a warning lurk behind them?

'As I was saying. The purpose of your visit home is not just for rest and reconnection. The Kin have a very specific task they want you to carry out, because you are uniquely positioned to do so.'

I straightened up in my chair. This was more like it. A thrill of excitement crept up my spine, making me forget all about my turbulent guts. 'Really? A job that only I can do?' I could feel the smile spreading over my cheeks unbidden and perhaps I preened a little. This was it. The real thing.

Dara Martin was special, and the Kin were acknowledging it.

But he soon put a damper on that rush of exhilaration.

'Like I said, I really don't agree with what they are demanding of you,' he continued, his brow lined again. 'You see, there have been rumors of disquiet amongst the elves. With your connections, they need you to delve deeper into that, find out what is really going on.'

Oh, shit. Not that. I'd just promised the terrible Dark Elf king, Eldric himself, that our meeting was already forgotten, it didn't happen, I never saw him. The chocolate cake was making its way back up again, I could taste it on the back of my tongue, the sugar mixed with the sour acids of my stomach.

'Like, be a spy, you mean?' My voice was choked. 'Use my friendship with Brin to *spy* on him?'

He nodded reluctantly, and saw the pain written on my face, and his own face hardened.

'But that would be a betrayal,' I whispered through the bile. 'Brin's my friend.'

'Which is what particularly appeals to some members of the Elders.' His mouth twisted. 'You're being tested, to see if you have the moral fortitude to devote to your work.'

'They can't ask that of me.' My mind was whirling even more than my stomach.

'They're not asking. It's an order.' His fingers drummed on the table, and he added in a gentler voice, 'Besides, it's only a betrayal if he's doing something he shouldn't be.'

'But...' I was grasping at anything now. 'But how about if all they want is to remove the Veil? Perhaps the other elves have seen how Brin is thriving over here, and all they want is to remove the goddamn Veil, get rid of Alt, make the world more open like it is over in Britain? Where, I might add, those Elders live!'

He shook his head. He looked weary. 'It's not those Elders,' he said. 'It's the North American contingent, you haven't met them yet. They're far more... conservative in nature.'

'And,' he continued. 'If that's all it is, a peaceful movement, that will be good and everyone's mind can rest easy. We've already begun the process of lifting the Veil, at least here in Newfoundland. We can work with them, I'm very open to that.'

'But there's doubts?'

'Almost a certainty.' He leaned closer to me over the table, his voice was hushed. 'Willem wasn't acting alone.'

I could spit at the sound of that hated name. Willem, the Dutch sorcerer (failed) who had caused me so much grief in the past. Yes, he was the sole reason I had the magnified powers which came about through my prolonged contact with the Crystal Charm Stone back in Scarp, in Scotland, but his intentions were pure evil, even when he pretended to woo me onto his side.

'The Ice King,' Dad continued.

'But I took him down! I brought his castle down about his ears, surely he died in that,' I cried, unmindful of disturbing Mom who was somewhere in the huge house.

Dad shook his head. 'Please, lower your voice. If your mother finds out what the Kin are demanding of you... And never underestimate the Ice King,' he said. 'Word has it that his court escaped the fall. There was more than one route to the outside world from his stronghold.'

I remembered the maze of tunnels and channels we'd gone through to find that freezing court where my mother had languished for a decade. Of course there had to have been another way out.

'This is what they fear, that the elves have somehow gotten mixed up with this larger worldwide movement,' Dad said. 'And if that is the case, we have to squash this rebellion.'

I was still shaking my head in disbelief.

'You see, it's not a simple case of betraying your friend,' he continued, his voice heavy. 'The future of the whole world might be at stake here. Possibly. We don't know if this is connected to the larger sphere. We need *you* to find out.'

I said nothing. What was there to say?

'The thing is, if we find out their plans, there's a chance that we can talk, have discussions, to prevent what we fear,' he said.

'Can you not just lift the Veil?' I whispered. 'Then they won't have anything to rebel against.'

Of course that was too simple a solution.

'It can't happen that easily. There are processes, and precedents, and red tape, and we need to get the North American Kin as a whole on our side before we can lift it. That will take years.'

So that was it. My first assignment for the Kin was to infiltrate the ranks of the elves, and in doing so, betray my friendship with Brin. If I had any aspirations and ambitions for my future within the Kin, I had no choice but to do as they demanded. I turned an anguished eye on to my father, wondering if he really understood the magnitude of this request.

He did. 'I *never* wanted you to get involved with the Kin,' he said in a low voice, his face almost crumpled into itself. 'I tried my best.'

I excused myself to finally unleash the contents of my stomach.

As I half lay over the toilet bowl, my energy spewed into its depths, I didn't feel any better knowing that with Eldric involved, this was not planned as a peaceful movement. The Dark Elves were so far removed from the Normal world that they wouldn't care about the Veil, wouldn't even notice if it was lifted. There was not going to be a conference or discussion about everybody talking through their differences and wearing flowers in their hair and singing Kumbaya. This was going to lead to war and destruction. Brin had gotten in over his head, and I was being dragged along into it too.

And I was possibly the only one who could prevent it.

CHAPTER 8

What time was it in China? I didn't know, and cared less. That country was almost exactly half-way round the world from my home, so perhaps ten o'clock in the morning give or take a half hour either way, whether it was yesterday or maybe tomorrow. Didn't matter. I had to speak with Hugh, even if it meant taking him out of one of his endless meetings.

'Dara?' He sounded surprised to hear from me so soon.

'Yeah, can you hear me?' The connection was sketchy. 'Have you got a moment? I really need to talk.'

'Sure,' he said. 'I'm on a guided tour of the Emperor's Palace Museum in Taiwan. It's a gorgeous warm day here, and I can't tell you how beautiful, how astounding this garden is.'

'Taiwan?' My geographic knowledge was lacking, but I was pretty sure that was a separate country. 'I thought you were going to China.'

'Same thing, depending on who you're talking to,' he said. 'This meeting is part of the never-ending process to bring reconciliation, but you probably don't want to hear about that. What's up?'

Through the staticky line, I told him what had just been dumped in my lap. 'They sent me here to spy on my friend. What sort of shit is this?'

He gave a cynical laugh. 'This is Kin shit, Dara, this is what happens,' he said. 'But look at it this way – if Brin isn't up to anything, if he's not taking any part in elven politics, then there's no problem, right? You get to enjoy a visit home, and you can write in your report that it was a dead end. You'll learn the trick of this soon enough.'

But how about if Brin *was* involved, already enmeshed with the secretive Dark Elf king Eldric? Could I even say these words to Hugh? I tried to sort in my mind the best spin on this.

'I did wonder why Cate was pushing for you to return to Newfoundland,' Hugh mused while I thought. 'It's not like her to be concerned for your advancement. But she felt this would be a great start for you.'

'Cate?' I yelled into the phone before I could stop myself. Dad's wife, or soon to be ex-wife, was the reason I was here, pulling the strings to have me in the position of betraying my best friend? How evil. How perfect of her. What a very Cate thing to do.

'Why didn't you tell me this before?'

'Because I knew you'd react like this,' he said, reasonably enough.

I heaved a load of invectives against her down the phone line, thus proving his point.

'Look,' he said patiently, though the reception was beginning to break up. 'I wouldn't take it personally. If there are hints of elven political action in St. John's, who better to send in than someone who already has a tenuous connection to the community? Dara Martin is the sensible choice. And Cate has done you a huge favor, in case you aren't aware of it. A new employee, one who hasn't had much field practice, never gets assignments of this nature. She's actually helping you up the ladder of your ambitions.'

Cate. The mother of Sasha and my other half-siblings. Although Dad was the head of the Avalon Kin, his wife was a pretty powerful witch amongst the Kin in her own right. Their marriage had cemented the fusion of the two most powerful Kin families in this province; the de Teilhards, the old money in the east, and the Huxors who controlled the center and the west. Her family was descended from Swedish witches who'd arrived a few hundred years ago, claiming the wilderness for their own as they searched for, and found, the elusive magical element adamantite. This metal was prized for its powers and only to be found in the very oldest of rocks in the world, and they held a virtual monopoly on the supply for western society. The Huxors had also made a tidy profit off timber and other mining rights, making them as rich and as powerful as the de Teilhards.

Cate. My nemesis. The woman responsible (I was pretty sure) for sending my mother into the clutches of the Ice King for the past ten years. Was it possible that she was really helping to advance my career within the Kin, or was she purposefully putting me in a position where I had to betray my friend? Given our history, I chose to believe the latter option, and my heart burned for the revenge I would take on that witch. Some day.

Our connection broke off before we could discuss this further, and before I could tell him of meeting Eldric, and that was a good thing. I was going to keep the whole Eldric thing under my hat for now until I figured out what I was going to do. Yes, I would somehow advance my career while not betraying my friend, but I was determined to find a way to bring Cate down while I did so.

....

Mom started at me the next morning, bubbling away just like the coffee percolating on the stove top.

'We need to begin preparations for the Solstice dinner.'

'You're celebrating that?' I reached around her for my favorite mug.

'All of us are, silly. There's a big do at the Temple every year.'

'But I thought it was just supposed to be Kin...'

'It's Kin and *family*,' Dad said as he entered the room, still adjusting his tie. Mom handed him a glass of juice.

'But...'

'No buts,' Mom said. 'This family is going.'

'I can't.' No way. I couldn't imagine a more excruciating way to spend an evening than to be surrounded by the Kin and their offspring, who all hated me.

'I'm afraid you don't have a choice,' Dad observed. He poured up coffee for himself and me.

'You can't tell me what to do.' And cursed myself as soon as the words had left my mouth. Why did he always make me feel and behave like I was five years old?

He heaved a sigh and ignored me, and Mom stepped up to the plate.

'No one is *making* you do anything,' she said. How she could be so reasonable and bright this early in the morning, I would never know. 'You're working for the Kin now, you have to go. It's that simple. Part of the job.'

'But why are you going?' This was directed toward her. 'If it's only Kin?'

'And *family*,' Dad repeated himself.

'Seriously? You're going to what, just fling it in Cate's face by bringing Mom to a Kin do?' I sat down across from him, hardly able to believe what they were saying. Nobody there would welcome her presence. Cate's side, of course, would see it as the hugest insult that he would bring his mistress to one of their stuck-up do's, and even the rest of the Kin would frown on it. I shook my head. 'You're not going to be welcome there, Mom.'

'What do you call this, then?' She took a card from the fireplace mantle and tossed it down onto the table so I could read it. 'I call it an official invitation.'

The cream card was fancy, heavy cardstock die-cut into lace around the edges with gilt lettering, and it was addressed to Dad, Mom and myself. Not just as 'plus-one' or 'plus family', but specifically by name. To each of us.

I had no choice in the matter. I had to go.

'I'd sooner poke needles in my eye,' I muttered, pushing the card away from me.

Mom laughed and rested her arms around me. 'But just think,' she said. 'We get to go shopping for dresses. You get to be a girly-girl for one evening. And I know exactly the thing for you, saw it the other day at Estelle's. Oh, you are going to be the belle of the ball!'

'Estelle's? Is that place still around? She must be, what, ninety by now.' I didn't say a word about the ludicrous prices in that shop. I'd seen them in the window. Years of poverty slammed an automatic barrier up at the thought of spending so much on something I would wear once in my life, to an event I didn't even want to attend.

Her face fell a little. 'Well, *I* thought it was charming.'

'Mom, there's no sense getting me a new dress for this, not around here,' I said, a little desperately. 'I have a dress. I think there's one in my closet. Or I can wear one of your old ones. Or even better, we can look up in the attic – there's trunks and wardrobes filled with dresses from years of Martin ladies – I bet we can find something cool up there.'

'I want to get you something new, to celebrate,' Mom said. Her lower lip was stuck out. I had a suspicion that I looked much like that whenever things didn't work out the way I envisioned.

Dad said nothing at all, just unfolded the morning paper and bent his head toward it. But I could have sworn I saw a smirk dance across his face.

··········

Sitting out in my garden in the morning sun with a fresh coffee, I put the matter of the Solstice out of my mind in order to concentrate on more pressing matters, like the Kin's request for me to betray my friend. I couldn't do it, could I? Actually spy on Brin and report everything back to the Kin. Especially as I already knew he was having talks with the Dark Elf king himself.

I searched for a way out of this. Perhaps it was innocent enough, at least on Brin's part. Perhaps they were seriously just at the talking stage and planned to, what? Bring a lawsuit or a petition to the Convention. The more I thought about this, the better I felt. My elf friend would never in a million years align himself with violence of any nature, that was the whole reason he'd been so desperate to hop the Veil in the first place.

Yet no matter how much I thought and poked and pulled, I was not able to twist this argument enough to account for Eldric's involvement, for I could conceive of no legitimate reason for the Dark Elves to be interested in removing the Veil. According to legend and rumor, they were stuck away in their eyrie in the Wilderness, and had nothing to do with anyone else at all.

Before I made any moves, I had to find out more about the depth of Brin's involvement, and he would be busy at work right now. But there was still Alice. I was determined to squeeze out every bit of information she might have, things she may not even know she knew. So I texted her and suggested a picnic out at the lighthouse.

Alice and I rode our bikes to Fort Amherst not long after that, the perfect excuse for us to hang out again after months apart. We climbed through the wire fence barriers erected to prevent tourists from falling off the rocks into the surf, down to our little nook ten feet above the ocean. It was mid-day in June with the sun beating down on us in this sheltered grassy spot, the water below us calm and blue. A rare day, indeed.

Mom had packed us a picnic of wraps filled with veggies and cheeses, leftover chocolate cake and bottles of her home-made pink lemonade. Alice's eyes bugged out when she saw the feast.

'Oh my God,' she said, hefting up a bottle to let the sun shine through it. The drinks had been thoroughly chilled before we set off, and the glass was slick with condensation. 'I'd forgotten about your Mom and how she can do things like this. And are those real cloth napkins?'

I tossed over a neatly rolled cloth with a fork tucked away inside, and I let her get through lunch before beginning to grill her.

'So, I dropped in on Brin last night,' I began casually enough. 'I was surprised you weren't there.'

'No, he had a meeting,' she replied as she dug out the last of the grapes in the bowl of cut fruit. 'He's gotten really involved in his political stuff, and it's so wonderful that he's found something to be passionate about. I have to say I'm quite relieved.' She popped three of the little fruit into her mouth at one time and gave a groan of pleasure as she bit down.

'I was worried that he'd be bored, or lonely, with me so busy with classes and labs,' she continued. 'He's shy, like me. But he's found a community.'

'About that,' I said slowly. 'Do you have any idea who his new friends are?'

'No, I haven't met any of them,' she said, then paused as she thought a moment. 'Although I don't think they're of this... I mean, I think they're in Alt. Not humans, I guess is what I'm trying to say.'

'Alt!' I stared at her, unable to take in the meaning of her words. Brin had been desperate to leave that place behind when he crossed over, and sworn he would never return.

And no one could get through the Veil unless they were a witch. 'How can...'

'Yeah, he told me he was given a thing to get him through the Veil.'

'Thing? What do you mean a *thing*?'

'I dunno,' she replied, looking a little offended at my tone. 'Just something which helps him cross over so he can meet with the others.'

'Other elves?' I was still trying to wrap my mind around the idea of Brin going willingly back into Alt.

She shrugged. 'Yeah, I guess. And dwarves, too. And I saw him coming out of that creepy house with the turrets down the road from me.'

'The vampires,' I said flatly. 'He's meeting with that crowd. In Alt.'

I was confused, unable to piece together this information with the Brin that I knew and loved. At his home the other night, I had assumed that like me, he'd been forcefully sucked into Alt by the power of the Dark Elf King. Yet now Alice said he was purposefully re-entering Alt and holding discussions with the scariest of beings over there. And dwarves? That group kept to themselves whenever they could. I shook my head. None of this was making any sense.

Besides, how could any item help him through the Veil? What was its nature? And even more important, *who had given it to him*?

Alice couldn't, or wouldn't, tell me anything else, so I would have to go direct to the source and soon, even if it meant lurking outside his house until he got home from work.

·········

But I didn't have an opportunity to corner Brin, not that evening and not for another twenty-four hours, for no sooner had I returned home than I was ordered to pack an overnight bag.

'We're going to Montreal!' Mom danced and kissed Dad on the cheek.

I could only stare at the pair of them.

Dad laughed. '*You're* going to Montreal,' he said. 'Keep me out of this.'

'What?'

Mom smiled with glee. 'You were right about Estelle's, Jon agreed.'

'But...'

'For this occasion, you need to make a splash,' she said and her eyes danced back to Dad's. 'So we're going to do what the rest of the witches do, which is go dress shopping in the right place.'

She noticed my distinct lack of enthusiasm. 'Unless you'd prefer New York? Jon, is it too late to change the tickets?'

He shrugged. 'You can do anything you want. I told you, it's your money too.'

'I can't,' I said abruptly. 'I have things to do. Tonight.'

I made eyes at Dad to let him know I was busy doing Kin business.

'Nothing is more important than your big night,' Mom said decisively. 'The Solstice Ball is your first official Kin function.'

And there was to be no more arguing. Within two hours I was on the airplane, Business Class no less, sharing champagne with Mom for our whirlwind trip through Montreal, the dress capital of Canada.

CHAPTER 9

We spent less than twenty-four hours in Montreal, but Mom sure packed a lot in. A late night cabaret, a night at a luxury suite, then up early the next morning to wander the markets. Lunch was taken not in a five star hotel, but at a little diner off one of the main drags. It was definitely rough around the edges, the leather on the stools worn and faded, but that didn't faze Mom one bit. She and the proprietor greeted each other like old friends, which they were.

I'd never known Mom used to come here. How had I missed her absences when I was growing up? But there was no time for wondering about that, for we had to find The Dress.

And after we had perused no less than ten shops, there it was in a tiny atelier on a laneway between three-story buildings, lots of wrought iron stair cases and little balconies just as if we were in Paris. The dress was blue like our eyes, with velvet and net and satin, and felt far too sophisticated for me. It was really more Mom's style, she had the aplomb to carry it off, but she insisted.

I had my own stipulation, only one. 'There has to be a pocket. I need my phone, and I refuse to carry that stupid little clutch purse all night.'

Mom rolled her eyes, but the short French owner of the shop agreed. 'All *les jeunes filles* demand this. You will find it there, just inside your waist, so. It is standard now, in all of my creations.'

And yes, so cleverly designed that the bulk of my phone, slim as it was, would not be visible. I smiled at Mom in triumph, but she was now busy looking for the matching sandals. As she stepped back to take in the effect of my fancy dress, she smiled. 'You'll outshine Sasha any day,' she muttered, her voice thick with satisfaction.

Which was the whole point of the trip, I realized right then.

Soon afterwards, we flew back home.

The upshot of this whole Montreal excursion was that I didn't get to corner Brin until that evening. I wanted to speak with him, badly, to find out the answers to all the questions that Alice's information had raised in my mind. There was also the little matter of my assignment from the Kin. Not that I had any intentions of actually reporting to them on Brin, however, it wouldn't hurt if I could offer them real information on the activities of the Dark Elf king, if in fact he was planning anything.

We got home around five o'clock, but before I could do anything more than stuff a sandwich in my mouth to tide me over, Dad cornered me.

'Your trip went well? I hear it was a success.'

I nodded, chewing.

'Marian always loved her little trips out of town,' he mused. 'I'm glad you went with her.'

I swallowed down the turkey and cranberry sauce sandwich. Mom had toasted the homemade bread, and with a load of butter melting through it and the swiss cheese soft and goopy, it was way better than anything served on the airplane, even in Business Class. Since my return from Scotland, Mom had been feeding me as if to make up for the past ten years of Edna's peanut butter sandwiches. I was going to have to up my exercising.

He looked around the kitchen a little furtively, but there was no need. We could both hear Mom upstairs unpacking her stuff. 'I believe you've already met with Brin since you've been back from Scotland?'

'Yeah,' I said, then drank down the last of the glass of milk, avoiding his eye. Did he have prior knowledge of the meeting with Eldric? Is that what began this whole spy business?

But no. They already had that role assigned to me before I even came back home. I tried to relax my shoulders.

'You should really go see him again this evening,' Dad urged, his voice low and persuasive. 'Get as much information as you can gather. I think we have less time than we thought we did, it may become an urgent situation.'

Which was precisely what I had planned to do before I got whisked away to Montreal. 'I'm actually on my way over to see him now, to meet him when he gets off work,' I said. I bent to place my dishes in the dishwasher, partly to cover my eye roll.

'Good, good,' he said. 'And can you get a report ready? I'll need it in a couple of days. Shall we say first thing the day after the Solstice? In thirty-six hours time. Before I leave for the office.'

'A report!' I whirled around to face him.

'Of course,' he replied as he shrugged off his suit jacket and loosened his tie, finished his own work for the day now the last order was given.

'What kind of report?'

He looked at me oddly. 'An informational report, of course. A factual record of all data. The conversations held, other things you may notice, everything that can draw the clearest picture.'

Including the bit about me interrupting the visit of Eldric on his rare excursion out of the Wilderness to meet secretly with Brin. It dawned on me again how big this scope was. This would blow the Kin's socks off. And Dad would definitely question why I hadn't told him about this immediately, and not in a gentle loving way.

Yet I'd sworn Brin to secrecy.

I didn't even notice Dad leaving the room, I was thinking so furiously as I paused, my hand still on the dishwasher door. It wasn't fair that Dad was my boss in this matter, the Kin should have assigned me to report to someone else. There was no way I could tell anyone about Brin's connection to Eldric, not yet, because I knew someone would come down all heavy handed and mess this up for me.

Someone like Dad. He wouldn't trust me to handle the situation as I saw fit. I drew in a deep breath.

Okay. I would go to directly to Brin's, which I'd been planning to do anyway, and I would pump him for more information. Like what sort of *thing* allowed him access to Alt, and who he'd gotten it from.

That was the really important bit. Who. I needed to trace the trail to find out who was behind all this. Brin might believe he was merely working toward getting the Veil dropped for the benefit of all, but I had a feeling in my gut there was something far more sinister happening.

Especially as Eldric was involved.

··········

I immediately flew over to his house on my bike again, and I lurked on his stoop until I spied him coming up over the hill. He must have been deep in thought because he didn't see me until he was almost on top of me.

'Dara!' His open face battled between expressing polite pleasure at seeing me and very real dismay at seeing me right at that moment. He tried to glance at his watch surreptitiously, but it was big and gold and old-fashioned looking and hung on his wrist below his too-short sleeves.

'Going somewhere?'

'Yes,' he sputtered, and he looked around nervously. 'No. But... but this isn't a convenient time.'

'We'll make it quick, then.' I was glad I hadn't wasted a moment in getting here. Sitting on his steps, I was at eye level with the elf, and I used this to my advantage. 'So,' I said as my eyes bore into his. 'We need to talk.'

He shook his head, his straw like hair flying off in every direction and his eyes darting back and forth like a wild animal. 'Nu-uh. Can't, not right now. You need to go. *Right now*.'

I ignored this. 'Alt. How do you do it?'

He waved his hands at me, palms up as if he was shushing me. He was terrified, but of what? My butt remained firmly on the stoop. I crossed my arms over my knees and continued staring at him, waiting for an answer, but all he did was stare over my shoulder and swallow loudly, his already huge eyes like saucers.

And then it happened again, the involuntary shift into Alt, but this time I fought it. It was to no avail though, my efforts only made the transition more unpleasant.

It was like being inexorably squeezed through a jelly tube, all slippery sides and sliminess, there was no purchase for me to hold onto to stop the flow, the sucking and pulling until I was finally spit out the other end to find myself still sitting on Brin's stoop but in Blackler's Lane, Alt.

More offended than afraid, affronted at this rude treatment against my will, I looked at Brin, ready to let him have the full force of my displeasure. If he had done this to me, with his mysterious *thing*, I was ready to...

But his eyes were cast down and his narrow shoulders slumped. He hadn't been the cause of my forceful transition into Alt. No, that had been initiated by the two elven warriors on either side of him.

Their perfect pale skin glowed, lending light into the shadows of Alt and they were very unhappy to see me, if elves could be presumed to have emotions. One drew his sword out immediately and advanced toward me, but Brin threw himself between us.

'No, you can't! It's Dara, remember,' he said. 'Dara de Teilhard.' He gulped again and threw back at me, 'I tried to warn you.'

'What's happening, Brin?' I stood up on the stoop, towering over even the warrior elves, keeping a close eye on them as I did so.

'She'll have to come,' the one on Brin's left said. 'We're not allowed to kill her.'

'Come where?' I asked, but in my sinking heart I knew.

Brin stared at me, apprehensive, and he bit his lip before he spoke. 'Rhovan Palace. To meet with Eldric.'

I didn't have time to acquiesce or react, let alone throw up a protective shield around myself before the other elf grasped me in his long arms and we were gone. This, then, was how they had disappeared the other night. It wasn't a process of winnowing or any other kind of instant teleportation from one place to another, it was wingless flight at a speed that I couldn't comprehend.

One moment we were all standing on Blackler's Lane Alt, and then the next we were high in the air above the old town, heading southwest. We quickly left the harbor behind in the shadows of the lowering sun which glowed through the coral clouds far to our right.

Yet the wind didn't touch us, nor were we positioned aerodynamically to cut through the currents. I was upright the whole time and my hair caught only in the slightest of breezes. Perhaps with my innate power I could have stopped the process, but I didn't want to test that theory out, not while I was a thousand feet up in the air.

Yes, I had the power of flight, Meg had taught me that, but I hadn't had much practice and was not going to risk my life. God alone knew what dark forces lurked beneath us within the interior forests of Alt.

Instead, I forced myself to relax and go with the flow. The elf had me in the lightest grasp as we headed towards the Avalon Wilderness, the rumored stronghold of Eldric and the Dark Elves. I would never, ever have an opportunity like this in my life again, and I was probably the only witch to ever have this chance. If I made it back alive, the Kin would be very interested in my knowledge. What a report that would make.

CHAPTER 10

I could see it fast approaching from the distance, the land of Eldric. Legendary Rhovan, which no mortal or witch had ever before laid eyes on. The circle of sharp mountains rose all pink and gold in the fire of the setting sun, above the shadowy depths below. The stone peaks were bare and cold, I could tell even from here, the ice capped shards of rock frozen and glittering in the last of the evening light. Eldric dwelled somewhere amidst that stronghold.

The Wilderness below us was like nothing I'd ever experienced before. If I'd ever thought about this land, like everyone else I'd assumed that the Wilderness was a land of barrens and ponds and bogs and boulders, fit only for the caribou herds who wandered those empty spaces long ago scraped clean by glaciers, a kind of unwelcoming tundra hinterland. But it wasn't like that, not at all. It was forested with ancient pines, untouched by logging and clearcutting, with deep ravines and gorges and mighty water ways below us. It was a mystical, magical place untainted by humans.

But that was the thing about the Avalon Wilderness, at least in real time. It managed to be completely ignored, even in these days with satellite imagery allowing us to see every corner of the earth. Nobody even thought about it, those hundreds of square miles smack dab in the middle of the large peninsula, with highways skirting every side of it along the shores and coasts. It was as if there'd been a spell cast on it long ago to make the mind slide away from the idea of this big land, to prevent anyone's curiosity from glomming on to it and desiring to explore its depths.

Now that I'd opened my mind to this idea, I could actually feel the resistance of that ban, like a thick wool cloak as we passed through it, just the slightest tug trying to push us away like a magnet's resistance. This most ancient piece of Africa which had drifted over all those millions of years ago was soaked in magic, and someone, some very powerful being, must have decreed it remain so.

Flying at this incredible speed, we soon passed through the mountain ranges surrounding a deep, deep valley. These peaks were the homes of eagles, I could see their great wingspans as our movement disturbed them, the gimlet eyes of one huge fellow hungrily following us as we passed as if deciding which of us would make the better meal. But they left us untouched, perhaps because they recognized the insignia of Eldric's forces. I wouldn't give much for our chances if we didn't have this elven guard.

Once inside the circle of sharp peaks, we gently slowed and lowered to land on a flat courtyard at the base of a great waterfall. The warrior elf let go of me as soon as the paving stones met our feet as if the touch of me was distasteful. I automatically drew closer to the shelter of Brin's taller form as I stared all around.

Incredibly enough, the movies had almost gotten it right. Almost, but even the big screen hadn't been able to portray the true majesty of this land of the Dark Elves. The peaks of course towered above us, and the thundering of the waterfall drowned out any other sound. The water itself was lit as if from within, even in the dusk, like the phosphorescence sometimes seen at the ocean's edge, and the huge sprays created mists that spread this light all around us. From this point on the valley's floor I could see the trees and other greenery that grew tall in this warm, moist place, they looked like nothing that had ever grown in this province of rock and bog and sea salt. No, these were a form of cedar, like the kind from an oriental painting with soft drooping branches reaching down to the life-giving water.

The patio we stood on was hewn from the solid rock, as smooth as polished concrete but the natural jewels within the ancient stone shone through. We walked on a floor of solid Labradorite, that beautiful stone of black and glittering blue so prized for jewellery.

The stone walls of this ravine were also the Palace, with doorways and windows and balconies carved from the very mountain itself. Lights glowed from within and silk curtains fluttered in the mists from the waterfall.

I was so in awe of these surroundings that I'd quite forgotten the fearsome creature who ruled them, but I was quickly, and rudely, reminded. One of the elves, I couldn't tell which one for they both looked exactly the same right down to the pale blue outfits they wore and the glowing whiteness of their skin, one of them grabbed my arm to turn me to face the largest doorway leading out to this terrace.

I automatically tried to place my barrier shield around me, for I didn't like his cold touch any more than he wanted to feel the warmth of me, yet I couldn't summon my own power. Me, the witch kissed by the Crystal Charm Stone, I could not find my own magic inside me anywhere. Panicked, I tried to twist out of his grasp but couldn't shake his hand off.

'Your magic won't work here,' he whispered in my ear as he dug his long strong fingers in deeper into my arm. 'Witch.'

That one word left me in no doubt as to his opinion of me. As he hadn't properly introduced himself, I would hereon refer to him as Bitch One. The other could be Bitch Two or not, he didn't seem as unpleasant as the one who held me in his grasp.

And then I looked up to gaze upon the wrath of Eldric. He stood framed in the large doorway, his lavender skin tones not warmed one bit by the gentle light from the mists surrounding us. He was a fearsome sight yet there was no emotion displayed on his face, only the glints flashing from his eyes hinted of his rage at my unexpected presence in his palace.

'What reason?' His eyes flicked to the elf who held me.

'You said no harm to her,' the other replied coldly. He held himself haughtily even in the presence of the king. 'She was there. We had no time to waste.'

Eldric then turned his fearsome eyes on to Brin and waited for an explanation of my presence in his hallowed palace.

'It was a mistake,' Brin blurted out. 'I didn't request her to come. I was running late, and she had dropped by my home...'

'How was I to know this?' The warrior elf stared at him glacially and cut off his protests. 'You were there at the appointed time. The appointed place. It was your mistake in allowing her to be present, not mine.'

Brin should have known better, could have picked his words more wisely. He more than anyone would know that imperfection was a stigma of shame amongst the Elven breed, and to point out another elf's error in front of the king, no less... Brin had made an enemy for life.

'You could have asked,' I added spitefully. The elf had it out for me anyway, why not heap on the shame while I could.

'Silence,' Eldric commanded. 'She is here, it is done. Brin, do you vouch for her?'

'By my inner light, I swear,' my friend answered fervently. 'Witch may she be, but she has known what it is to be an outcast among her kin. We have spoken a small amount about the Cause, and she has shown herself to be sympathetic.'

'A de Teilhard, they are not the worst of the witches,' Eldric said as he rubbed his chin, looking at me all the while. 'But they are intertwined with the other Kin.'

'Not the Huxors.' I stepped up, refusing to be talked about anymore as if I wasn't there, as if I was too insignificant to have a voice. 'I have no business with Cate or that line, or indeed with most of them.'

Eldric gave a small, twisted smile. 'Is that so? And you think we can trust you on that account? Because the Kin show weakness in division?'

Hugh had said that Cate was the force behind my return to St. John's, bringing me back here in order to infiltrate the Elven unrest, to betray my friend. Now that I'd been so rudely and abruptly transported to Rhovan, I intended to make the most of it and gather what information I could. I still believed then that Brin was innocent of any evil intent, and that I could somehow excise him from my report to the Kin. I didn't give a thought that I might be getting mixed in too deeply with forces beyond my control.

'Yes.' I answered him as boldly and honestly as I could.

'Interesting,' Eldric replied, still staring at me as if trying to peer deep inside my heart. 'We will see.'

He barked orders to his warriors, then he and Brin walked further into the huge open door of the palace. I made to accompany them, but was held back by Bitch One.

'You don't think He trusts you that much, do you?' This was said with such a sneer in his voice that his face almost cracked a grimace. 'You'll stay right here in the courtyard.'

Frustrated, I could only watch as Brin disappeared into the depths of the hall.

··········

I had no way of knowing what plans were being discussed by my friend and the king, I could only bide my time in that beautiful ethereal outdoor space.

The beginning of the waterfall, the source of the magically lit mist all around us, was too far up for me to see. The water fell in a steady, graceful stream. It was a narrow slip of water, I saw as I examined it more closely, nothing like the giant of Niagara Falls, just a steady outpouring of water as if from the ewer of the Gods, yet its tremendous height lent it force enough to cause the mists and spray all around.

We waited there for hours as the last of the light slipped from the sky far overhead, beyond the circling peaks, and the night grew still. I wasn't offered any refreshment, nor did Bitch One move his stance one iota the whole time.

The stars were cold above us, yet the evening here held no chill, as if this deep valley held its own unique biosphere. Was it Elven magic that caused this, I wondered, or was it the protection offered by the mountains against the sharp northern winds that swept the island? I never did find the answer to that question.

They returned to the courtyard, Brin and Eldric, and stood before me. Only the king would meet my eye.

Eldric spoke first. 'Witchling, you are in a very privileged position. Few outsiders have ever entered my palace of Rhovan, and fewer still have lived to tell the tale.'

He paused. 'De Teilhard you may be, but a betrayal will cost you dearly, both you and your Elven friend here.'

Brin was pale, and he flashed his eyes at me, nodding vigorously. He knew Eldric, and knew this wasn't an idle threat. Here in the middle of the Avalon Wilderness, our lives depended on this king's whim. No one would think to look for our bodies here if we didn't return home tonight, and not even my father's name could save me from the wrath of Eldric. I straightened my shoulders and stared levelly back at the king, for we had nowhere to run to.

'As assurance for your fealty, you will assist our cause.' The king was speaking slowly and clearly so that his intent would be fully understood by me. 'You have close ties with the Kin. You will gather information as I require, and other duties as the need arises. You will, in fact, be an agent for the Elves within the Kin.'

Bloody hell. Now I was to act as a double agent for the opposing forces of which, I was becoming to realize, was not just a soft political movement to lower the Veil and give freedom of movement to those trapped behind it. Eldric wouldn't be demanding my assistance in endless bureaucratic talks with the Kin, he wouldn't need the negligible help I could offer in that arena. What was going on here, what were they planning? A full scale Elven rebellion? I turned a beseeching eye to Brin, who merely hung his head, staring hard at the polished stone at his feet.

The ghost of a smile appeared on the king's face. 'Rather a peculiar dilemma for you, I would imagine,' he remarked. 'Still, from what I have heard of your exploits, I don't believe the Kin have done you any favors over the years or earned your loyalty. Brin tells me you are sympathetic to our cause.'

'The lowering of the Veil?'

He nodded.

'And what else?'

That small smile returned. 'That remains to be seen. But I am sure you will step up to the plate when the time comes. After all, the health of your friend depends on it.'

Brin looked miserable. Perhaps he was only now realizing what he'd gotten himself mixed up in, although he should have known better. He was an elf, after all, and had given up everything to avoid that heritage. Now he was stuck in the middle of it, just like me.

'Till we meet again, then.' Eldric nodded to Bitches One and Two. As they grabbed us and prepared for takeoff, he lifted his hand to stay them a moment.

'Oh, and do give my regards to Cate.'

CHAPTER 11

The flight back was lit by the path of stars above our heads, the wide swathe of the Milky Way with its thousands and millions of pin pricks like a white road leading us out of the Wilderness and back home. The return trip seemed shorter, and in no time at all we were standing again in front of Brin's home, roughly deposited in Alt before the two elves whisked themselves away again without even a farewell.

Alt faded around us as they left, and Brin and I found ourselves staring at each other. Bleakly, with no need to speak of what had just happened. Our lives were at stake, and yes, it was all Brin's fault, his idealism and naivety and his search for a better world had landed us in this.

'Do you still believe you're on the side of right? After that?'

He stared at me in the unlit gloom of Blackler's Lane and then gave a decisive nod.

'Yes,' he said although his voice quavered. He swallowed, the Adam's apple of his long neck bobbing, then spoke more firmly. 'Yes, undoubtedly. The Veil is an anachronism, it has no place in our lives. The Kin refuse to lift it, and they refuse to give freedom to those trapped behind it.'

He gave a bitter laugh. 'All those talks that Jon promises? They will achieve nothing. Nothing will change. Things will remain the same for the next hundred years unless we act now.'

'Then, that's it,' I replied slowly, still trying to feel my way around this abrupt change in circumstances. 'I guess I'm forced to go along with this, to become a part of it, to betray my own kind. In order to save my life, and yours.'

'You have to take a stand at some time in your life Dara. And this is important. What do you owe the Kin anyway? After all those years of abuse, do you really feel you belong with them?'

His question stung me but I tried not to show it. Of course he was right. The Kin, my own father and his family, had rejected me for the past decade. I really owed them nothing.

Except. I still wanted what I could achieve within their structure. To use my power and develop my magic and live the lifestyle of the fabulously wealthy. Like Hugh did. My ambition burned in me stronger than ever.

And Brin had no idea that I was now a double-agent. I nodded, which he took for acceptance and he let out a sigh of relief.

'It will work out, Dara, you'll see,' he said, almost like a question as if he was asking for reassurance. 'You won't be sorry.'

·····•·····

I left him then, hopped on my bike and just pedalled, pushing myself up hill and down with no direction in mind, cutting in front of cars on the main roads and leaving a stream of blaring horns behind me. If I could have managed to have an accident, perhaps I would have, for that would put me out of commission and solve my immediate problems. But I didn't. I sailed between the vehicles as if in my own little safety bubble, though I had no recollection of creating a shield around me.

Give my regards to Cate. Eldric's last parting shot, but what did this mean? How was she mixed up with the Dark Elf king, of all creatures? And for what purpose?

Cate again. My mind seethed with disquiet. I was caught blindly in a spider's web of intrigue with my father's ex-wife lurking at the center. She had brought me here to spy on my friend's political activities, so was it possible she had ties with the very being who was planning to overturn the Kin?

All the magic and power I had summoned but been unable to use to protect myself at Rhovan, it had come back with a vengeance as if on a delay timer and I was unable to stop the flow, and that's why I pushed myself, trying to work it out before the anger and confusion inside me caused me to do something I would regret, to harm some innocent in the expulsion of this force which ran through me like lightning.

Down King's Bridge Road, then a turn to travel on the rocky pathways surrounding the lake, illegal to take a bike on but I didn't care. There was hardly a living soul to see me at that hour of night and in the darkness of that unlit path, no one save a few lost creatures huddled round the used-needle bin, and they had other things on their minds.

At the far end of the lake my bike leapt off the path as if it had a mind of its own, and I turned down to the tiny harbor of Quidi Vidi. But I didn't stop to sit by the water. Panting by this time, still I forced my legs to climb up the steep hill towering over this little inlet, up and up until I found a new wilderness, atop a rocky cliff overlooking the ocean with no sign of humanity around me in any direction. I was alone, and it was safe to let go.

Out of breath yet I still summoned the voice to scream my anguish out over the vast expanse of the peaceful water. I let loose with all my power, flushing it out of me, hoping it would be soaked up by the nothingness before me, willing this action to clear my channels so I could think clearly once again.

As I screamed, that primal yell, I grasped the lapels of Mom's jean jacket, the better to force all the magic and air out of my lungs. I didn't even notice the bejewelled dragonfly still pinned there securely, the metal cutting into my fingers, I was so lost in this purge. I was going on instinct alone, I had no idea what was going on with me or how else to try to achieve a balance of power within myself.

I hardly noticed the warmth of the jewellery, or how it gleamed with a power of its own, the largest blue sapphire shining and likewise the rubies and emeralds and yellow diamonds until it became like a beacon of bright turquoise shining far out into the heavens.

At last, spent, I could allow myself to stop and watch the stream of my anguish let loose in clouds of colorful magic float away, sinking down to the water, caught purple and green in the rising of the almost full moon on the horizon. It drifted slowly out to sea, that cloud, hardly dissipating as it moved with the wind. How far across the North Atlantic would it travel before melting into the eddies? I wondered. I had no way of knowing what I had just unloosed, or what its effects would be, and I didn't care. I could only stand there and watch and let the ever-present wind flow through me and cleanse me.

I became aware of her presence by my side, slowly. First the slightest warmth, then the rustle of silk in the breeze. I turned my head, knowing it was her. Margaret Forsythe.

'You called?' Her voice was sardonic, and she laughed. 'That's one way to do it, but remind me to show you the proper way to flush the system, one which won't cause the cows in Ireland to bark at the moon.'

Her face no longer held the paleness of her enforced confinement in the dungeon in Edinburgh for those many years. Instead, I could see even in the moonlight that Meg was healthily tanned, her red hair burnished with golden streaks and she wore, not the Edwardian gowns I'd last seen her in, but a soft, barely-there confection of printed silk almost like a sari, belted with a thin golden chain around her slim waist. It matched the tiny sandals on her feet.

'And I might add, there are better, less painful ways to call for me.' She rubbed her ear and gave a shiver. 'Christ, it's freezing here, worse than Scotland. To what barbarous land have you called me?'

She opened a tiny shoulder bag and managed, by some tugging and huffing, to pull out an object a great deal larger than the original container. Once out, she shook it, and I could see it was a coat of some kind, a black one, stiff yet thin. Margaret dropped her arms into it and shrugged it onto her shoulders.

Coat? That was hardly the word to describe it. This was an exquisite garment, form fitting and made of the thinnest midnight fur, with a high collar that served to emphasize the length of her fine neck. She fastened it in front with a satin and pearl clasp, and the line of it was perfect. I could never have dreamed of such a creation.

She glanced over at my expression and smiled with that wide generous mouth of hers.

'Vintage Simon Chang,' she noted as she brushed down the length of it with her hands. 'I must say, I am loving the twenty-first century so far.' She flashed her easy grin at me.

Of all the people I could ever want to be like, Margaret Forsythe was at the top of the list. Sophisticated, confident and of course, powerful. Like me, she'd been bold enough to touch the Crystal Charm Stone, although her stealing the lodestone had not been a theft at all, but her attempt to demonstrate to the Kin how strong a female witch could be. She'd been in the act of bringing it to the Kin in Edinburgh to show them what was possible when, alerted to the disruptions she'd caused in the ley lines, Nachtan had rode out to arrest her.

I'd never understood how he could have tricked her and locked her away in the depths of the Vaults. But he had, and the story between the two was not yet ended despite her present freedom. She said she would tell me that tale, some day. When I was ready.

There was so much I needed her to teach me.

'How did you do that, just appear out of thin air?'

'I had no choice, with you squeezing my call bell so hard.' She flicked her hand at the brooch on my lapel.

'That's why you sent me this?'

'You thought it was a memento to remember me by?' She trilled her silvery laughter. 'As if you could ever forget me.'

That was true, but I pressed on. 'Seriously, you must have been somewhere on a beach, somewhere warm, and that could be nowhere close to here. You were thousands of miles away. How did you get here so quickly?'

Even the flying elves wouldn't have made such speed.

She didn't answer me. Instead she frowned and threw a question right back at me. 'What are you doing here?'

I shrugged. 'I'm home for a bit of rest and relaxation. Orders of the Kin.'

'You say that with such a straight face, as if the Kin truly have your well-being at heart,' she replied crisply. 'One of my many super-powers (and yours, you will find) is that I can smell a lie. So tell me, why are you here and not in Edinburgh furthering your education?'

She was right of course, but before I could think of a sharp retort, she looked all around us and gave a shiver. 'Can we not get off this God-forsaken mountain and find a more comfortable spot?'

I pointedly looked at the dainty sandals on her perfectly painted toes. 'You'll need hiking boots, or at least sneakers,' I said. 'The path is really steep and rocky.'

'Never mind me, I'll manage. Just bring me somewhere warm, preferably with a fire lit, and a snifter of brandy.'

CHAPTER 12

How she managed to make it down the scree slope, I'll never know. But she did, effortlessly, and then she somehow found a little restaurant in the tiny village of Quidi Vidi that happened to still be open despite the late hour. It had the requisite log fire burning brightly, although we were almost into summer.

'That's more like it,' she said as she wriggled her toes to take in the warmth. We were now ensconced in deep comfy chairs and sipping our brandies. 'So. Why were you sent here?'

I didn't answer her right away, I was still just a tad annoyed that she'd dismissed the possibility that my new employers, the Kin, had lied to me. What did she know? She'd been stuck in a dungeon for a century. Things had changed since her time. I removed my phone from my jean jacket pocket and idly glanced at it out of habit. Hugh hadn't called, or texted.

'What is the fascination with this box?' she muttered, and reached over and snatched it out of my hand. She stared at it intently, seeing only the colorful apps against the background photo of me and Hugh at Edinburgh Castle with the setting sun behind us. I'd thought it a very artistic compilation. Margaret merely screwed up her nose in distaste and tossed it onto the table between us.

I told her the whole story of why I was here, from the flight and finding Mom and Dad together again, and Dad's revelation of my real purpose in being sent back to Newfoundland. How Hugh had let it slip that Cate was behind it all, and then I told her my experiences with Eldric. She sat back and took it all in, only moving once and that was to flick her hand at the server to bring more brandy.

'And you are continuing in this charade. Why, exactly?'

She took me aback with that question. I looked at her searchingly. How had she missed the salient points?

'Brin is my friend,' I replied. 'And this is my future at stake.'

'Friend.' She tasted the word. 'Not much of a friend if he gets you mixed up with the Dark Elves.'

'I think he didn't realize what he was getting himself into.'

She shrugged. 'That's his problem, surely. You don't need to make it yours.'

A cat appeared from the shadows, a large black one with golden eyes. It leapt onto her lap without asking permission and she idly stroked its fur as she turned her gaze on me, waiting for my reply.

How could she be so cold, so heartless? The century in the dungeon must have sapped the humanity right out of her, or perhaps it had never been there in the first place. 'He's in danger,' I said simply. 'I can't leave him.'

'And your future? Why are you tying yourself to the Kin?'

'Are you kidding me? This is what I want in life! I've finally found a place where I can excel, I can grow, I can be important. I belong. And I'm learning,' I continued with passion. 'Learning how to use my power. And, oh my God, the fringe benefits of working with the most powerful organization on earth? How can you even ask?'

She thought about it as she continued to look at me haughtily, then shook her head. 'But you don't need any of this.'

'Where else am I going to be trained?'

'Come along with me, I'll show you a trick or two.'

'I don't want tricks, I want an in-depth magical education. I'm being taught by the Venerable Nacthan, and that means a lot. It's really prestigious, I'll have you know.'

'Venerable, is he now?' She snorted in a most unladylike fashion. 'He wasn't so venerable when he was trying to get into my skirts, the dirty old dog. So tell me, how is this *prestigious* education working for you?'

I opened my mouth to snap back a reply, then shut it again.

'I thought so,' she said. 'Filling your head with theories and not showing you a damn thing that's practical. Do you know why? He doesn't know anything! He's got as much power as you and me, and what does he do with it? He sits on it like a throne, and lets all the lesser Kin be in awe of him. That's no way to live your life.'

She'd had the benefit of a magic education from a young age, unlike me who had to start from Ground Zero. 'I *need* to learn the basics, before I can go on to the higher learning.'

'And you actually believe that shite? All you *have* to do is be yourself. The right teachers will come along when you're ready. It's quite easy if you let it.'

Margaret also came from a background of extreme wealth and privilege. She would never understand the insecurities seeded deep within a person's soul by early poverty.

'It's not just that,' I said, brushing my hand in the air. 'There's so much more the Kin can offer me. I'm going to go to China.'

She blew a raspberry. 'The only thing of interest in Zonguo are the dragons.'

'Security. A pay cheque.'

Margaret looked over at me like I was speaking a foreign language.

'Wealth, Margaret,' I said through my teeth. 'I want money. I want luxury and the lifestyle. I'm so sick of being poor and having to make do and pretending it's okay. I want to be rich, and working with the Kin... It's a fast-track to all my desires.'

She sneered. 'So you'll spend your life and energy chasing after the golden carrot on a stick, your life dictated by the whims of the Kin Elders, for what?'

I took a deep breath to try to calm myself. 'Not all of us were born wealthy, Margaret, not like you and your father, what was he, an earl?'

'A duke,' she reminded me, her eyes rolling just slightly upwards at my North American ignorance.

'Whatever,' I continued. 'You've had buckets of money all your life, he even left you a trust fund for when you got released from the Vaults. You don't have to worry about anything.'

'But you can have all this without the Kin, don't you see? That's what I'm trying to tell you.' She huffed, most uncharacteristically and sat up. The cat sprang off her lap and retreated back into the shadows. 'You're wasting your time.'

She stared at me intensely. 'You and I are the same, Dara. We're different from anyone else, any other witch, don't you see? You need to take responsibility for your own tremendous power. The Kin can't control you, they are taking advantage of you, letting you believe they actually have something to offer you. Fortunately for you, they don't yet know everything you're capable of.'

'No,' I sputtered. 'I need this, I need to have...'

'You're simply looking for justification,' she said, pointing her long index finger at me. 'You're looking for their approval, like a child searching for love.'

'But they are teaching me...'

'What?' She almost barked this out. 'What is my dearest Nachtan teaching you? He's stuffing your head with his fusty old theories, that's all. You're not learning to harness your energy and passion, you just showed me that, up there on the cliff top.'

I was so angry with her, partly because I knew she was speaking the truth about my education and I didn't want to admit it, for then I would be forced to take, as she insisted, responsibility for myself. I flexed my hands with frustration, and blue fire sparked out of my fingertips. It had no direction or intent behind it, so it merely flickered harmlessly around before fizzing out. I looked up at her.

'So can you teach me more? Perhaps you could stick around instead of flying off to some beach resort, perhaps you could make yourself useful!'

'For that, Dara,' she spit out as she stood up, sending the heavy armchair back with the force. 'For that, you will need to renounce the Kin and their false offerings, and come with me.'

'I'm not doing that! I have a life, and Hugh, and friends and family and my future.'

'Hugh, of course. Is that your plan for life then? Start sprogging and never have to make another decision again? The Kin will have you in their clutches well and truly, and they'll never let you go. What a perfect plan to absolve yourself of all responsibility for the rest of your life.'

'How can you say such rotten things?' I stood up too, banging my shins on the coffee table. The pain hardly registered. 'He loves me! You know what your problem is? You've never been loved. You're a cold and lonely and bitter witch.'

'Oh, I've been *loved*,' she sneered. 'And look where that got me. Stuck in a dungeon for more than a century.'

She shook her head. 'Fine, then, you make your choices. But I'm warning you, you will never, never reach your true dreams and potential unless you cut the ties with them, all the Kin, Hugh included. Stay in this spot, and you'll just get the same back to you.'

Margaret held out her hands and the server appeared out of nowhere to help slide her arms through the sleeves of her vintage Simon Chang. 'And I will say only this, for your own good. Even if you won't take the chance and come with me, stay away from the Kin and their business. No good can come of it for you.'

She gave me no opportunity to reply, for with that, she whisked out of sight, taking the last word with her, leaving me sitting in front of the dying embers with the waiter looking at me dazedly. He would have no clear recollection of what had he just witnessed.

'Uh, we're closing now,' he said as he flicked on the overhead lights. 'And here's the bill.'

I took it in my hands, speechless with rage. So much for Margaret Forsythe and her fine words and advice. Daughter of a duke, recipient of a trust fund which had grown exponentially over the past century. Not only had she refused to help me, she had stiffed me with the bill for the brandy.

CHAPTER 13

I was still furious with Margaret the next day, but I didn't have an opportunity to sit and stew about it. It was the morning of the twenty-first of June, and the Solstice celebration was that night. Mom had me up and out of bed before the nine o'clock news.

'We've got so much to do,' she exclaimed as she pulled my curtains apart, letting the sunlight pour in and smack me square between the eyes. 'We have an appointment for us both at the salon. Your hair really needs some work, you've got a whole rainbow in it, yet your roots haven't been touched for months. And I haven't said anything before this, but we've got to do something about that fringe on your forehead.'

It was true, I hadn't done anything with my hair for ages. I used to bleach and color it, and Edna had given me too-short bangs, cut on an angle by mistake. But since going to Scotland, I hadn't bothered even to get it trimmed.

But it was too early in the morning for such thoughts.

'So, eat, shower, hair and then nails,' Mom said, then she disappeared back downstairs. I wished I could feel a quarter of her enthusiasm as I dragged myself to the bathroom.

There was no way to avoid this day, I knew as I drank down the first coffee. Dad was right, if I wanted to be a part of the Kin I had to show up and be seen, even if I'd spent the past ten years trying to be invisible to them. That would be the only way to get accepted and to further my advance within their ranks.

I submitted to it all. The preening, the cutting, the polishing – because I knew it was a necessary evil. Just another rung on the ladder of my future.

When it was all done, the person who looked back at me in the mirror was hardly recognizable. I looked like the early photos of Mom when she was all dolled up to go out on the town, but different, and I don't mean because of the change in fashions. No. This new person was elegant and poised, haughty and perhaps even beautiful with all that makeup subtly shading and highlighting her eyes.

The deep midnight blue of my long gown was reflected in my eyes, and the mascara on my lashes and the smoky shadows on the lids caused them to become like deep pools, I could hardly tear my gaze away, like Narcissus in his pond, fascinated by this new me. I wanted to believe in this new woman so badly, even though I knew it was all fake, merely a skillful illusion.

I almost pinned the dragonfly brooch onto my dress. It was a habit I'd gotten into, to bring Margaret's gift with me at all times for its comforting presence. But my gown didn't require any more embellishment, and besides I was still narked at her, so I left it behind on my dresser. I tucked my phone securely into the hidden pocket of the dress.

Even Dad's eyebrows rose a notch in appreciation when I walked into the kitchen.

'You are the spitting image of your mother,' he breathed.

Mom lightly jabbed him with her elbow. 'She has lots of you in her, don't forget. The stubbornness, the idealism...' But she broke off because tears came to her eyes as she looked at me. 'I'd hug you but I can't disturb your hair.'

She gathered her tiny reticule, then looked up again at me. 'It's all so perfect. Let me take a picture to send to Hugh.'

The mention of Hugh stung a little. Yes, I was missing him, but something was niggling me. It wasn't that he'd sounded a little impatient with me the last time we spoke, no I was used to his ways and didn't take that personally. But it felt like something was coming between us, and I searched inside myself for whatever it could be, but came up empty handed. If something was bothering him enough, he would tell me, surely.

Right now, I needed to garner my strength to face the entire Witch Kin clans. I was glad to have Mom and Dad by my side, because their first public appearance together would take the heat off my entrance. I wasn't naive enough to think that just because I had more power and was accepted by the Kin elders in Scotland, that the local Kin were going to turn around and welcome me with open arms. Prejudices died hard around here.

Unlike many of the Kin, Dad never bothered with hiring a driver to bring us to the Temple. We just piled into his dark SUV, the three of us, although I found it an inelegant struggle to hoist myself up into the back seat. I was nervous about the evening ahead of us, so I chattered inanely all along the way up Allandale Road and then on to the hidden laneway to the Temple in the middle of Pippy Park.

And I found that when I wasn't speaking through my grudges, Dad became an almost likable human being.

'Why didn't we take the Batmobile? That's a way cooler car than this truck.'

Jon laughed. 'Because it only fits two, if you recall. You'd have to leave me behind, and that's not fair.'

'I should get my driver's license while I'm home.' My mind was flitting along from topic to topic like a butterfly. I could hardly sit still with nervousness. I wouldn't know many people at this thing except Sasha, my half-sister, that was about it, and I'd spent the past few years hating her and her friends. 'Would you let me drive it if I did?'

'Not a chance,' he pretended to growl. 'I'll get you a nice sensible Tesla.'

The drive didn't last long enough. We were soon pulling into the Temple grounds.

Not many Normal people know about the Kin Temple. It's located in the middle of Pippy Park, an old estate donated to the city by some wealthy geezer, a Kin of course. The building itself sits directly on the convergence of ley lines, in a tiny dale in the untouched boreal forests of the parkland, with only an unassuming narrow unpaved lane leading to it. It's warded to keep Normals from stumbling on it, much like the Avalon Wilderness must be, and is to all intents and purposes invisible to their eyes.

The vehicle turned a corner, and I peered through the front seats to get my first sight ever of the Temple. It was Grecian in appearance, with long white columns holding up the portico, and the huge building looked to be created from marble. It glowed in the light of the full moon, sparkled with an ethereal light and I could tell there was no Veil here. No need of it, for there were no Normals here to protect.

Not even as servants, for that class was made up of those super naturals whose appearance was deemed acceptable to the Kin, meaning there were no trolls or goblins in attendance.

Discreet lamps served to showcase the magnificence of the structure, and to light the pathways in the gardens.

A lot of fancy cars and limousines were already in the parking lot to the side, and the Kin offered a valet service for those who required it.

We exited his vehicle, me trying my best to be graceful as I hopped out of the back in those foolish high heel sandals. I'd spent the better part of an hour that day taking a crash course in walking-on-stilts, and I just about had my ankles under control. I did wobble a little as I looked up at grand bevelled glass doors thrown open wide, and the beautiful witches who thronged inside.

'Chin up,' Mom whispered for courage for both of us. Her eyes were glowing and she seemed to be in her element, and so she should be. She had no reason to be nervous. Marian was truly beautiful tonight in her violet-shot silk gown, and even more than the skillfully applied make-up, she was lit from within from her joy and love for Dad. Yes, it was her first time here too, and she didn't even technically belong, but she was walking in on the arm of Jon de Teilhard and no one would dare argue her right to be there.

Yet I, who had his blood coursing through my veins, I was the one who had to force myself to approach the grand doorway, for I'd spent too much of my life terrorized by the very people who waited inside. Overcome with reluctance, I trailed behind my parents as if to hide behind them, but at the last moment Dad turned and brought me forward so that we entered as a united family group.

There was an almost imperceptible pause in the flow and chatter when we presented ourselves at the head of the shallow wide stairs leading into the main room. Eyes flashed toward us, fans flicked before mouths, even the musicians reached a tiny moment between the movements of their etudes.

It lasted not longer than a blink of an eye, though, and then part of the throng broke off to welcome Dad, and thus Mom and me, into their midst.

It was a face I vaguely knew from election posters, some elected official in the government. The political heads were mostly all Kin, at least the Conservatives were. His toothy lopsided smile and long nose were now jawing on to Dad and Mom about how it was a great night for the Kin, how the Cons were planning on developing the oil fields and bla bla bla. Who really cared?

I looked around in apprehension, searching for Sasha but not really wanting to see her. Yet I knew no one else here, and I hated the thought of hanging around with my parents for the whole ball. How pathetic would that be?

There she was, her and the other Kin kids grouped around the bar. All adults now of course like myself, but inside I was still that quivering high school kid.

CHAPTER 14

'There's Sasha,' Mom pointed out to me, almost pushing me in her direction. 'God, she's turned out as gorgeous as her mother, hasn't she? Whyn't you go on over and reconnect?'

I stubbornly stayed firmly in place, in as much my heels would allow. Sasha was standing with her crowd, the very same ones who had been prepared to kill me last September, her French boyfriend Seth leading the pack. I shivered involuntarily. They *had* killed that poor half-blood, Tracey, they'd all participated in it even if it was Seth who had plunged the sacrificial knife in her heart. I didn't really have much to talk about with them.

Not to mention the fact that my own mother's return had effectively split up Sasha's parents' marriage. I was not expecting a warm welcome from my half-sibling. I gulped as Mom gave me a firmer shove between my shoulder blades and then I tottered over in their direction with as much poise as I could muster.

Their conversation died as I drew near. All twelve of them were there, Seth had been the thirteenth witch in their coven, and this dozen had always been a tightknit pack. I saw the beginnings of a sneer on the face of the guy who wore his hair in a quiff. For the first time, I noticed his weak chin and the beginnings of pudge around his middle.

I wondered how he looked without his glamor applied, and I remembered the face looking back at me in the mirror. This witch hadn't needed spells or glamors to make her beautiful, so I threw my shoulders back and to lend me strength, I pretended I was Margaret Forsythe. I was a far more powerful witch than any of them now, I'd been chosen to study under the Venerable Nachtan, and while I didn't have a trust fund to soften my life, I had a brilliant future ahead of me in which I would travel the world and really be someone.

In twenty years, I might even be an Elder, while they would all still be here at the Avalon Temple, still gossiping amongst themselves, growing fat and lazy and living the exact same lives as their parents. My pace perked up.

'Hi, Sasha,' I said, gracing only her with my greeting, and I sniffed in the direction of the others.

'Hey,' she said, eyeing me up and down. 'Look at you. You cleaned up nice. Lost some weight, too.'

Had I? I glanced down at myself then immediately realized my error when she laughed. Okay. It was going to be like that then.

'And Montreal, I presume?' She nodded her head toward my dress. 'It's gorgeous. I was thinking of buying that model last year. Good thing I didn't! That would have been too embarrassing, eh?'

The group around her were starting to break out in smiles hidden behind their hands, taking their lead from Sasha.

'Though, of course,' she continued smoothly. 'You wouldn't have known. This is your first ball, right?'

And last one in the Avalon Temple, if I could help it. The heat rose in my face. I comforted myself with the thought that if I wanted to, with a flick of my hand I could blow them all against the far wall. But of course I wouldn't do that. Any show of magic at the Kin ball would be in extreme bad taste. Only a child unable to control herself would do such a thing. I took a deep breath and swept past Sasha toward the bar, forcing the pack to break up to let me through.

'What's the house champagne?' I asked airily. 'Dom Perignon?' I nodded to the vampire behind the bar.

I could act as rich and fake as anyone. I was fuming inside, although I was pretty sure I was hiding it well. I inclined my head at Sasha, ignored the rest, and walked carefully across the room, praying I would not make a misstep in those bloody heels.

Feeling sick to my stomach by this time, I found a large potted palm to lurk behind as I sipped the chilled champagne. I'd better make myself comfortable for I'd probably be hiding out for the rest of the night. The air was cool here, with the French doors flung wide open behind me and the heavy smell of lilacs perfuming the air.

From this spot I could keep an eye on Sasha and company, for they had seen the direction I took and were conferring together. I tensed, preparing myself for a quick getaway if the occasion demanded.

The music had started into a waltz, and the center of the room came alive with bodies gracefully dipping and swaying and swirling. It was just as well that no one would ask me to dance, for I had no clue how to perform on the dance floor.

Hugh should have been here by my side. In his arms I could have learned to dance the steps, allowing him to lead. The Midsummer Solstice was one of the biggest celebrations in the year amongst the Kin, a time to welcome the summer and life and continuing prosperity. You were supposed to be with your nearest and dearest.

But he was in China, or Taiwan. He'd chosen his career over my needs, and that was right, I told myself. We
were going to be a power couple in the Kin.

I gazed at Mom and Dad, joyously sweeping through
the room, no thought of anyone else, nothing in their
heads but their own happiness. I felt bereft.

'Looks like I'm not the only one left abandoned.'

I whirled around at the familiar voice, tensing and
automatically bringing up my mental armor all around
me.

Cate lounged elegantly against the pillar, her darkness
in contrast to the white of the marble. So much like her
daughter, but so much more in every way. Sharper, more
beautiful, more sophisticated and even more confident.
Her raven locks flowed into her black gown all covered
with tiny diamonds, shining like the very night sky itself.

'Relax,' she drawled. 'And drink up. What is left for
us rejects, but to get stinking drunk?' She upended her
champagne flute and swallowed it all down. I did the
same, to give me courage.

At a wave of her wrist, a waiter came by and she put
her empty flute on his tray, and relieved him of two full
ones. I placed my empty next to hers, and she handed
me the fresh glass.

She flashed a smile at me, her black eyes dancing. It
almost looked genuine, but I remained tense, anticipat-
ing the first of her daggers.

'I hear good things about you,' she said. 'You've ex-
ceeded all my expectations.'

Her expectations? The only things she had foreseen
for me was a quick extermination on the historic bon-
fires for half-bloods.

My eyes darted left and right, looking for an escape,
but all I could see was the deep red of Sasha's gown as
she and her coven slowly followed the path I'd just tak-
en. I was cornered, the potted plant and column behind
me, my enemies on every other side.

Cate's glance followed mine, pausing as she watched her daughter making her insidious way toward where we stood. The narrowed eyes of my dreaded high school enemies belied their laughter as they searched the crowd for me.

The older witch's gaze was now on me and I was forced against my will to look up at her. Was that sympathy in those dark eyes? Surely not. I must be mistaken.

'Come, let's leave this dreary crowd of happy people,' she said lightly, turning to the French doors behind her, opening up an avenue of escape for me. 'It's a beautiful night, and I don't believe you've seen the Temple gardens yet.'

I didn't have a lot of choice in the matter. I could stay where I was and be cornered by the coven, or follow Cate's advice and go with her through the open doors and hope to lose myself outside.

I cautiously followed, throwing a glance over my shoulder in hopes that Mom or Jon was looking my way, so they'd know to come rescue me from Cate's clutches. But they'd danced themselves to the far end of the room by now, lost in their little world of two.

Why did I go with Cate? Why didn't I ditch her the moment I hit the open air? Curiosity, I suppose, and I knew even she wouldn't dare hurt me, not here, not tonight at the Solstice Ball. She'd never extended the slightest invitation or welcome my way before, and that alone would have made me curious as to her motives.

More important, I wanted to find out why she had advised the Kin to send me back home to betray my friend, and why Eldric had specifically sent his regards. I wanted answers from this witch.

The walled garden of the Temple was lit only by the full moon's silver beams. The center of the space was given over to formal gardens laid out in a circle, divided in a cross, full of every sweet smelling plant that grew in this northern hemisphere. The almost sickly perfume of peonies and lilac still, the harbingers of summer, but beneath those were lower tones in a full rich palate. Herbs, yes, rosemary and oregano and mint. It smelled green and floral like a hothouse.

But I couldn't linger there, for she'd disappeared into a small opening in a cedar hedge to our right, not pausing to see if I followed. Pale statues loomed out of hidden niches, small bowers behind curtains of flowering clematis to hide secret trysts, and still she walked on. The only way to track her was by listening carefully for her lightly tapping heels on the flagstones.

It took some time for me to realize that Cate unerringly led me into the heart of a maze for suddenly, there before me the narrow hedge-lined path opened up into another square, this one tiny, with only a statue of Diana in the center.

Diana the Huntress.

I stood at the exit, still shadowed by the cedars, and watched as she sat on the central stone bench. She was like a shadow herself, a dark smear with only the diamonds splashed across her hair and dress catching the light.

'What do you want from me?'

She laughed, a genuine enough sound. 'Oh Dara, let's let bygones be bygones. What is done is in the past, and we have only the future ahead of us.'

Cate patted the bench seat next to her. 'Come. Don't hover over me as if you're about to take flight. You'll never find your way out of the labyrinth, not by yourself. It's specially warded, we use it to teach the kids.'

It was easier to walk now, perhaps the champagne had something to do with correcting my balance, and I moved gracefully toward her, my head held high but on full alert.

She settled in as if for a long comfortable chat. I couldn't believe that I was sitting next to Cate of all witches, without her slicing me open with her words and barbs. I perched on the edge of the bench, ready to take off the moment she started in at me. I swallowed nervously, we were alone in this labyrinth, there were no witnesses. I wondered if anyone had seen us go off together.

My phone, while it fitted perfectly into my dress and was invisible when I stood or walked, dug into my waist line once I sat down. There wasn't much give to the fabric. I dug it out and held it loosely in my hand

'So I hear you and Hugh are quite the item now,' she observed.

I tensed even more. Last fall she'd wanted to match Hugh with her daughter, and had told me in no uncertain terms to back off from him, that he'd never want to be bothered with a humble halfling like me.

'Yes,' I managed to say. 'We've become... close.'

'That is simply marvellous,' she purred. 'He's an up-standing member of the Kin and with him on your side, all doors are open to you.'

I waited for the knife jab about us both being half-bloods, but it didn't happen.

'Yours is a very different situation,' she observed. 'You had a rough start to it, with Jon not giving you all the advantages you deserved.'

That was because of you, you bitch! I screamed in my mind, but I said nothing aloud. My hands were clenched so tight my newly manicured nails were almost breaking through the skin on my palms.

'But you've come so far in such a short time.' She turned to look at me, forcing me to also turn my head and meet her straight on and I was shocked at what I saw in her face.

Or what I didn't see. There was no meanness, no narrowing of her eyes in spiteful anger. Cate was relaxed and gazing at me with... pride?

'I thought you hated me,' I blurted before my mind caught up with my tongue.

Her expression became unreadable for the briefest split second of time, a bland mask automatically lowered and then just as quickly it lifted again and she was laughing merrily.

'Oh, to be young again and so full of passion.' She shook her head wryly. 'Our families are so intertwined, you're like one of my own, just... removed a little.'

I couldn't believe the words I was hearing. Had the fairies taken the real Cate and switched her out with this pleasant, kind woman? I hoped fervently that they would keep the old one locked underground, if that was the case.

'But you don't resent Mom and D... Jon, getting back together again?' I had to ask it. It might appear rude, but I had assumed that my mother and I would be headliners on Cate's 'to-kill' list, yet she was acting so friendly and warm towards me. It just wasn't natural.

She smiled wryly. 'It threw me for a loop at first,' she admitted. 'But then I realized that by them confirming their love and commitment, they had bestowed the greatest blessing on me. They showed me that it's important to be happy, and their actions have freed me to be all that I can be. I'm no longer chained to being a mother and the wife of Jon de Teilhard. I can be Cate Huxor again, and resume my life where I left off all those years ago.'

She slid her eyes to me. 'You planning to marry Hugh?'

I shrugged. 'We've talked about it.' I smiled a little, my pride showing through. He hadn't wanted Sasha, he'd chosen me. 'He wants to give me the family engagement ring.'

She shook her head vehemently before I'd even finished my words. 'Don't do it! Don't accept it, at least not yet. He'll just be binding you to bear his heirs. And once that starts, you won't see Dara de Teilhard for many a year.'

I could only gape in shock at the force of her reaction. If I could have ever in a million years prior to
this evening imagined this conversation, I would have
known without a doubt that Cate's discouragement was
only for her own gain. Yet, her words were all about me,
not her or her daughter, and concern for my future. Any
rebuke I might give her flew out of my mind.

She was quiet for a moment. 'Why do you think his
mother wants to pass on the ring to you?'

'She says it's ugly and clunky and she doesn't want to
be responsible for it anymore...' I swallowed quickly and
added, 'But she was joking.'

'Was she?' I felt Cate's eyes sidle over to me again. 'Or
does passing the ring on to you mean she would then be
free of its burden? Once you start bearing the children,
then she can pick up the pieces of herself again.'

I started, because Hugh had in fact talked of beginning
a family. It had been quite cozy, the way he put it, we
could be all settled on his family estate and bringing up
a brood of magical youngsters. I hadn't thought about
my career or aspirations for life in the light of the rosy
picture he'd painted.

'Be careful, that's all I'm saying. With your heightened
powers there will be many who want to use you,' she
said, staring unseeing at the hedges in front of us. 'Who
will be jealous of you. Him included.'

'He's not jealous...,' I began but faltered. Hugh had
been short with me, impatient. I'd noticed a spark of
something, that last evening at Edinburgh, and had told
myself that Hugh Sabiston would have no reason to be
jealous of me. Perhaps I'd been wrong.

'Men, even the most brilliant of them, tend to feel
threatened by a more powerful woman,' she said bitterly.
'But I'll say no more on that matter. This is something we
all have to learn the hard way.'

CHAPTER 15

My mind was reeling by now. It was as if she had held a lamp over the murky bits of my mind, the thoughts that I desperately clamped down on because I couldn't bear for them to be true. But Cate Huxor of all witches had lifted them out of obscurity, held them up and let the moonshine and champagne wash the muck off them and shown them in their own legitimate light.

'Never mind all that,' she said, with another sidelong look at me. 'I'm just an old woman nattering. I really brought you here to talk about you and your future.'

I mentally shook my head to clear those unwanted thoughts out of it, and tried to pay attention to the conversation's new turn.

'I can tell you've matured a lot since you left,' she observed. 'This is a good time for you to choose to return, for there are things happening, things brewing. You can be very useful at this moment in time.'

Choose to return, indeed. I was here solely because she had demanded that I be returned, in order to use me and abuse my friendship with Brin. I wasn't afraid to reveal to her that I knew the depth of her treachery.

'Why did you encourage the Kin to send me back home?'

She smiled as if taken aback at my abruptness. 'You were the obvious choice,' she drawled. 'You have an acquaintance within the Elven community, one who is quite enmeshed in the political movement we see rising in the future. The elves are well-known for keeping to themselves, not allowing outsiders in. Who is better placed than you to find out the extent of their work?'

'To spy on my friend,' I said flatly. I wasn't going to let her pretty words disguise what was really required of me.

'All information is valuable,' she said softly, then she paused to sip her champagne. 'Tell me, what do you think of their motives?'

'Motives?' I clutched my own glass. How much did she know of the Dark Elf Eldric's involvement?

'What they're requesting. A lifting of the Veil, freedom for all super naturals and even the humans caught behind it.'

The official Kin line was that the Veil was a necessary evil. After all, it profited the Kin, and that was the sole reason for it being put into place in the first place. Anyone who voiced otherwise would be branded a rebel, a misfit, an outcast, and I'd had enough of that to last me all my life. Anything said to Cate, even in the privacy of this secretive maze, anything could and would be used against me, twisted to fit her devious purposes. I chose my words carefully.

'The Veil keeps the Normals safe from the threat of the super naturals.'

'Oh well done,' she replied. 'That's straight from the text book, word for word. Quite proper.'

She turned her head, twisting her long neck to look at me. 'Now. Give me your honest answer,' she said. 'You've been in Scotland. You've seen firsthand that it's possible for both to live side by side in relative peace. And you've seen the conditions behind the Veil here in our little part of North America. I can assure you, you may think it's horrendous here, but wait until you visit New Orleans. Middle America. The Florida swamps.'

She leaned in to whisper. 'Alabama.'

I could feel the softness of her breath on my exposed neck. She didn't need to expand on her words, for the pictures she suggested sent chills up my spine. Take the worst of the worst in human history, and multiply it by a hundred, and that's what you'd get behind the Puritanical Veil. I swivelled my head to look right into her eyes.

'How can we continue to say that this benefits any living creature?' Her whispers were so quiet as to be almost swallowed up by the surrounding hedges.

I couldn't believe that this was Cate sitting here next to me, speaking such forbidden thoughts aloud. Cate, hardened, vicious Cate, the scion of a line who had benefitted more than most from the Veil. She was bordering on treason right now, and taking a big chance speaking these words to me. I was no longer a nobody, a despised half-blood, I was now Dara Martin de Teilhard, latest favorite of the Kin, someone who was going places. And if I chose to turn her in, well...

She leaned back against the stone bench. 'I know you are sympathetic to their cause. As am I.'

We sat in silence for a couple of minutes. I had to let this sink in. Cate would have no reason to lie to me, but where was she going with this conversation?

'You are in a unique position,' she continued at last. 'To help this groundswell of movement, to bring about lasting changes in the way things are done. To change the very course of history. This can be done without bloodshed.'

But it wasn't just a popular movement, as she seemed to think. Eldric was heavily involved and that would not auger well for a peaceful transition. How much did she know? How much could I tell her? How much *should* I tell her?

I swallowed. 'I thought the Kin were in talks already with the super naturals about lifting the Veil.'

She laughed. 'Yes, and you know that will take years, decades, even longer before anything changes. We need to act now, to help the movement achieve its goals.'

I made up my mind. Even if this was Cate and we'd never had a happy history, it felt right at this moment, and I wanted this burden lifted from me, but still I spoke cautiously, feeling her out. 'It's not just the super naturals who live in town, you know. There are others involved.'

Cate became still. 'You mean Eldric,' she said softly, her voice carrying only as far as my ears.

I nodded. She knew already. 'So I've heard.'

'Yes,' she said as if reading my mind. 'Eldric. I've been in contact with him, and despite his rather overbearing manner, he does not have a fullscale rebellion in mind. Not, that is, if he can achieve his ends in a more peaceful manner.'

Thank God I didn't have to confess to the two meetings of Eldric myself. I could keep that a secret, for no one needed to know the extent of my involvement. But that relief was short lived.

'I know you have met with him,' she said, still under her breath. 'And I also know you haven't told a soul, not Jon at any rate. And I believe that is for the good.'

She drew a deep breath then continued. 'You see, Eldric's involvement could be... misconstrued in the eyes of the Kin. And your silence about those meetings with him, well, that could also be misinterpreted by those who don't hold you in esteem, your enemies, and despite your acceptance into the Kin, don't fool yourself. You have many.'

I lifted my eyes to meet hers straight on, hardly believing my own daring. 'And you, Cate? Do you count yourself among them?'

There was no guile in that perfect face. 'We've had our differences,' she said slowly. 'But that was not of your doing. I believe we are united in this common cause.' She smiled, such a sweet unexpected expression on her porcelain perfection, yet it was tinged with pain.

'I can only ask, no, beg of you, do not breathe a word of Eldric to Jon in your reports. I, more than anyone, know the ways of the Kin. If they find out you've been consorting with the likes of the Dark Elves, even in the line of duty, then your very tenuous position will topple. The future you dream about will become ashes, even with Hugh by your side. And along with this will fall everything we've built so far.'

She reached out and took my hand. I visibly flinched at the coolness of her touch, yet she lingered, her gaze insistent.

I nodded dumbly, for I recognized the truth in her words. I'd been an outcast from the Kin for too long to truly, deep down, believe in their total acceptance of me, and the worms of self-doubt had burrowed inside me for too many years for them to be fully excised. My shoulders sank. 'But, what will I put in the report for Jon?'

'You need only tell him of what has passed between you and your friend Brin. He won't be looking for anything further, he doesn't expect much else. Be honest with the information you give him, just omit any mention of Eldric or your visit to Rhovan. What he doesn't know won't hurt him.'

She smiled and stretched then, gracefully got to her feet, and I stood up too. Glancing behind us, she reached back down to the bench. 'Your phone,' she said. It flashed to life with the movement. Her face twisted into a smile when she looked upon the photo of Hugh and me taken in a more innocent time. Had it been less than two weeks ago? 'Can't be without that.'

I took it back without a word, concentrating on avoiding her cool touch.

'So,' she said, quirking an eyebrow at me. 'The Venerable Nachtan. Learning lots?'

'Theory. Lots of the theoretical aspects,' I said through gritted teeth. 'Which is the necessary basis of everything, right?'

She laughed, that silvery tinkle like the moonlight itself. 'Come round to the house sometime. I think I have some practicalities to show you, to help you navigate your future within the Kin. It's not things you'll learn from the textbooks, believe me. You deserve that much.'

I stopped short and turned to her. 'What?' I blurted out before I thought. This single word was not a request for further information but an expression of disbelief. Had I heard correctly, an offer of assistance from my hither-to dreaded enemy Cate?

But she took my question at face value. 'Politics,' she answered decisively. 'The ways of the Kin.'

'Not magic, then?'

She shook her head. 'There's little I could teach you in that respect, although... But it's a harsh, cruel and cold world out there, and you'll need a map to get you through.'

'Really? You're offering to help me, without making demands on me?' My voice was flat, the disbelief still present. Not even Margaret Forsythe, the witch I'd come to look upon as my mentor, not even she was willing to do that. No, Meg had demanded I leave everything I held dear in return for her tutelage.

Cate faced me. The moon was at her back, so all I could pick out was her outline and the diamonds in a shower across her hair. 'I know you recognize the importance of keeping quiet, about Eldric, about us meeting in this manner. The Kin have wronged you in so many ways, Dara,' she said softly. 'I will try to make it all up to you. You are, after all, our future.'

She led me out of the maze without another word.

CHAPTER 16

'Where have you been all evening?' Mom broke off the dance, leaving her partner as she skipped over to the French door. I had just entered by myself, Cate having slipped off after we'd exited the maze. She hugged me. 'Ooh, you're chilly.'

She in contrast felt warm, almost feverish in her gaiety. This was perhaps her evening even more than mine, and she had every right to be ecstatic. After all those years, her and Dad were now officially 'out', he'd presented them as a couple in front of all the Kin at this oh so important social occasion.

'Yeah, I was out in the garden,' I said, still dazed from my encounter with Cate and our conversation.

'I'm so glad you're getting re-acquainted with people.'

I gave a start. How could she know? But then a few of Sasha's friends came through the doors behind me, and I relaxed. She thought I was bothering with those idiots. Well, I'd let her continue to think that. She wouldn't be too happy to know I'd spent the past hour speaking with Cate.

'How is your night going?' I asked her as I linked arms and drew her back into the ballroom.

Mom giggled, high on champagne and love and her apparent acceptance into the Kin. She didn't see the occasional lowered brow or frown sent her way behind her back, but I did. I'd been attuned to this for so long, it was second nature to me to be aware of threats from all angles. After all, I'd been a half-blood witch who'd successfully lived through high school with the Kin kids.

I was a survivor.

'You haven't danced yet! How can you not dance at your first ball?' Without warning, she pulled me onto the floor and attempted to sweep me into the waltz. But she hadn't reckoned on my complete lack of internal rhythm and inability to place my feet into the accepted movement of the dance. That was one big difference between us. I'd never learned to move my body smoothly to music, at least not to match with another person. Guess I'd always had a different drummer beating in my head.

I couldn't take a step without squashing her elegant sandals, and we lasted no more than a couple of minutes on the floor, before she collapsed, giggling at the pair of us.

She took my arm as she led me back out of the center. 'No matter, there's time enough to learn. But it looks like the dining room is open now,' she said. 'I'm starved! Let's go see what kind of spread the Kin have for us.'

Before we could approach the food, however, my father intercepted us, smiling at Mom's exhilaration. He took my other arm and hooked it around his own elbow. 'You'll eat later, Dara. It's time for the service now.'

Mom screwed up her face. 'Oh, Jon, does she have to? I was looking forward to showing off my gorgeous daughter to the Abernathy's.'

'Nothing is compulsory,' he said, and turned to look at me. 'But I think it would be a good idea. To show your allegiance to the Kin, to prove you're committed to the ideals.'

'This is the first I've heard about any kind of service.' I looked around the large ballroom. The majority of the dancers were flowing towards the dining room where I could see vast quantities of every kind of food laid out on linen topped tables. There was another large door opposite the one where the food was held. It too was open, but it was dark inside and few were giving heed to it.

'Not everyone attends,' he noted. He shot a glance towards Sasha and her crowd. By the looks of them, they'd already imbibed more than their share of champagne, and were loudly pushing through the crowd to be the first to get to the delicacies on offer. At least they'd temporarily forgotten about terrorizing me. The lines round his mouth tightened just a little. 'It's a sign of respect, to give thanks for all we have. I'd like you to come this first time. You can decide afterward if you choose to attend again.'

I got the message loud and clear, and I pulled myself up a little straighter and let go of Mom's grasp. 'I think I should, Mom, just to see.' And finally, at last, for the first time in my life, I had the chance to be the good daughter, the one who did what was expected of her, the one Jon could be proud of. My heart was thudding in my ears. I finally had the chance to win his approval.

'Me too?' Mom asked.

He shook his head gently. 'Sorry, Marian. Only Kin witches.'

She breathed a sigh of relief and leaned over to kiss my cheek. 'Thank God for that. See you later, sweetie. I'll save some of the best dishes for you, I promise.' And she floated off in the direction of the dining room.

Me and Dad looked at each other for a moment, then he smiled. 'Come on,' he urged, leading me toward the darkened doorway opposite.

I held back a little. I'd never been to a *service* before in my life, for neither Mom nor my aunt were Christians, and both had refused to allow me to enter the hallowed grounds of churches. I had no idea what to expect. 'What is this all about?'

'Like I said, it's a service to give thanks,' he answered. 'There are some who think this is an outdated anachronism, superstition if you will. I'm afraid the Solstices and Equinoxes have downgraded into an excuse to party four times a year, but there was a time... A time when the Kin understood their position in the world, and they respected that a far greater power than any individual was behind the very essence of life, and I still believe it behooves us to recognize this.'

He watched then as a food fight broke out in the dining hall, some teenagers throwing buns and hors d'oevres for the hell of it. No adult was checking their behavior, and his mouth tightened again. 'If nothing else, it keeps us humble.'

'Will I... will I be expected...?' I wasn't quite sure how to express my fear. From watching TV and movies, I knew that services often entailed responses and singing, the participants already knowing their parts. I was afraid I was going to stand out, look like an idiot for my ignorance.

He grinned. At me, with me and I melted inside. It had been so long since we'd been alone together and not screaming at each other. I felt at that moment I would do anything to keep that smile on my father's face as he looked at me.

'You'll be fine. No one'll be expecting anything from you.' He drew me inside the open doorway, and then it shut behind us. All sounds of the ball and music and laughter were immediately cut off.

'It's called the Drawing of the Moon,' he whispered in my ear. 'It's not the main ceremony, that's just for Elders, later on this evening. This is a simple service, but I hope you feel it.'

It wasn't so dark in there, not when my eyes adjusted to the different level of light. Sconces burned all around the dark panelled walls, they appeared to be gas lit, not electric, I could tell by the faint flickers of the flames behind the protective glass globes. They gave off just enough light for me to see the outlines of the space and the people within.

It was a far smaller room than any I'd yet seen in the Temple, but the ceiling rose way above our heads to a circle, which then stretched up like a tube, or a steam ship funnel, to end in a huge circular skylight through which I could make out the Milky Way. The round space we stood in was totally empty of furnishings, no altar or pews.

The few people in attendance were hushed. Dad reached into a closet by the door and handed me a robe, a black silk robe much like that worn by the Elders in Scotland, and I put my arms through it and shrugged it on my shoulders till it was sitting comfortably. Despite the lightness of the fabric, the garment had a heavy weight to it as if years of tradition were woven into the weft of the silk.

I proudly took my place in the circle of Kin with Dad at my side, my back straight and head held high. I was the only one of Jon's children to attend with him that evening.

The ceremony itself was, as Dad had said, very simple, so much so that even I could participate. At a given moment, the ring of witches began to softly hum, each with a different note according to the pitch of their individual voices and a split second later a sliver of the moon appeared far above our heads. I easily joined into the harmony, letting my voice naturally attune to the others in the fellowship of our single notes.

A woman began a soft chanting. Her age was revealed through the lines in her voice. I didn't understand the language but it was lilting and flowing like the ocean waves, building, then falling, then building and falling again. All the while the entire group watched the disc of the moon imperceptibly travel, inch by inch over the skylight until it completely filled the circle.

The congregation paused as if in wonder at that moment. I know I did, feeling an incredible lightness of being and fulfillment at the completion of the disc, the moon's light shining down upon us like a spotlight from the heavens. We all drew in closer to each other to stand in that silvery light, to bathe in it.

How could I find words to describe this feeling? It wasn't magic as I knew it, that prickly blue energy, it was something deeper, more basic, more internal to the soul. Perhaps it was my very soul itself singing. All I knew was that as the moon's circle passed, slowly, out of the skylight, I was left with a feeling of replenishment and joy such as I had never experienced, as if I'd awoken from the soundest of sleeps or I'd been cleansed of sin by the purity of the moonlight, and I only wanted to sing my praises of the earth and all who dwelled upon it and whatever force had created this wonder.

As the last of our notes faded softly away with the final passing of the disc from the skylight, the room was left again in the dimness of the flickering gas lamps. Nothing had changed, but it felt like everything had changed. Dad turned to me, I could see his love for me in his eyes, and I knew my own must be reflecting it right back to him.

'You felt it.'

I nodded, unable to speak.

And then an unprecedented thing happened, he reached out and hugged me, and it was as if the past decade of hurt and pain had never happened, washed away in the tide of the moon. It lasted only for a moment but it was enough.

The group had broken up by now, the main door reopened and the lights of the ballroom streamed in again. He hung up our robes and we walked together into the bright lights and noise.

'I'll need to attend the deeper service now,' he said. 'One day, you'll be inducted into that. But I just want to thank you.'

'Thank *me*?' I almost squealed, but there were no squeals or excited highs in me, I was so energized with the good feelings of the service. 'This was amazing. I've never felt...' How could words describe it?

He nodded. "I'm glad it affected you this way.'

'You do this every Solstice?

'And Equinox,' he replied.

Where ever I was in the world in three months' time, I vowed I would experience this again.

Mom found us, a plate in her hand all piled with goodies and pastries. 'Come on, sweetie, time to eat!' She handed me my dish and suddenly my physical hunger was overwhelming.

'I'll see you back at the house.' Dad was speaking to Mom. And then I felt him turn to me. 'Don't forget the report. I'll need it tomorrow morning,' he murmured casually into my ear. Then he left.

I nearly choked on the mushroom turnover, the flaky crumbs of pastry inhaled and setting me to sputtering and coughing as I tried to loosen them from my throat.

The report, I thought miserably to myself as Mom fussed and handed me a glass of water to wash it all down. The report of the happenings amongst the elves, the one which would omit any mention of Eldric, of my forced visit to Rhovan.

I had to lie to my father and to the Kin, even if it was a lie of omission. My future, all my ambitions were at stake. I looked up and through my tearing eyes I could see Cate standing a small distance off, a smile on her face and a warning in her eye.

It went against every grain inside me to trust Cate. Yet, she was on the side of good, of peace, of freedom, while my father inevitably was on the side of the Kin.

CHAPTER 17

A limo had been arranged to pick us up, as Dad had to stay for the 'deeper' ceremony, whatever that entailed. When we got home, I pleaded exhaustion and ran to my room.

But I wasn't tired, nothing like it. Energy raced through my veins and the moon was still on the horizon, fat and thick, and I needed to sort out my head. Too much had happened in too short a time and I had to help settle my mind.

So I went for a midnight bike ride. It was quite late as I rode my bike through the dark streets, few cars on the roads at this hour. There was far too much to think about and to sort out and I needed to expend my physical energy so I could bring order to my mind. The whole hour I raced and put my consciousness only to the physical and pushing myself, and it was only after I had purged this did I turn my mind back on.

Dad wanted a report in the morning on anything I'd learned thus far. I laughed bitterly as I coasted along the flat of Warbury Street, my body relaxed now and catching my breath again. I could tell him, I supposed, I could tell him of his newly favorite daughter being whisked away to Rhovan, that mythical land in the depths of the Wilderness, and how our lives had been threatened, mine and Brin's, if I didn't go along with Eldric and his demands to turn double agent for him.

But Cate had begged me to say nothing of the Dark Elf, and said she would fix it with him. Why the hell would I trust Cate, of all people? I had always thought the witch despised me because of the accident of my birth, yet tonight she had been warm. Charming. Open. Real. On the side of freedom by working behind the scenes for a peaceful removal of the Veil.

I'd been flattered by her attention, I would be the first to admit, but her words were true. I *was* special. I *was* headed for great things. Margaret might claim I had no need for the Kin and their 'golden carrot', but she'd never known what it was like to experience poverty. I needed something real to hold onto, not the floaty claims of asking and knowing I would receive if I had no idea of the source from which I would be getting. I had to know what I was trusting.

It was all too tangly. And I had no one to talk it over with. Margaret was pissed at me for not going along with her airy-fairy ideals. Hugh – I caught my breath. Cate had warned me that he was jealous, and I knew in my heart that she'd been correct.

I cocked my head as I replaced the bike back in the tidy garage. I could, of course, tell Dad everything. That would probably solve all my problems. In the past, most of my troubles had come about because I simply didn't share information that the Kin needed to know. I could tell Dad, and he would take action, without a doubt. But what would the nature of this action be? I sat down heavily on the back step before entering my home, trying to sort out the gnarls in my mind.

The Kin believed something was up with the elves and wanted me to act as an information gatherer on their actions and plans. Knowing my previous connec-

tion with Brin, they'd brought me back home under the
excuse of rest and relaxation in order for me to pump
my friend and spy on him. Hugh hadn't thought this was
a serious matter, he'd just advised me to kick back, see
what I could find, give it to the Kin and enjoy my vacay,
knowing I was furthering my career and earning brownie
points with even this small amount of work. Neither of
us had believed that Brin was capable of treachery or
anything more political than a peaceful demonstration
and endless nattering.

Yet look where that had gotten me thus far. Being in
the wrong place, definitely at the wrong time, I'd been
whisked away to Rhovan and quite frankly, I was in
over my head. I owed the Dark Elf king, and I had no
idea what he was going to demand of me. Pulled in all
directions with no one to give me the advice I wanted
to hear, only Cate who told me to look out for myself.

I made the decision. I would write the report based
only and accurately on my interactions with Brin and
what I had learned directly from him. My elf was harm-
less, he would never act on direct rebellion or warfare.
That would satisfy Dad and the Kin and Hugh, and Cate
and Eldric too. Then I would sit back and not be involved in any of it anymore.

....

Of course things didn't work out to be that simple. They
never did. What had I been thinking?

Not five minutes after I'd sent the report to Dad's Kin
email through my laptop than a request for a video chat
popped up. It was an unknown email address, a Kin one
I could tell. Unlike most large organizations, they didn't
go for the personalised tags. Everyone had a different
number for the Kin.org addresses.

I looked at the address nervously before opening it. Was it the bureaucracy of the Kin telling me they were unhappy with the report, that they knew I was leaving out vital information? I had to look, for to ignore it might be suspicious.

'Hello?' My voice was too quavery. I quickly swallowed and said again with more assurance, 'Hello.'

Cate's face filled the window. Her perfect smile was warm and her eyes bright.

'Dara.' Her low, smooth as velvet voice was unmistakable. 'So glad we made contact last night. Are you free for a little tennis today?'

I stared at her, trying to keep my face blank. What the hell? 'I don't play the game,' I said slowly.

'What are you talking about?' She laughed playfully, so relaxed. 'Everyone plays tennis, or at least they should. It's the easiest thing in the world. Come up to the house and I'll teach you. Our court is sadly underused these days. Two o'clock. And after that, we'll have tea in the gazebo. Oh, and wear your tennis whites.'

I had to go, if even just to tell her I wanted to remove myself from all the politics, that I just wanted a peaceful life. I'd gone along with her request not to share the Eldric business in my report, but now I wanted to withdraw from the whole thing. I would even make up some story about a disagreement with Brin to excuse myself from further involvement. Everyone knew what touchy creatures the elves were.

Tennis whites. I stood in front of my crowded closet, searching in vain for anything that was white or even pastel in color. But I'd been semi-Goth in my style for the past five years of my life in St. John's, partly through finances and the rest from attitude, and there wasn't much to choose from. I settled on a pair of cut off jeans, Mom's old Rolling Stones t-shirt and my grungy sneakers. Nowhere near tennis whites but it was my summer uniform and would have to do.

At the appointed hour I arrived at the entrance to the estate in the center of the east end. The iron gates gleamed in the sun. I pushed my bike past them, my butt and thighs now achy and sore from last night's long ride. The sweat was quickly drying from my t-shirt.

I remembered from my few visits to Dad's estate years ago that the tennis court lay behind the mansion, shielded from the pool by a trimmed hedge. I'd always wondered how such perfect angles and straight lines were achieved from a living bush. I guess with the magic of money you could do anything.

She had just strolled onto the court from the direction of the house when I emerged through the bushes. Cate smiled at me like we were the oldest of friends and beckoned me over with her racket.

Dad's wife sure had the tennis costume thing down pat, dressed in the skimpiest tunic which barely brushed the tops of her thighs. Her long tanned legs had not an ounce of fat on them and were muscled just perfectly, nothing over developed, but lean and strong. Cate wore her raven black hair tied in a simple ponytail with a visor over her forehead to shield her from the sun. As she turned to greet me, I even saw a flick of lace below the tunic.

'Here's a racket you can use,' she said, as she proceeded to explain the rules of the game without any of the usual social niceties or greetings. This woman meant business.

'You have to learn this game,' she said as she was showing me how to hit front hand and back without straining my wrist or elbows. 'If you're going to move up and fit in with the Kin. It's a social ritual, same as golf for the men. I can teach you that too.'

She smiled at my dazed look. 'Politics is not played in the Cabinet Rooms,' she said. 'But in the activities of Class. Bet the Venerable didn't teach you that, did he?'

I swung my hand through the air just like she showed me, over and over until at last, satisfied, she said we would commence the game.

'But first,' she caught herself. 'Where are my manners? I'll introduce you to the Umpire for the day, but I believe you're already acquainted.'

And with that, a short little figure hopped out onto the court. I almost recognized the way he walked, but I told myself it couldn't be.

Instead of the rags I'd last seen on him, he was dressed in summer whites, a brand new sparkling linen suit. His feet were clad in white shoes with spats, very fine, not like the red boots I'd bought him in the Edinburgh charity shop which he'd worn with such pride as he tip-tapped down those ancient cobble stones. His old ragged wool cap had been replaced with a straw boater. He could have stepped out of the novel, The Great Gatsby.

Except he was a goblin.

'Trevor?' I blinked twice, but it was unmistakeably him. Much cleaner and shinier than when I'd last seen him in the Ice Kingdom, but still with the greenish tone to his skin despite his fine new clothes. And his head was attached to his body.

'Hello, Dara,' he smirked as he sent a leering glance at me. 'Surprise!' His fingers played with the scarf gaily tied around his scrawny neck. It must have been hiding a hell of a scar.

'I thought you were... I mean, I saw you die! How did you ...' It had been terrible after I'd let loose that volley of magic, with the ice crashing down all around our heads and panic and mayhem everywhere. We'd barely escaped with our lives, me and Mom and Fiona. And Willem, who was now securely locked up and strictly warded in punishment for all his evil deeds against the Kin.

'After you left me there for dead, y'mean?'

'You *were* dead! Your head... the dogs were eating your body, weren't they?' I couldn't believe he was here. Alive. Arguing, well, yes I could believe that. 'How is this even possible?'

'What, don't you know nothing dies in the Ice Kingdom?' He sneered. 'Ye're still a fat slag and stupid as ever.
'

I could have run over and smashed him with the racket, but I held back. He was, after all, here as a guest of Cate as I was myself.

'Trevor was a lost soul,' Cate intercepted smoothly. 'I found him on my travels and gave him the assistance he needed. And he's turned out to be a loyal associate.'

I found that hard to believe. The Trevor I'd known had only ever been loyal to his own wallet.

'But that doesn't explain how you got from there to here,' I insisted. There was no way I could let this go, and I found it difficult to understand how Cate, that sophisticated and very powerful witch could not see through the little bastard.

'With a little help from friends,' he said with a leer, which turned into a simper when he directed his gaze toward Cate.

She smiled fondly at him, then turned to me. 'The Ice Realm is a land of illusion, Dara,' she said softly. 'Even more so than our reality. You have much to learn. Over time, I will show you.'

A second later, she flicked her head, impatient to begin. 'Let's play the game,' she barked out, already heading to her end of the court. .

'It's none of your business anyway,' he whispered spitefully, determined to get the last word in. 'Ye auld cow.'

Our hostess already had her racket in the air and was about to serve. I had to scurry to get in place and attempt to volley back to her.

It being my first game of tennis ever, of course she won. And the three sets she insisted on playing after that too. I might have performed better, but my mind was still trying to figure out the puzzle of Trevor's continued existence and how the hell he got there. And why. I didn't buy Cate's claim to be the patron of the down and outs, no, not even with last night's revelation of the bright new side of her that I'd never suspected before.

No. Cate must have a good reason for bringing the goblin close to her, though what benefit he could be to her, I truly couldn't see. And I didn't trust that goblin one inch.

As I ran back and forth chasing the green ball, my mind worked overtime. Trevor hurrahed each time Cate scored and jeered whenever I missed the ball or screwed up. He was useless as an umpire, but I had a feeling that wasn't the real purpose for his presence. Cate was parading him out for me to see, a deliberate action on her part. Was she warning me, or letting me know she trusted me?

CHAPTER 18

I was huffing and puffing from my work out by the time she finally took mercy on me and called it quits. She hadn't even broken out into a sweat, her whites unstained by perspiration, her pale face barely even glowing. Of course, I recognized that she had controlled the entire game, hardly moving from her place on her side of the net as she unerringly sent the ball to the opposite side of the court I might be on at any time. A couple of times I had her on the run, though, and I was confident that with time, I would master the physical aspect of this peculiar game and learn to play it on the psychological level, just like her.

The gazebo was, thankfully, a shaded oasis in the heat of this summer sun, and she had a full afternoon tea awaiting us, a repast on the scale of the teas served in the finer hotels of London and Edinburgh. The white painted iron chair was cool on my overheated back, and I gladly drank the first glass of iced lemonade right down.

Trevor got stuck right into the cake. I could only watch with fascinated disgust as he gobbled the delicately scented lemon dessert, not bothering with a fork, but using his fingers to stuff it into his gob. He looked up to see me watching him.

'Watcher lookin' at?' He asked, crumbs spraying everywhere. Then he opened his mouth wide and stuck out his tongue at me so I could see right into his maw with the soggy chewed up cake. He didn't pay much attention to oral hygiene. I tore my eyes away from the horrible sight.

'Remind me again why you're here?' I murmured to him as Cate busied herself with topping up our refreshments.

'To bring peace into the world as we know it, stupid,' he said. 'What do you think? Although I cannae see why she brought the likes of you on board, for ye've never been much good at anything that I can tell.'

'Behave,' Cate told him absently, then she addressed me. 'So. I saw the report you submitted. Well done.'

I couldn't help but shoot a smirk at the goblin, who ignored this praise for me and helped himself to a fistful of macaroons. I couldn't bear to watch him destroy those fine delicacies, so I turned my full attention back to Cate.

She must have caught the look of disgust on my face, for she turned to Trevor. 'Be off now, you vile creature. I'll call you when you're needed.'

He looked askance, his jaw hanging open.

'Do you not have work to do?' She stared him down. He soon shut his mouth again and after shooting me the dirtiest look he could, slunk off out of the gazebo and through the hedges. I was liking Cate more and more.

'Now. The game. What did you learn this afternoon?'

I looked straight into her black eyes and knew she wasn't referring to the lopsided physical tennis matches we'd played with the goblin crowing every time she won a point. My right arm was aching and sore as I told her my observations on the psychological aspect of the game she'd played, positioning herself in the center of her side and how she had lobbed the ball constantly into different corners of mine, keeping me on the run to keep up with her.

'Brilliant.' She sat back and there was genuine pleasure on her face. 'You'll go far.'

Cate took a small sip of her lemonade. 'You realize that a lot of magic, practical magic, is like that too.'

She obviously wasn't finished her thought, so I stayed silent. 'I don't mean every day magic, spells, wards, and all that. I'm talking about defending yourself using magic.' She looked up sharply. 'I don't suppose Nachtan or Hugh...'

I shook my head. 'No. Not... as such,' I told her. 'Although at Scarp I picked up some things.' Shields, ice balls, fire bombs, but these were all child's play, literally. Any witch could do them. I felt a frisson creep up my spine, and I liked the way this conversation was headed. Cate was treating me like an equal, the powerful witch we both knew I was, and she was willing to take on my education, to teach me the things I needed to learn.

'Yes, the defensive arts are all about psychology,' she mused. 'You have to position yourself to your advantage, wear your opponent out. It's all about confidence and knowing and believing in yourself.'

Wait now. Wasn't this similar to what Margaret had been jawing on about the other night? I sat up straighter in my chair.

'I believe you haven't gained the confidence you require, despite the wonderful things that have happened to you, that you have caused to happen,' she continued. 'And yes, I'm talking about the whole Crystal Charm Stone episode of course, but also the other things.'

She leaned closer to me over the table. 'I truly believe you have gotten a raw deal from life, and I want to help you overcome all the wrong things you've picked up along the way. All the self-hatred, perhaps, not believing yourself worthy, the lack of confidence. You can overcome all those false ideas. I want you to shine and be everything you should be.'

Her words cut into my soul with their truth, as if they lifted me out of the artificial box that had been labelled 'Dara Martin', and I saw with immediate clarity the stultifying framework with which I'd defined myself for so long, a self created to keep the world and its hurts at bay. There was no way I could move on until I swept away the detritus of the old, took control of the reins of my life and began to really believe in the power of myself.

Margaret had also insisted this, but she hadn't offered to help me achieve it, not without the stipulation of giving up on my dreams and ambitions, of renouncing the Kin and the life I foresaw for myself. Cate understood, for she was of the Kin, was an important member of them. Cate knew what I needed, and knew how to help me get there.

I nodded slowly. My heart was beginning to sing in a way it hadn't for a long time. At last, someone understood my needs. The needs of Dara Martin. That this someone was Cate, this was the oddest thing, but odder things had happened during the life of Dara Martin.

'That's what I want, too,' I breathed.

She continued to stare in my eyes as if she was trying to spy into my very soul, then gave a funny little smile and nodded. 'Why don't we work together? You'll help me as I try to advance the removal of the Veil, and we'll work on getting you to the point where you will be a far, far more powerful witch than I can ever be.'

Despite the history and all the shit between Cate and me, she cared. Unlike Margaret who had stormed off when I refused to do exactly as she had advised.

'You need to accept right from the first, I'm not an easy teacher,' she said severely. 'There will be times when I demand things of you that it may not be in your nature to do. Knowing you...' She smiled to soften her words.

'Knowing you, you will be tempted to run amok and do things your own way. Understand right now, from this moment on, that is not acceptable. I am the Master at this game, and only through working closely with me, and observing what I do will you grow. And so we will assist each other in this process.'

I was ready to shake on it, but she didn't offer her hand.

Cate smiled with a warmth I had never imagined she could possess. 'Just one more thing,' she said. She hesitated as if searching for the words, then shook herself and plunged in. 'You really need to get in better shape, for I fear you lack the necessary stamina for what may be... required of you.'

'Oh, I'm good,' I assured her. 'I ride my bike every day, these hills are a great workout.'

She shook her head slightly. 'I mean strength training. You should be going to a gym every morning. One, even two hours with the weights and core work. I'd let you in on my membership but, well, it's better that we don't have a paper trail connecting us.'

I grimaced. A gym. Even a short term membership wouldn't be cheap. Besides, what did this have to do with practicing magic? I was young and fit enough already.

'Every morning at eight o'clock,' she repeated firmly. 'You'll find it's good mental discipline, it will strengthen you not just physically. And also...'

Her voice slowed and trailed off here, as if she was treading on uncertain ground. She sighed, and pushed on. 'Also, in the past, I haven't been... well, I haven't always been the best person I could be, quite frankly.' She inclined her head and shrugged in a self-deprecating manner. 'So, Jon and Marian. It's probably best you don't tell them of our partnership. Not just yet. They might not understand.'

I nodded slowly. Yeah. Too true. Even though both my parents claimed the break-up between Jon and Cate was amicable, there were still a lot of undigested grudges and wounds from the previous twenty years. I remembered the satisfaction in Mom's voice in Montreal when she saw the perfect dress for me, the one that would help me outshine Sasha. I knew Mom still held onto her grudges because, well, because she was just like me.

'In fact, feel free to pretend you still hate me,' Cate continued genially. 'Otherwise it would just lead to awkward questions. Jon, Goddess bless him, he is so idealistic and truly believes that his endless discussions will actually see movement in the lowering of the Veil in our lifetimes. Hugh, also.'

She paused again all while keeping my gaze. 'I know you love him. That's natural. But it's important that you keep him at bay for the next little while. It's not difficult to do right now as he's still overseas. Remember what I said last night. There's jealousy lurking deep inside that man, as there is in all males. His ego won't want you to shine your brightest, no matter his words. You need the space to truly grow into your potential.'

I left the estate that afternoon a changed witch. Now I had someone on my side, someone I could respect who believed in me and more to the point, was willing to go out of her way to help me achieve all my goals.

No matter our past history as enemies. Cate was proving that, more than anyone else in my life right now, she was fighting for me. As I waited on my bike for the light to change to green, I smiled. Nothing but the best, for that was what I deserved.

I rather thought Margaret would be proud of me, if she could see me now. I was gaining confidence by the day, along with my inner expectations. Wasn't that how she said I should be?

....

When I got back to the house there was a surprise waiting for me.

Hugh materialized at the back door as I approached our house. I could only stare at him, drinking in the sight of him, those gorgeous green eyes with the flash of gold deep within them caught by the lowering sun, that tousled head of curls like a fifties movie star, and those strong arms. I didn't waste a moment before I jumped right into them. Damn, it felt good to hold him, although it had been only a week since I'd last seen him in Edinburgh. It felt like a month.

'Why didn't you tell me?' I finally managed to gasp out, then I reached up with my mouth and wouldn't let him answer.

After a moment, or an hour, he broke off our kiss and gave me another deep squeeze.

'Tell you?' He stood back and held my upper arms in his hands. 'Why didn't you answer my phone calls or texts? I've been trying to reach you since yesterday.'

'I haven't received anything,' I said as I took my phone out of the back pocket of my shorts. 'Look.'

But it was dead, there was not a bit of life in it, no matter how much I tapped the glass or clicked the side button. 'That's so weird.'

'You forgot to charge it?' He looked hurt. 'Has your life gotten that exciting that you'd forgotten I might want to be in touch?'

'No! I wondered why I hadn't heard from you.' I tried to think back to the last time I'd even looked at the phone. This morning I'd just hung out with Mom, then left to meet Cate as we'd arranged. Yesterday perhaps? But that had been so busy with getting ready for the

Solstice Service, I hadn't had a chance to even think about the phone. I shook my head.

'I don't know what to say. It's not like me to let it run down.'

'Anyway, I'm here, you neglectful creature.' He held me back into his arms as if he could never get enough of me, and I wasn't going to argue.

'So *why* are you here? Not that I'm not extremely delighted to be graced by your presence.'

'Change of plans,' he said. 'The Taiwan talks fizzled out. and then everyone wanted to take off two weeks for the Chinese Solstice celebrations, they do things differently down there, and I thought I'd rather be here,' he continued. 'With you.'

I rested my head on his chest and breathed in the smell of him. He had been travelling for a day non-stop, but he didn't have the stale smell of airline dinners or re-cycled air about him. No, his shirt had that unmistakable odor of fresh starch, like he'd just unwrapped it from the plastic cover of the dry-cleaners, and the scent of his soap still lingered on his body. I sniffed at him again. 'You don't smell like you've been travelling.'

He laughed, that deep rumble coming from his chest. 'I took the Kin jet direct, of course,' he said. 'Otherwise it would have taken me days. Much more comfortable this way.'

I stayed leaning against him. The Kin jet. One day, I too would be able to travel in that style.

'Sorry to have missed your first Solstice Ball,' he whispered in my hair. 'Did you dance?'

I giggled into his arms. 'Only with Mom, and that was a disaster,' I said. 'If I'm going to get the hang of this moving to music thing, I'll need a good teacher.' I squinted up at him.

'I consider that a challenge,' he said. And he waltzed me back to the house, humming his deep tenor and twirling me as we danced along the paved pathway.

My phone's mysterious death continued to haunt me, though. I plugged it into the charger for a couple of hours that evening, but nothing happened, no matter how hard I clicked the side button. The last time I remembered using it was two days ago. I'd had it in Montreal, we used it to find the small dress shop. After that, nothing.

But then I remembered. Margaret had touched it that night, she had picked it up from the coffee table. Looked at it and put it back down in disgust.

This realization made me gasp out loud. What had she done to my phone? She'd somehow caused its death. Had it been a deliberate action?

I remembered again how she'd warned me about Hugh and the Kin, advised me to make a clean break, couldn't understand why I wanted so badly to become a fully functioning worker of magic and not become an outlaw like herself. Had she killed my phone out of spite? I was so busy being pissed at her for everything, that I didn't remember who else had touched my phone. In the Temple garden, on the night of the ball.

CHAPTER 19

H ugh was staying at one of the boutique hotels downtown. There were spare bedrooms at my own house, but I was glad he chose to be more in-dependent. I was still trying to adjust to Dad having moved in, although we were getting along much better. It just would have been weird having Hugh sneak into my bedroom like we were kids.

He ordered a new phone for me, a brand new IPhone compliments of the Kin, the fanciest cell I'd ever owned. I flashed it every moment I got, but actually I only used it for texts and measuring my steps, so it was sort of wasted on me.

I began Cate's recommended routine the very next day. I purchased a short-term membership at the gym up the road in the mall, using the last of the cash in my bank account and I'd researched what seemed like a good workout plan. The two hours passed painfully slowly, the clock hardly moving between sets. But I was determined not to disappoint my new mentor and I forced myself to stick with it.

Hugh and I met for coffee at the hotel afterwards. I was still sweaty despite the bike ride down the hill which had cooled me off. My hair had long lost its beautiful sheen achieved by the salon on the day of the Ball. I really wasn't feeling at my most glamorous, and I hungrily eyed the last pastry on the plate.

'You? Working out in a gym?'

I didn't like the disbelieving tone in his voice, so I reached out and snatched the blueberry scone with defiance.

'What's brought this on then? Since when have you become fitness minded?' He was ready to bust a gut laughing.

'I need to,' I told him earnestly between bites. 'I have to be at my most fittest in order to accept the challenges which lie ahead of me in my new life.'

'But I like you just the way you are,' he said. 'You're not really one of the hard-body types.'

I glared at him as I swallowed the last of the delicious buttery pastry.

'Who's been filling your head with this nonsense?' he continued relentlessly, then a deep sympathy formed in his eyes and his face softened. It stung. I didn't need his, or anyone's, pity. 'Sasha?'

'No! Cate...' I shut my mouth quickly.

Hugh nearly choked on his coffee, and ended up spitting in on the table on front of us. I crossed my arms and watched as he mopped it up with his napkin. He was trying hard not to laugh.

'What?'

Finally he looked at me, his eyes were crinkled at the edges. 'Cate. Cate Huxor? Seriously? I thought you hated her. But all of a sudden you're taking her advice? When did you two even start speaking?'

'Things have changed.' I bit my lip. This wasn't the time to share the news of my new alliance with Cate. Yes, we'd had our differences in the past, me and Dad's wife, but she was the first one to reach out to me, to really understand what I wanted and needed in my life, that I had to build my life according to what I wanted, and not what someone else wanted for me.

'I guess it's just time to grow up and let bygones be bygones,' I said airily. 'Mom and Dad are happy with their new arrangement, and Cate seems delighted enough to be free to do her own thing.'

'That's certainly an about-face.'

'Like you pointed out, she's responsible for me getting my first assignment,' I said. 'And I appreciate the encouragement.'

He looked at me with a peculiar expression on his face. 'Are you sure she's not ... planning something?'

He put up his hand to stop my flow. 'I only say this because I know Cate,' he continued. 'Not well, I admit, but she's never struck me as the selfless, nurturing type.'

'I guess their marriage was never as perfect as she pretended,' I said slowly. 'And now, like I said, she's free to be herself. And she knows the difficulties a woman of power faces, even in the Kin today.'

He reached over the table to kiss me. 'Well, I'm glad the air is cleared between you,' he whispered. 'She's a dangerous woman to have as an enemy.'

Hugh sat back again with a smile on his face. 'So, have you found out anything about the elves?' This was asked casually, but I was immediately on alert.

The elves. Brin was regretting his political involvement, although he couldn't tell me of any concrete plans. Yet Cate had assured me she had it all in hand and I had to trust her in that, for there was that little matter of Eldric that I hadn't reported. I waved my hand in the air as if to brush it all aside. It would be dealt with.

'As you said, if there's something happening, Brin doesn't know the details,' I replied. 'So perhaps I can go back to Scotland when you do?'

That would really be the best case scenario, I decided. Leave St. John's and all this messy business behind, and then I could claim all ignorance by the time it was cleared up.

'I'll be here for another week or so,' he told me. 'I may as well stick around for the clearing of the ley lines.'

'The what?' I sat up. 'You're talking about those magnetic lines underneath the earth? Aren't they natural – why would you need to clear them?'

'Yes, they are naturally occurring, but because of... well, because of Kin action in the past, it's something that needs to be done at times, but very rarely,' he hastened to add.

I sat at the edge of my seat, my arms on the table. 'Tell me.'

'Nachtan didn't get that far with the ancient history, did he?' Hugh looked uncomfortable.

I shook my head.

'Okay. Well.' He cleared his throat. 'The ley lines are seams of natural magic running through the earth. They interconnect and, you know all that. They've always been present, since well, forever.'

'And what do the Kin have to do with them?'

'The Kin were born because of them,' he continued, looking out the window at the harbor down below as he gathered his thoughts. 'Some ancient humans were sensitive to magic. Not able to use it, of course, not then, but they were able to divine the seams. Until, one day, there was a human, a genetic abnormality, who was stronger than the others and actually figured out a way to tap the energy of the ley lines.'

'How?'

'The whole story is lost in the mists of time, and happened long ago, way before the Greeks arrived on the scene,' he admitted. 'But it happened one summer's day somewhere in modern day Persia, in an area prone to dry lightning. This is also a land where the ley lines run close to the surface. This particular human, let's call her Eve, she was curious about the ley lines and the power she sensed from them, and dug down to find out what they were about.'

'And in the midst of doing so...'

Hugh nodded. 'Yes, she was caught in a lightning storm. Survived it, but was genetically changed. She was the first Witch.'

He sighed. 'She was able to harness this energy, and learned to use it for her own ends. The so-called history of mankind, the first civilizations, they were all brought about by this ancestor of the Kin.'

I thought about this new bit of history. 'But if they were so powerful, more powerful than their neighbors, say, then why didn't they continue to thrive, these bright new cities?'

He laughed, but it was a cynical sound. 'History repeats itself, over and over and over again. Kin kind would get greedy, and leech more magic from the ley lines to give themselves yet more advantages over those around them, to use them, enslave them, conquer them.'

'So what would happen to take them down?' I asked, but I thought I knew the answer already.

'Basically, they screwed up these wonderful, natural seams of magic, causing blockages. You know how the Middle East is largely dry and much of it taken over by desert? Well, in the time of Babylon and Mesopotamia, these areas were lush and full of vegetation and life. But when the power got clogged up, the living energy wouldn't flow through the ley lines, and turned the whole area into desolation. The Sahara Desert, too, is another example. Once upon a time it was all green forest and savannah. It's never been able to recover.'

He shifted his legs. 'We have since then learned how to undo some of the damage before it gets too serious,' he said. 'Although some places may never regain their life force. However, the original leeching over so many years did change the whole ley system, so sometimes, every half century perhaps, the ley lines in all areas require cleansing.'

'How is that done? Is it not dangerous?'

'Very,' he said, nodding. 'It is done with great care. The witches involved must be strong and also pure of heart, for it would be very easy to disrupt the process and use the magic for their own ends.'

'How do you mean, use it?' I repeated myself. 'You mean they can harness the ley energy?'

'By... by drinking the ley lines,' he said. 'Siphoning off the magic when the lines are opened for cleansing.'

I leaned back, trying to picture this. 'Sort of like a vampire?'

He nodded. 'Exactly like that,' he agreed. His voice had a hard edge to it. 'Drinking the very life of the lines in order to increase one's own personal power. Siphoning off the magic. Can you imagine being arrogant and selfish enough to threaten the very ecosystem of your home? The Kin have learned finally, and are very, very cautious of this. Cleansing the lines is not an easy task, it takes a high level of control to work the lines in this way and not accidentally touch them. It's a really dangerous task.'

A dangerous job, one which called for extreme power and strength. Like mine. My spine straightened and my shoulders came back. This! I could help with this, having the power invested in me by the Crystal Charm Stone. I could make this my place in life, one where I could be useful and necessary to the Kin and not have to bother with the politics and the wrangling side of it all. I could be making my name, doing something practical.

I looked up at him, he must have seen the excitement on my face.

'No, most definitely not,' he said, shaking his head firmly. 'We're all agreed on that. Never, not with your track record.'

'My track record!' I sputtered, trying to find the words to express the offense I couldn't help but feel at his words. 'You really believe I would do something as ... as *heinous* as to drink the magic from the ley lines?'

I was pretty much seeing red by then. They had me right here on the spot, and I could assist them like no other witch ever. Except perhaps Margaret, but she would never have selflessly offered to help the Kin, not like I was doing. And yet, Hugh and the higher ups couldn't let go of my past. Couldn't see that I had undoubtedly matured by leaps and bounds, and that with a bit of practical education, they could use me?

What bothered me even more was what I suspected lay behind his words. Jealousy, Cate had said. Jealousy of my increased power.

'Hold on a moment,' Hugh said. 'Don't lay into me like that! I'm just repeating what the Elders have said, you think we haven't already approached them with the idea of training you for this? I don't want you to get your hopes up. It'll never happen.'

He paused a moment, to allow me to speak. When I remained silent, he continued. 'You have to look at it from where they stand. You're an unknown measure to them. Your actions thus far have not shown you to be the most trustworthy individual.' He held his hand up to stem the flow that now threatened to burst from me. 'Despite your intent. I know your actions weren't motivated from evil, or self-serving in nature, none of them. Jon knows this too. But, you have to look at the timeline of events thus far from an outsider's point of view. Until you prove yourself, prove that you are trustworthy, they simply can't allow you anywhere near the ley lines.'

I sat back in the uncomfortable little chair.

'Look, you're on the right course,' he said. 'Doing small jobs like the elf briefing, that's great. As time goes by, you'll complete more and more important assignments, until one day you'll have a name as being steadfast, and then, and only then, can the Kin allow you to be involved in more delicate matters.'

What could I say to that, how could I argue against that logic? Especially since I was already halfway into mucking up my very first assignment by omitting mention of the little matter of Eldric's involvement with whatever the elves were planning.

Dammit. I swallowed. 'I understand where they're coming from,' I said. My voice was small. And faint.

'What?' Hugh asked in disbelief. 'Did you actually just agree with what I said?'

I nodded, and allowed my eyes to meet his.

'That's what I'm talking about,' he said, a smile breaking out. The sun had moved since we'd sat down, and was now shining in his eyes, sparkling off those intriguing gold glints among the green. 'Humility. The ability to view the larger picture. This is what they want to see.'

He reached over to take my hand and smiled so tenderly, I almost broke down and confessed. In fact, I even opened my mouth to speak but he interrupted.

'I know exactly what you're going to say. You want to learn more about the ley lines, don't you?' He smiled proudly, probably congratulating himself inside for understanding me and my needs.

My confession died a quick and painless death as I grasped what he was offering. 'That would be cool. Yeah, I do want to know more.'

He nodded. 'Tonight, after dark,' he said. 'I'll show you how to see them. How to open your eyes to them. Sound good?'

It sounded very good indeed. Dang, yes.

CHAPTER 20

T he last of the light was fading from the sky as he picked me up that evening from the house, driving the Bat Mobile no less.

'How come? Why does Dad let you drive this but he won't give me lessons on it?' I climbed in and he closed the door behind me.

'Trust,' he reminded me after he started the motor to its smooth purr. 'Besides, do you even know how to drive a car?'

'Yes, Mister I'm-So-Clever,' I said. 'Mark gave me a few lessons. There's nothing to it. You start the engine, put it into gear, then aim to where you're going.'

'That's how you drive an automatic,' he said as he pulled out onto Shaw Street, steering with one hand and moving the gear stick with his other. Mark's old Toyota had less pedals, and once it was in drive it stayed there. 'But do you know about standard transmissions? About using the clutch with your foot to change gears?'

'I won't know until someone teaches me,' I said, then turned to him with hope. 'Why don't we...'

'No. Absolutely not,' he said. After a pause he continued, 'Jon would have a conniption.'

I smiled in the dark, holding onto that pause. I'd plant-ed the seed, Hugh would find a way to teach me on some other, less valuable car, and then some day, when I'd gained enough trust with Dad, I might get my chance to drive this fancy car. I mentally patted myself on the back, for I was learning to play the long game.

We drove up to the top of Signal Hill. From this height, at the foot of the stone tower, we could see the city spread at our feet, the old downtown ringing the harbor, and then the lights spreading off west and north. Off to the other side, the ocean stretched away into darkness. Tiny lights twinkled away in the distance, ships either coming or going across the sea routes.

This was one of my favorite spots to come and sit and contemplate, at any time of day or year. There was space here, space to breathe in this large vista, not even a horizon to limit the view, for the boundary between sky and ocean did not exist, the two merely merged at some point between the everlasting fog and mists from the ocean. It was clean here, the salt air always present, the wind too, blowing right through your mind and clearing out the muck that life accumulated in it.

We walked up the slight incline to the tower, and then just beyond it till we were in a naturally sheltered spot where we could sit on the granite face of the hill, with our backs against the boulders.

'Why here? We're overlooking the harbor. I want to see the ley lines in the earth.'

'Have you ever noticed them? Ever sensed them, picked up on them?'

I shook my head. Never. I hadn't even heard of them till last year.

'There's a reason for that. You need to become sensi-tive to them first. And the best place to do that is in Alt.'

'Are we going to...' The first time we'd been up here on Signal Hill together, he'd introduced me to flying with the mind. At the time, he'd strongly advised against flying this way in Alt. Which I'd ignored, of course, when I had been looking so desperately for Alice, and I'd paid the consequence.

'You've proved you can do it already,' he murmured. 'So what the hell?'

I grasped his hand hard. 'What are we waiting for?'

With that I shut my eyes halfway and let the Alt blinders fall away from my sight. It was easier to do these days, more natural to slip behind the Veil. The lights of the harbor below softened, gas lamps casting their soft glows over the city's cobbled streets, candles in the windows of the wooden buildings. Alt St. John's was a lot smaller than its real time equivalent. Entire neighborhoods of houses disappeared, leaving only the faintest evidence of life in the outlying areas, the farms and woods in their places. He came alongside me, I could feel it.

I looked expectantly at the distances, out to the Goulds, the farmlands stretching to the west, but I couldn't see any evidence of ley lines. Perhaps, I thought, perhaps I needed to look closer to home, up north where I knew for sure the lines converged on the Temple.

But nothing.

'We need to fly,' Hugh said. 'You remember how?'

I gave a small smile. Remember? In this arena, the student had long passed the tutor. Hugh's version of flying was simplistic, to send the mind out over the landscape, to project astrally, but this witch could fly with her body. However I didn't want to show off so I held back on that, and I joined with his mind as we soared over the Alt city.

I looked and I looked in all directions, but all I could see were the mean hovels of Alt, the roads and laneways and cow paths with poor houses strung along them, but nothing that suggested magic or straight lines.

Hugh was right next to me, still holding my ethereal hand as he led me north, up towards the Temple.

Remember the ley lines on the map?

I nodded, and I picked out the point from the edge of the cliff over Portugal Cove, and looked down at the Temple below us. It was dark tonight, no activity, no lights shining through the glass ceilings. Still nothing.

Look below the surface. Look deep within the very earth itself.

I didn't know quite what he meant, but I adjusted my sight and suddenly, they appeared. There they were in all their glory. Bright spring green and gold, almost neon in their glow, like highways of magical life running through the earth.

I see them!

And once seen, they could not be unseen. How could I have never noticed these before? I followed each one in turn with my eyes, straight lines, but there was no grid pattern here, not like the latitude and longitude lines seen on a map. Instead, I realized as I flew a bit higher to get a larger picture, the ley lines formed triangles. And something clicked in my head.

Triangulation. Pythagorus. This was why Nachtan, that venerable, this was the very reason he had yammered on and on about the importance of the old Greeks. Thales, that was the other guy's name, the one who had mapped out the cosmos wholly in triangles. The skies above, yes, but also the ley lines below. Everything was made of triangles.

I flew even higher, the better to see more. Hugh dragged at me, warning me to stay with him, but I shook him off and darted up toward the heavens. There, that was better. I followed the lines across the land, the south west toward the Wilderness. If I wanted, I knew I could follow that line and it would bring me directly to Eldric's palace in his hidden mountains. And then I turned to the wide expanse of ocean to the east. Yes, those lines diverging and crossing, way, way out to sea. The shipping lanes followed them intuitively, even the currents were affected by the magic life lying far beneath the sea.

We have to go back.
Not yet, I have to see.
Come back now, we can't leave our bodies too far behind.

I sensed the worry, the panic in his thoughts and his mounting fear, and I felt my frustration at his lack of faith. I could have gone on for miles, straight to Ireland, I knew this, without harming my poor physical self at all. But I gave in to his urging and allowed him to guide us back to our small nook within the granite of the hill.

Once landed back in the physical, I opened my eyes to the bright city lights below. They now appeared so shallow, so artificial, so unimportant compared to what I had just witnessed, as if a strong breath of wind could cut off their source and they would be no more. Mere electricity kept these lights burning, a facsimile of life compared to what I'd witnessed in the glowing, pulsing forces within the earth.

'What the hell was that all about?'

Man, he was pissed. I brushed him off, I didn't want him raining on my bliss. 'That was incredible. Absolutely out of this world.' I needed time to really digest all that I had seen and the realizations that had clicked in my mind.

'How could you endanger us like that?'

'What danger? We were perfectly safe. We could have gone a lot further,' I barked at him.

I looked out over the land, trying to find the ley lines again with my physical eyes. There was something, the barest wisp of power flowing under the rock, but it was more like I could sense the movement rather than see the magic lines like I had in Alt. I needed to concentrate.

'That was the most reckless, immature action,' he went on. 'You had no idea what you were getting us into, or the consequences...'

'Shut it, would you?' The *geometrical loci*, that was the term Nachtan had used.

'What did you just say?'

I glanced over at him. His face was red in the reflected light from below. I'd never seen him this emotional. 'I had it under control. You were safe with me.'

'We could easily have been snapped away, you realize this kind of travel is like an elastic band, you can only go so far before it breaks?'

'There was no danger, I tell you,' I bit back at him. 'You need to push your limits sometimes.'

'And how about our physical bodies sitting defenseless in Alt? We couldn't even see them. Anything could have crept up on us.'

'When did you turn into such an old woman?' I muttered, low enough that he couldn't hear me over his own panicked reactions.

'I just feel like I don't know you sometimes,' he said, calmer now he had that out of his system. Perhaps he felt a little silly at his overreaction, not that he would call it that. He sat back down with a thump next to me.

'I want to go higher,' I said. 'I want to see the whole loci of the earth.'

He shook his head.

'Well, do we have satellite images or something?'

'Of the ley lines?' He sounded incredulous. 'No, not that I'm aware of...'

'Why not? We've sent people to space. Surely one of them was a witch, and they could have had a quick gander at the lines, noted them down, seen how they all interconnect.'

He let out a deep huff of air, right from the bottom of his lungs. 'There are... maps. In the Bodleian library, in England. But why?'

I shook my head. 'I dunno,' I said. 'I just want to know more about these. The lines and their angles, it's all so fascinating, like I need to... to know them better.'

Yes, they fascinated me. I wanted to touch them, swim in them, immerse myself deep within them.

Or drink of them? A small inner voice asked. Shocked, I denied it, tried to push that thought out of my head. But the idea wormed itself up again. Throw myself down on them and lap directly from the Source. Drink of the life magic like a person who'd crawled through the desert approached an oasis. I slowly brought my hand over my mouth as if to keep my hunger down.

This, then. This was what the Kin tried to prevent. Because anyone who gave into this urge would surely burn out like a fireball. This was why the Kin could not trust me.

The force of that desire scared me. To think that such a dark hunger lived inside me. I hadn't known it existed till I saw the lines.

I crept closer to Hugh and sought his embrace. 'I'm sorry,' I whispered. Whether I was apologizing for allowing myself off the tether, or for actions not yet committed, I wasn't entirely sure myself.

My body was shivering, and he placed his arm heavily around my shoulders to let me soak in his warmth and comfort.

'This is what happens when you go too far,' he whispered. 'Your body has gone into a kind of shock because you stretched the leash too much. Stay safe with me.'

He was talking about the mental flying, about leaving our physical bodies too far behind, but I could only see it as a direct warning against following my inner urges.

'I fear for you,' he said, his breath warm against my ear and the delicate skin of my neck. He hugged me tighter. 'Stay with me. Marry me. Let me wrap you up in a safe blanket, like a cocoon.'

And help protect me against myself. Having seen that desperate hunger deep within me, how could I ever trust Dara Martin? I clutched my arms around him. Yes, why not take the easier path, one that wouldn't expose me to the depths of my own treachery? I needed Hugh as a shield against myself, and I nodded into his shoulder. 'Let's do it.'

I pushed away the echo of Cate's words. Tried to. Along with the memory of that heavy ring meant to keep me grounded, but which in fact would only weigh me down. I ignored the memory of Margaret's voice as she urged me to leave the Kin behind, to follow her in her lawless life of expansion and growth. Yet even as I tried to submerge those echoes back into a place deep within myself, my body refused to allow it and reacted directly against this, against my own falseness of mind.

'Really?' Hugh grabbed me by the arms as he turned me to look at him, straight on. 'You mean, you're agreeing to marry me?'

I opened my mouth to say yes, and that happy light in his eyes only dimmed a small bit as I gave into my body's urges, as my supper made its way back up my throat and I threw it up all over his spanking white t-shirt.

Purged, I could only stare at the steaming mess, panting as I realized the impact of what my body was telling me.

'That's what happens when you push yourself too far in Alt,' he said flatly, letting go of my arms and allowing distance between us as he pulled his t-shirt away from his body and surveyed the hot damage. 'This is the effect.'

I let him tell us that, even as I knew the difference, knew that my body was viscerally rejecting the idea of hiding my light behind Hugh's ring. I let him believe that he was right. It was easier that way.

CHAPTER 21

Hugh refused to tell me anything more about the lines or the ceremony to cleanse them that night. Perhaps he was in a snit because I'd upchucked right down the front of his pristine t-shirt, or perhaps he suspected that my body's reaction had nothing at all to do with me stretching my limits in the mental flying.

'I'm not part of it,' he said finally with a scowl. 'That is kept for far wiser and more trained minds than mine, okay?'

I tried to leave the ley lines aside, to get on with the business of daily living. I continued to go to the gym every day. It felt good to be living so physically, not just the way I looked in my clothes, but I began to feel energized, ready to take on life, even able to ride my bike straight up the hills without getting out of breath. I had never before been so fit, and I liked this feeling.

But they continued to haunt my thoughts, the ley lines, an obsession I couldn't let go of. Their beauty, their allure, calling me every time my thoughts wandered, like a compass needle always bringing me back to them. As I walked the streets of St. John's I would find myself listening for them, for that faint whisper of tinkling like crystal, single notes and chords all chiming together like the music of the spheres. I would picture in my mind's eye where the lines ran, the ones we'd seen, and I would find myself walking their paths, searching for the slightest hint of them.

I admit I even went into Alt a few times on my journeys, and it was easier there to follow the lights, to seek them out, but I didn't do this often because of the company I found there along the lines. The burned out, hopeless cases, human and super natural alike, they knew the lines were running beneath their feet although they'd never seen them, not like me, yet perhaps they too could hear the music and hungered for their beauty and power. Unable to reach the magic in those lines, these poor souls self-medicated with alcohol and other drugs, a poor substitute for the beauty they dreamed of, yet still they hung about the lines, those sad dreamers, hoping beyond hope that someday they might attain the magic deep within the earth.

These pathetic druggies showed me, by their very existence, what I had to fear from the lines and I stayed well away. Except when I couldn't. But I knew enough not to delve deeper into them.

Cate became my new source of information. I couldn't hide my fascination for the magical seams, and she was happy enough to impart her knowledge to me.

But that came later. First she wanted her own curiosity sated. She wanted to know what my power entailed.

'I don't really know,' I told her as we sat on the bench along the side of her tennis court. I was improving my game, and learning much from her. I'd even had her on the run that day. She was delighted with my progress. 'The Kin have told me that my powers are so great, but I don't seem to be using them for anything. They won't teach me things to do, anything that can help them.'

'What was it like at first?' she asked casually as she sipped her lemonade and sat back in the warmth of the sun. 'After you'd held the Crystal Charm Stone.'

I thought back to that evening on Scarp. I had brought the stone all the way from the stone tower, the Broch, to the water's edge where Willem waited with the boat.

'I glowed,' I told her. 'There on the beach of Scarp, everybody sort of backed off away from me because I was glowing. And then the full moon hit, I was short circuiting the WiFi and all the phones, so they packed me off to Edinburgh. By ferry.

'That part of it was short lived, though,' I added. 'The cycles of the moon don't affect me anymore, and I no longer mess with the electricals onboard planes, so it's safe for me to fly again.'

'How strange it all is,' she mused, then she eyed me speculatively. 'Can you sense things?'

'Like what?'

She shrugged. 'Magic. Seams of magic?'

'You mean the ley lines? Yes! I saw them the other night. Hugh showed me how to see them, in Alt. Aren't they the most beautiful thing?'

'They are, indeed, the most wondrous of all natural phenomenon.' She drew in a breath and leaned closer to me, her hand coming unbidden to her mouth. The gold and diamond tennis bracelet sparkled on her wrist. 'Can you... did you try to touch them?'

'Oh, God, no,' I said quickly. 'As much as I would have loved to. Hugh said to not get too close to them. Especially me, with my history.'

'And why is that? Did he give an explanation?'

'Just that they are extremely powerful. I get the impression they might sear through my brain and leave me a babbling idiot or something.'

She leaned back. 'There's always that possibility,' she murmured, her fingers still on her chin. 'But I think the Kin fear something far more dangerous from you.'

I looked at her, waiting for her to expand this thought.

'With your history, as Hugh says... You've already strengthened the power in yourself. And if you were to touch the lines, then they probably wouldn't have the same effect on you.'

I didn't know what she meant.

'I mean, your magic conduits are already strength-ened beyond belief. Instead of burning you, the touch of the lines would infuse you with a power far greater than has ever been known. Even greater than Margaret Forsythe's.' She leaned back, watching my reaction.

'So you're saying the Kin are not afraid *for* me,' I said as her words sunk in. 'They're afraid *of* me.'

She nodded, then her body relaxed and she dropped the whole subject of the lines. 'But with regard to your so-called powers, what can you do?'

I thought some more. 'Well, I haven't really explored it all. No one's encouraging it. Hugh and I had a bit of a showdown, back at Tomnahurich that evening, and without even trying I sent him flying back into the bush-es.' I gave a little smile to think about it. He'd been shocked at the evidence of my growth, and I was still rather proud of that. It wasn't like I hurt him or anything, just punched a temporary hole in his ego.

Cate waved her hand like that wasn't really much of an accomplishment. 'Anything else?'

'Well, I...,' I thought for a moment. What evidence of my powers would impress the high and mighty Cate? 'I can call up storms.'

She shrugged. 'Meh. Weather magic.'

'And I made a cloud dragon over the skies of Edin-burgh. It was very realistic,' I boasted.

'Why would you do such a thing?'

Why indeed, I asked myself. Everything I had done with my powers, my oh-so-increased powers, all of that had been accidental, a direct result of my mood and thoughts. Nothing had been purposeful. I was a little embarrassed to admit this even to myself. There was only the one time, with Margaret, that I had actually done something.

'I can fly,' I said as I turned to face her.

'That's just mind travel. We all learned to do that at a fairly young age.'

'No, I mean I can *fly* fly. With my physical body. As if I had wings, but of course I don't.'

That made her sit up on the wooden bench. 'No. That's against the laws of physics. Only elves can... . I don't believe that. What instrument do you use to achieve this act?'

'What do you mean, like a broomstick?' I laughed. 'No, it's just me. I'll show you. I did it before, I should be able to do it again.'

It was as safe a place as any to try this, for we were completely hidden from anyone else's view by the tall hedges. I hadn't practiced this skill at all, and wasn't even sure I could do it without Margaret at my side, or without the added impetus of danger spurring me on. But I stood up and closed my eyes, trying to remember how to put my mind into the action. But I didn't feel myself budge. I tried jumping into the air, to help, but I just landed back on my feet.

'Maybe,' I said, climbing up on the bench beside her. Margaret had urged me to jump off the cliff and have faith, that night on the Fae hill, and perhaps I needed to relive that. 'Maybe, this will do the trick.'

Cate leaned back and watched me, not saying a thing.

I took a deep breath, closed my eyes again, and called the power from the depths of my being. Lightly, not attaching myself to it. Allowing it to be. And I stepped off.

There was only the sound of Cate's gasp. No flopping of my sneakers on the gravel, no wrenching of my ankle as I hit the ground. No, I was in the air. I opened my eyes and smiled down at her in triumph.

'Can you move around?' she whispered as if afraid to break the spell or whatever was keeping me aloft.

'Of course,' I said, smoothly moving to my left. I led with my arms and my head, where I wished to go, my body followed. It was almost a swimming action, but without the need to flap my limbs to move me along, I could move by flicking my body. It was very different from the flying evinced by the warrior elves, I realized.

It was quite tiring though, so I soon settled myself back on the ground. Cate was staring at me with a peculiar expression on her face.

'I had no idea,' she breathed. 'Is anyone else aware of this talent?'

I nodded. The Kin had seen me flying that first night, when I'd had to in order to fight back the dark forces of the rogue elder.

'And they've said nothing to you? No one has addressed this?' She sounded incredulous.

'No.' That was rather odd, now I came to think about it. No one, even Hugh, no one had brought it up. 'I wonder why they didn't ask me about it?'

She looked off into the hedges, sunk in deep thought, and tapped her right hand lightly on the bench arm. Finally she spoke again. 'One of two explanations. Either they saw, and are hoping this power of yours will go away if it's not nurtured, or... Margaret Forsythe cast some sort of spell to wipe that from their minds.'

I thought back to the time. Could Margaret have done such a thing to Kin Elders, without their knowing?

'Odd as it seems, that's the most logical explanation,' she continued. 'Which means...'

I sat on the bench next to her, waiting for her to finish that thought.

'Which means, they have no idea.' The pupils in her dark eyes widened as she stared at me, and I swore I could see a new respect for me on her face. She placed her elegant arm around my shoulder.

'Dara, we are going to train you. You deserve to be the most you can be.'

'Yes,' I breathed.

'Your powers are far beyond mine, but you need to be nurtured,' she continued. Then she cocked her head as if thinking some more. 'But it's got to be secret. We can't tell the other Kin. Otherwise...'

'What?'

She shook her head. 'They won't accept it,' she said. 'They'll stop us.'

Cate spoke the truth, I couldn't deny it. For all the Elders appeared to be warming up to me, they still didn't trust me, didn't offer me a practical education. But my father's ex-wife understood, and was offering.

And so began my rigorous training by Cate Huxor, of all witches. I kept our new bond hidden from the other people in my life, as she insisted, not a difficult feat at all. Jon and Hugh were off every day doing their Kin business, while Mom had her own life to live. Brin and Alice, too, were busy with their lives, so I was able to sneak off every afternoon for practice with Cate in the privacy of the estate's hedges.

It was exhausting, but with my daily work outs at the gym and this practice, I could feel myself becoming more adept at flight. I took to practicing at night, too, so that I could fly higher without attracting attention from the Normals. I rode my bike and hiked to the farthest flung areas I could reach, the cliffs over the ocean and the hidden valleys by the shores and there I taught myself to turn and increase my stamina, and soon I was even learning to use the wind and the currents to help me glide.

I flew first with the seagulls, and then the eagles who inhabited those lonely shores.

I was finally learning to use the practical aspects of my power, and it was Cate who was pushing me to this extreme, Cate who cared enough to nurture my talents, unlike any of the other witches in my life. I had cause to be grateful to this woman, my former sworn enemy.

CHAPTER 22

I was dedicated to my practice, yes, but Cate had advised me not to speak of any of this to my friends and family, for they might not understand. I still had to navigate around the other people in my life, forced to spend lazy hours with Mom when I was itching to get up and move and push myself. I spoke no word of Cate to her, for although she believed the separation had been amicable, she would not have been able to grasp that Cate and I had become true friends in such a short space of time.

Or Dad. I didn't dare breathe a word to him. We were getting along better than we had for so many years and I didn't want to burst that bubble of good feelings. And yet, he was still pushing me for more information from Brin.

'I gave you the report,' I grumbled. I was only on my first coffee of the morning, and it was way too early for him to be nagging me. 'I haven't seen too much of him lately. He's busy.'

'With what?'

'I dunno, work? Alice? His new house, which you helped him rent. It needs a lot of work, by the way. What else does an elf get busy with?'

'I wouldn't press you, but there are rumors that the elves are in a state of unrest, that there's a lot of political activity happening. I need you to have your finger on the pulse of the action.'

I sighed, but I agreed to do it. What choice did I have? I couldn't suggest Jon go discuss the matter with Brin himself, because my elf friend would undoubtedly let slip the fact of Eldric and our visit to his palace. It had to be me.

'Alright, I'll see him tonight and get a report for you.'

'First thing tomorrow, if you don't mind. I'll be busy with the visiting Elders.'

That caught my interest, with the automatic flash of guilt that the mention of this august body always caused. I hadn't been doing anything wrong lately, not really, but the thought of that black-robed, dour group still made my heart race. 'Elders are visiting? What for?'

'Oh, it's the cleansing ceremony,' he said, his head in the morning paper, already not paying attention to me now he'd given me my orders.

'The ley lines? The cleansing of the lines?'

'Umm-hmm,' he agreed absently, then as my question sunk in he looked up. 'Yes, as matter of fact. The semi-centennial cleansing ceremony. You've heard of it?'

'Are you a part of it?'

He nodded slowly, and was already decisively shaking his head when I opened my mouth again. 'No, you can't take part in it. Only the most trustworthy and powerful of witches are allowed to do this. Don't take offence. It's written in the Kin Constitution.'

I wasn't offended, for Hugh had already explained it to me. But I had to test him. 'Hugh can't either?'

'Correct. At this point in time.'

'How about Cate?'

He'd resolutely returned his attention back to the newspaper, but shook his head again. 'No, she's expressly forbidden to take part.'

This took me aback. Cate was, in her own right, way up there in the Kin power hierarchy. What reason?

Perhaps he felt my eyes boring into him, for at long last he continued that thought. 'She's the head of the Huxor Kin,' he explained, lifting his eyes to mine. 'They control the adamantite extraction and production in this province. So she's not allowed near the ley lines. It would be a potential clash of interests.'

'And how does she feel about that?'

He shrugged. 'It's an accepted fact of life,' he said. 'She knows the rules, and she's not the kind of witch to waste energy whining about it. I'm sure she prefers having control of the adamantite trade over being forced to partake in rather dull ceremonies all over the world. It involves a lot of travel, you know. It's why I'm so often not around.'

··········

So after supper I made sure he saw me set off to Brin's on my bike in my quest to pump the elf for information. There was no hint of Alt on Blackler's Lane that evening, I was very happy to note, because it meant the area was clear of Eldric and his Dark Elves. I was even happier to find Alice hanging out in the home, too, because that was the perfect excuse not to get too involved in a political discussion.

The atmosphere in the small house was charged, unsettled even though Alice didn't appear to notice anything amiss. She chattered on in her way, yet Brin sat on the beat-up sofa in quiet agitation. He was restless, tense and unhappy. A picture of misery.

'I'm getting ready for my trip,' she announced. She was grinning from ear to ear with excitement.

'What trip? You never go anywhere.' I felt a flush of guilt at having neglected my best friend so much lately. Surely I should have known if she was planning to travel. I eyed Brin as he stared back at me as if he was trying to communicate something to me, but I had no idea what it could be.

'My summer job,' she said. 'It's part of the work for my thesis. We're spending two weeks on Miquelon, studying seals on the beaches.' She was flushed and evidently excited at the prospect of visiting the tiny French island to the south.

'You and Brin are going?' I asked, brightening. This could be very good. Brin would be removed from the political situation and I would no longer have to fear that he'd tell Dad anything. This was excellent news for me, and it solved the issue quite nicely. I hadn't finished congratulating myself when she spoke up again.

'Brin on the ocean?' She guffawed out loud. 'No, this trip is for biologists only.'

He opened his mouth, then shut it again as he darted a glance at Alice. She didn't notice, but kept jawing on about the finer details of seals and their eating habits. Surely he wasn't upset about her leaving?

'I've been meaning to ask,' I jumped in when Alice stopped for a breath. I directed my question at Brin. 'I've been dying to know how you manage to get through the Veil. Alice said you had a thing...'

'This!' He finally exploded into action as he dug around in his pants pocket and slapped a little bit of metal onto the coffee table. He wasn't getting any calmer. 'Take it, I can't stand to have it on me any longer!' He darted glances all around him as if fearing an invisible onlooker, yet there was only the three of us present.

Alice looked at him and sighed audibly.

I shook my head and kept my hands firmly on my lap. I didn't even want to touch it by accident, not until I knew what the thing was, but I leaned over to examine it more closely.

The object was circular, like a coin with a hole in the center, but thinner and plain, no writing on it. It looked more like a washer actually, a boring industrial bit of metal, but it was black and dull, as if it sucked in the lights around us rather than reflecting them.

I sniffed the air around it. The thing had magic infused into it, but I'd never felt the like of it before. Could it be forged from that mysterious magical metal adamantite?

This had to be Elf magic. I shook my head again. 'I'm not touching it. You'd best return it to where ever it came from.'

With a quick sharp movement, he swept it off the table. 'I'm done with it. I'm done with them all.'

'Well, I am *so* happy to hear that.' Alice said as she stood with her hands on her hips. 'Honestly, you're out every evening with meetings and whatnot and it's not making you happier that I can see.' She bustled away to put the kettle on to boil in the old fashioned kitchen, leaving us alone in his front room.

'I need to speak with Jon!' He whispered as soon as she was out of the room.

I hemmed and hawed and shrugged. 'What's the matter?'

No way would I let Brin get near Dad.

'The elves,' he burst, unable to keep it in any longer. 'They're ramping up the action!'

'What exactly are they going to do?' I kept my voice calm and pitched low. I wasn't worried. Cate was in charge of this, she'd never let Eldric do anything really terrible. She'd control him, like she controlled so much.

Alice passed back into the room. 'What's that you're talking about?'

Neither of us answered.

'You'll take good care of Brin when I'm gone, right Dara? Keep him away from those politics.'

I forced a smile on my face. 'It's probably a good idea to loosen the ties,' I suggested to him, very pointedly.

'Yeah, they sound like a bunch of troublemakers, actually,' she said seriously. 'And Brin still only has landed immigrant status, he hasn't received his full citizenship yet. I don't want him to jeopardize the process.'

'Good point,' I said and I turned to address him. 'You *should* back away from it all. This might be a good time to cut off the contact.'

'It's too late for that,' he muttered, then he paused as the kettle began to shriek and Alice went back to make the tea. He stood up and began pacing.

'Calm down, Brin,' I said. 'What's the matter?'

'Calm?' he shouted. 'How can I be calm? It's a disaster. Eldric is...'

'Lower your voice. What's going on?'

'Jon needs to know what is happening,' he said. His eyes were still wide but at least he was speaking more quietly. 'Eldric is false.'

That revelation didn't surprise me one little bit, but alarm bells were sounding clearly now. Brin was upset at something, yes, something that the Dark Elf had done or revealed, and something he felt Dad should know about. And if he spoke to Dad, then undoubtedly my omission in my report would be revealed and... Better not to go there.

'Now, tell me,' I said, keeping my voice low. 'What exactly is going on?'

'I can no longer go along with this,' Brin said, still quivering with emotion. He sat heavily back on to the armchair.

'It's getting out of hand,' he continued. 'This is much larger than me. I had hopes, dreams, and I thought he shared them. But he wants...'

'Yes?' My voice was terse.

'He plans violence,' Brin whispered. He glanced around although we were quite alone in the small space. Alice was humming to herself as she waited for the tea to steep, and I heard the metal scrape of a cookie tin being opened.

'How?' I began, then switched tracks. 'What? Why? How do you know?'

'I've suspected for a while,' he said as he looked at me sombrely. 'Especially after the other night. He threatened your well-being, as you know.'

I nodded. I'd been there.

'I've been given orders,' Brin continued, then he began to shake his head. 'I'm afraid he... he plans to directly attack the Kin. Dara, there's going to be violence, bloodshed, and I don't want any part of it.'

Brin was scared. Afraid enough to back out and run to Jon and confess everything about his part so far in the involvement with Eldric. And that meant he would tell Dad about how I'd been taken up with it all, reluctantly and more as an innocent bystander, of course, but that wouldn't excuse my omission in the report. Sure, Brin wouldn't rat me out on purpose, but I knew that elf. Once he started, he wouldn't be able to stop especially in the light of Dad's questioning, and he would spill the beans on everything I hadn't mentioned in my report.

Yet, Cate said she was on top of it all. Cate of all witches wouldn't allow Eldric to cause harm to the Kin, surely. My mind flashed back to the tennis court that first afternoon, how she had stood in the center of the court, not breaking a sweat as I ran hither and thither trying to match her game.

Control. She had been the calm center, controlling the game.

Brin,' I said again. 'I think you're over-reacting. Why don't you just tell me everything, right from the beginning?'

He gaped at me. 'Over-reacting? But the Dark Elves, Dara, they're coming, they're planning something...'

'What exactly is it you fear?'

'Mayhem! Murder! They won't stop till they've brought down every single one of the Kin!'

Cate was Kin. She would never allow that to happen to her own kind. I shook my head. 'No, that won't happen. Cate has it under control.'

'Jon's wife?' Now Brin's jaw hung slackly. 'You hate her. How do you know what she's doing?'

'We've had our differences in the past, me and Cate,' I said, a little annoyed at him for bringing up my ancient history. 'But we've smoothed over them, as mature adults do. We're...' No, I couldn't tell him that Cate and I were working together. Not with his loose mouth. Brin had lots of good qualities, but he would never be a politician, he was far too trusting a soul and a blabbermouth to boot.

'I tell you what,' I said as I leaned over the coffee table. 'I will look into all this, your claims. There's got to be an explanation.'

'You don't have much time,' he said. He was wringing his hands with anxiety. 'This is of the utmost urgency, for there's something planned very soon.'

A niggle of disquiet worried the back of my mind. 'How soon is soon?'

He shrugged.

'Tonight soon, or sometime later this week or month soon?'

He shrugged again.

'Well, do you have any idea what it is, this thing Eldric is planning?'

'There's mention of a bomb!' he hissed, his eyes wide. 'Something to do with the Temple, I wasn't close enough to get the details.'

Seriously? A bomb. That just sounded so... so mundane. 'Well, in that case, their calendar is a little off.'

I smiled at him and leaned back in my chair. 'They've missed the Solstice service. We have time to figure this out.'

'What can *you* do about it?' His eyes were growing large again, I could almost smell his fear rising. 'You're not a real witch, you're not trained enough. No, we need to tell Jon, the others, the ones in charge of everything.'

That stung. *Not a real witch.* What did he know? Brin had no idea what had happened to me over in Scotland, how my contact with the Crystal Charm Stone had increased my powers one hundredfold, or how if I ever learned to use that power I would be quite the force to be reckoned with.

But I swallowed my hurt ego. We didn't have a lot of time before Alice would return with the tea tray.

'So, what sort of bomb and where?' I asked him under my breath. 'And who's going to plant it? Eldric?'

'Or his horrible new worker. That Scottish goblin.'

'The Scottish...' I stared at him as the realization broke over me. There was only one Scottish goblin on this side of the water, or at least in this town. The irrepressible, unkillable Trevor. But he was working with Cate. What did this mean?

She was in charge of this whole mess, or so she claimed, and Trevor was working under her command. I was beginning to get a little nervous over the choices I had made.

But a bomb? That didn't sound like any super natural's choice of weapon. It was so... blatant. So Normal, so unmagical. There was something very wrong with this whole picture. I needed to talk with Cate. She would have the answers.

CHAPTER 23

I suppose I could have phoned her, but I needed to see her face to face when I asked the questions which were racing through my mind. Did she know that Trevor might be involved with the treasonous acts of the Dark Elves?

And seriously – how much threat was a physical bomb against witches? Sure it might damage their Temple, but it just seemed so out of place, so childish.

It took me quite a while to bike up to Cate's estate in the east end, but my body was hard and fit now so I was hardly out of breath even biking up that last hill. I left my bike right by the grand front entrance and ran up the stairs. I knocked, then walked on in as if I belonged there.

Dad's moving out hadn't changed things one bit here in Cate's house. The downstairs rooms still held the same chic yet comfortable furnishings, every chair a masterpiece of workmanship, a unique marvel hand crafted and upholstered in fabrics that weren't bought off the shelf at Fabricville. Every item, whether it was a coffee table, the long antique dining room set, even the simple vases by the balustrade leading upstairs, every piece had its own story and history, and that would never come cheap. No, the whole house had been furnished according to Cate's explicit instructions and taste. Maybe it had never really been Dad's home, despite him having lived there for most of his life. It had been his family estate, not hers, yet she had redone the whole place.

'Cate?' My voice echoed through the grand hallway, bouncing off the many closed doors and the stained glass windows lining the landing on the staircase. I heard a slight movement upstairs, but no answering call, so I set off climbing to look for her. At the head of the stairs, two corridors faced me. I listened, but heard nothing further. I knew Sasha's room was down the right hallway, the turret room, so I cautiously went down the other, shorter corridor. One closed door stood apart, the only entrance on that side of the hall, and I bet that was the Master bedroom. I knocked.

I heard soft footsteps on carpet, and then there she was. Her face broke into a smile when she saw it was me.

'Dara, what perfect timing,' she said as she opened the door wider to welcome me in.

The Master bedroom was more like a hotel suite than a private chamber. Inside the door was the first room, a large sitting room, the same white on dark theme that was evidenced in the rooms below. Pale velvet sofas on a neutral rug, dark wood furniture against the huge and colorful paintings on the walls. Various doors led off this room, and Cate led me through one.

As I followed her, I could only gasp at the dress she wore. It was a gown in every sense of the word. Sweeping low to the ground, rainbow hues flashed with every movement she made as if the silk itself were infused with magic. It shimmered, hugging her curves lightly but loosely, and her hair was piled up on top of her head in an intricate arrangement of curls.

'Sorry,' I mumbled. 'I didn't realize you were going out.'

'No,' she said. 'I'm in for the night.'

'It's just your dress and your hair...'

'Ah,' she replied, looking down and brushing the silk so it glimmered and glowed even more. She led me into her dressing room, a huge space of course, lined with closet doors and a three way mirror. She sat at a large make up table and waved her hand to the chaise longue, telling me to sit. 'I'm not going out, but I am expecting company. You're welcome to join us.'

I perched at the edge of the white velvet seat. I'd had these cut-off shorts on all day, working in the garden with Mom, then biking all around town. I wasn't dressed for the grand company she evidently expected. I watched as she fitted something amongst her elaborate hairdo.

"What do you think? She turned back to me as she asked, and the diamonds in her tiara caught the light and flashed like the brightness in her dark eyes.

'It's very regal,' I managed to say.

Cate grinned as she fastened bracelets around her wrists. 'It's important to dress for the job you want,' she murmured as she turned back to the mirror to give her facade the final touch ups with her lipstick.

'Just a joke,' she threw over her shoulder. 'But I'm expecting someone who thinks he's very important, and he would be decidedly unhappy if I didn't treat this occasion with all the pomp he feels he deserves.'

She stood up, and the full effect of her gown with her jewellery was amazing. Diamonds dripped from her wrists and around her neck, combined with the tiara, which now looked more like a crown. We left her suite and walked toward the grand staircase.

The heels she wore made her even taller than normal, and with her natural slimness and beauty, she looked like how Normals might imagine a dark Fairie Queen would appear. I, on the other hand, felt as insignificant as a goblin by her side, in my grubby day clothes, baggy t-shirt and Mom's jean jacket and my uncombed hair tied back with an elastic band.

'So this is an unexpected visit,' she reminded me as we reached the head of the stairs. Her hand lightly touched the ornately carved balustrade and she gracefully flowed downstairs.

I started, remembering why I was here. 'I was speaking with Brin, you know, the elf?'

'I'm familiar with Brin and his story,' she replied with a small smile.

'Of course,' I said. 'Well, Dad was pushing me to get another report for the Kin, and so I went over there to Brin's house, and he's told me something about a bomb! The elves are planning to blow up the Temple, he said.' I stopped there as the ludicrousness of my words hit me.

We'd reached the bottom of her staircase and she directed me into a small room off the great hall, the one next to what had been Dad's home office.

I'd never been in this room before. Like the rest of the house, it had Cate's taste all over it, but it must be her own office. A huge but elegant ebony desk combo took up an entire wall, and the fireplace opposite was surrounded in the same wood. Like Dad's room, tall French windows looked out onto the gardens, but the fine sheers were closed. The walls were adorned with, unlikely as it seemed, large maps in frames.

We sat in the matching white leather armchairs by the fireplace.

'A bomb,' she finally said, wrinkling her nose. 'Doesn't sound like an elf thing at all.'

I let out a big sigh of relief. 'I know, that's why I wanted to check with you first. It sounds kind of farfetched, don't you think?'

She was deep in thought and carried on as if I hadn't spoken. 'The only kind of bomb that would threaten the

Temple with all its wards and spells protecting it would be an adamantite bomb. And that's just too ridiculous to think about.'

'Adamantite can be used as a bomb?' This was news to me. I knew it was a magical metal used for all sorts of arcane purposes, but could one actually blow it up?

'Oh, yes. But the question is...' With this she turned to me, her eyes bright. 'Where would they get the metal?'

'There are seams in the center of the island,' I pointed out the obvious. 'But you control them.'

'Yes. The Huxors have a monopoly on adamantite. The extraction and production is a tightly controlled process. Every speck of it is accounted for.'

I thought carefully. She agreed it was unlikely, but in the worst case scenario that Brin was speaking the truth... 'If the elves did get their hands on some, and could make a bomb, what sort of effects would happen?'

'It would be devastating,' she replied simply. 'The Temple is built on the convergence of the ley lines. If you mix adamantite in with that, the seams would be broken, the magic would not flow. This has happened before in the world. This is one way that deserts are created. It takes years for the lines to recover, and even if they do, they are scarred forever. Which also affects the minds of the creatures living there. They're more prone to darkness, to bad thoughts, to violence.'

I gasped. 'Why would the elves want to do such a thing?' It was on my mind to draw similarities between the drinking of the magic in ley lines and the devastation caused by adamantite on them, but she was already speaking.

She shook her head bitterly. 'To bring down the Veil? To stop the Kin? Who knows the mind of a Dark Elf?'

CHAPTER 24

I didn't understand. I searched for the words. 'Adamantite and the seams, they're all magic, aren't they? Why would the metal have such a horrendous effect on the ley lines?'

'The magic in each are polar opposites,' she said. 'Because they are the same material, they can't align.'

She saw I didn't understand. 'You know magnets, how you can't bring some together no matter how hard you try?'

I nodded, harking back to middle-school science classes.

'That's what they're like.'

I shook my head. No, I wasn't getting it.

She stared at me for a moment longer, then abruptly stood up. 'Come,' she said, striding to one of the large maps on the wall. 'This will illustrate it quite nicely.'

It was a map of the island of Newfoundland, the familiar jagged coastlines and islands in evidence. Unlike most maps, though, it didn't just show towns and outports and the web of roads leading to them. It had them all, but they were sort of faded out, as if unimportant to the map's purpose. What stood out far more clearly were the bright green lines running in every direction. I knew these signified ley lines.

'These areas in red, they are the mines, where the metal is concentrated,' she continued, pointing her long bejewelled finger at a cluster of red masses in the center of the island. The Huxor adamantite mines, the source of Cate's family wealth and power.

'You also see the ley lines in green. Do you notice something about the placement of the mines in relation to the lines?'

And then I understood. The red masses were huddled into the centers of the triangles created by the criss-crossing green lines, squished together as if the metal deposits were trying their best to stay away from the ley lines.

'Yes,' she said, smiling at the dawning light in my eyes. 'Just imagine the lines were the wrong end of the magnets, and the adamantite deposits were iron filings.'

'So if the two were forcefully brought together in an explosion...'

'An adamantite bomb placed on a ley line?' She shook her head. 'It would temporarily reverse the charge of the line. But even a short reversal would cause untold hell for the land all around.'

She gazed at the map for a moment longer, then I felt her eyes move to me.

'And this is one of the reasons the precious metal is kept controlled. It's not a financial or power issue at all. We need to conserve our land.'

She flitted over to the wooden globe and her hands played over the antique pink, reds and greens of the old Colonial country delineations till the turning came to an end. Her right index finger remained over Manchuria. I watched as the ruby red perfect nail tapped on this land.

'Magic bombs,' she mused.

I swallowed, thinking of the desert areas like the Sahara. Were they really magically induced? 'Is there no way to correct the damage?' I burst out. 'Can it be cleaned up somehow? Or is there, I don't know, some kind of cure for the magically devastated areas in the world?'

'A cure,' she said. 'That'd be a nice thing.'

She shook her head. 'No, once done, it cannot be undone. Like a nuclear accident, we must wait out its time, and hope that nature will be kind.'

We both stared at the dry, yellow area of North Africa, then her long nail set to tapping again. 'The only thing that can be done in such an event, the only thing that can possibly save a land from the effects of an adamantite bomb...'

'Yes?'

'Is for three powerful witches to work together, before the damage sets in.'

'What would they do? How would they undo the damage?' This was the kind of thing I'd wanted Nachtan to teach me, or even Margaret. The practical aspects of how to use my so-called great powers. If I knew such things, if I was educated, then I could truly be of help to the Kin and satisfy my own need to be a contributing member of Society. To make a difference.

And Cate, of all my mentors, only Cate understood this need.

'One to hold the gate open, one to mend the path. And one to guard over to ensure no harm comes in.'

'Is that a spell?' I breathed. 'A spell to recite while doing it?'

'No, not at all.' She laughed. 'There's not really much power in words. That's just a little phrase to help you remember what needs to be done, for in the panic of the moment, your mind can go blank. It helps enormously to have little ditties like this drilled into the brain that can be hooked into. Do you remember 'Stop, Drop and Roll'?'

I nodded. 'Yeah, that was repeated so often in grade school,' I said slowly. 'In case we ever found ourselves in a situation where our clothing was on fire. We used to run around the playground chanting it, not even understanding what the words meant.'

'Exactly. But paired with the graphics you were given when they planted those three words in your minds, it would come back to you when needed.' She looked at me again. 'Hold the gate, mend the path, guard over all. Say it.'

I did as she requested, then asked, 'Do you really think I need to learn this?'

'Oh, this is a catch-all for anything that needs mending, not just for the unlikely situation of an adamantite bomb on ley lines,' she laughed again, dismissing the possibility and putting my mind at ease. 'Anything that is magical and has a force field around it. It'll be useful enough someday, I'm sure you'll find.'

'But,' I was so unwilling to let this go. 'You say mend the path. How would that be done? What are the... the mechanics of working with a seam of magic?' I visualized the ley lines, and what possible damage an adamantite bomb could do. Hugh had also instilled in me quite firmly the hazards of touching the magic in these lines.

All of a sudden she was by my side, her elegant hands holding both my shoulders, and her dark eyes stared into mine. 'You really want to know this?'

'Yes,' I sputtered. 'I want to know everything! Anything practical.'

She let go of my arms and unexpectedly squeezed me in a hug. 'Goddess bless,' she murmured, and then let go of me. 'I've tried to pass this knowledge onto Sasha, but she's just not interested, she's far too concerned with the physical and cheap glamors and sex. Finally, a young witch who wants to soak up the necessary knowledge.'

Pride washed over me and I straightened my shoulders. Was I finally to get my dearest wish granted? And of course, I couldn't not love that I was finally besting Sasha in something.

'Everything,' I said firmly. 'I want to know everything you can tell me.'

'Alright, come sit.'

We sat back into the comfy armchairs, and she began.

'If, in the very unlikely event such a thing would come to pass,' she began. 'To mend the lines, it's much like weaving strands, but these are strands of magic. You've seen the seams.'

I nodded fervently in agreement.

'I'd advise you to look closer at them, without actually touching the lines of course,' she said. 'Study them closely, and you will eventually pick out the individual... threads, so to speak, since we're using the weaving analogy.'

She watched me carefully the whole time she spoke as if she could make me understand better by the intensity of her gaze.

'If any of these threads are broken, as would happen with a hypothetical bomb or disruption to the ley lines, then it is a very delicate operation to weave the lines back in a flow, tying the ends together very carefully, securely. Just like electrical wires – but you don't need to scrape off the protective plastic coating on the copper.'

I thought back and digested what she was imparting, trying to picture it all in my mind, then nodded. 'It sounds simple enough,' I said. 'You've done this before?'

Her eyes opened wide and she barked a short laugh. 'Goddess, no! No, it would take a very powerful talent to be able to do such a thing. To begin with, holding back the wards, opening the gate? Not an easy task, it could only be done by someone who has the ability and confidence to not get herself, or himself, burned on those spells. And the weaving?'

Cate shook her head. 'There are very few witches living today powerful enough to take on that job. Li

Minh in China, perhaps, and a small handful of others, who may not even exist. They might just be legends.'

'Oh,' I said, feeling rather deflated. Still, it was good practical knowledge to have, even if I could never be able to use it. 'I guess that's why the deserts were never mended? Because there wasn't a witch who could do it?'

She shook her head. 'That's not the case at all,' she said firmly. 'The problem was the timing and placement. The witch would already have to be in close proximity in order to perform the operation, because there's a very small window of time in which the lines can be mended. The power flowing through them, if interrupted, will inevitably scar the lines, like melted plastic bubbling over, or even scar tissue in the human body, and it takes centuries, millennia even, before the power can find another route to flow and heal the land and the people living on it.'

'And the witches couldn't just fly to the spot when they were needed?'

Her face was in shadow, with just a glitter from her eyes in the faint light of the wall sconces. 'Flight?' she asked softly. 'There's very few witches who have mastered that art, who have the power to learn.'

A thrill ran up my spine as I stared into those fathomless eyes of hers. 'I have that power,' I breathed as the realization broke over me, and the impact of her words hit me.

'Yes,' she agreed, her voice barely audible, her eyes unreadable.

And pride reared its head again, deep inside me, a secret I could hold on to, only shared by me and Cate. And Margaret of course, but she had removed herself from the picture.

'How do you know so much of this, if you don't have the power yourself?' I had to ask Cate.

'I am the Huxor, and I take that role very seriously,' she replied. 'It's my job to know everything there is about the earth and its elements.'

She sighed. 'Yet I have no one to pass this mantle on to,' she remarked. 'None of my own children are worthy. Only you, Jon's daughter.' Cate looked off in the direction of the globe. 'There might be a way yet.'

Before I could really comprehend the import of her words, a clock struck, deep within the depths of the mansion.

'Come,' she said standing up and shaking off the atmosphere she had created. 'It is time to greet my guest.'

I came to with a start. 'No,' I said, looking down at the grubbiness of my person and then back to her stately perfection. 'I think I'll pass. I'm not dressed for the occasion.'

She laughed, a sparkling sound like the diamonds which dripped and flashed in the light of the room. 'Nonsense. Come with me.'

Cate opened the sheers and then one of the glass-paned doors leading out to the garden. As we stepped through, I felt a shimmer, a shift, as if we were passing through a force field.

The formal gardens looked different somehow, from the last time I'd seen them. There was an abnormal abundance of flowers despite the earliness of the year, I could make out full blooming roses and rhododendrons and others I couldn't identify, and they filled the air with the unseasonal perfume of deep summer. The stars overhead were brighter, everything was somehow more.

We had moved into Alt.

She led me down the slate path. The stones were surrounded by tiny plants, impossible to avoid, and as we walked we crushed them underfoot and the spicy smell of them wafted up. Finally, we reached the hedge surrounding her tennis court. With a secret smile, she ushered me past.

I entered the court, expecting to see the lawn and net in the light of the stars overhead, but the entire place had changed. I stopped with a gasp.

Burning sconces sat on stone pillars lining the hedges on all four sides, and by their soft glows I could see that it was still a court here in Alt, but not one meant for playing tennis. The entire ground was covered in black and white checkered marble tiles, like a giant chess board. Like the Red Queen's court in the book *Alice Through the Looking Glass*.

Along the center of one side where the umpire's high seat had been, now stood a majestic wooden throne, carved throughout with wondrous, terrible faces and beasts. A throne fit for a queen, to match the crown sitting atop Cate's head. I turned to ask her what was the meaning of all of this, but before I could utter a word a movement from the side took my attention.

Eldric stepped out from between a parting of the hedges, the Dark Elf king himself. He stepped boldly, his demeanor haughty, and as always was accompanied by Bitches One and Two, their paleness a foil for his lavender hue. Trevor was nowhere to be seen, and I wondered again at Brin's information that the goblin was playing both sides.

Cate and the Dark Elves met in the center of the court, and the two main players bowed to each other as if in a stately dance of equals. They were well matched in height and beauty, Cate's iridescent gown like a chameleon taking on the colors of Eldric's lavender, dancing with darker purples in the folds.

In these surroundings, there should have been a musical ensemble playing in the background, with finely dressed courtiers mingling in the open spaces, and servers laden with trays of roasted beasts and delicacies. Instead, there were only the five of us.

'Welcome, Eldric.' Cate's voice rang clear and true in the sheltered courtyard. She ignored the warriors on either side of her guest. 'I trust your journey was fair.'

He likewise ignored my presence. 'Cut the niceties. We need to discuss the matter at hand.'

'Everything's in place, as my missive described,' she replied. Did I imagine the trace of fear in her bearing? No, I decided, it must be a trick of the light, I thought as she calmly met his eye.

'We must have action, and sooner,' he said.

'Patience, my friend. Not long now.'

'I don't trust this change in plans,' he said, then he finally acknowledged me by darting a disparaging sneer. 'You've brought in too many uncertain elements. I demand to adhere to the original outline.'

My presence was inhibiting him from being more explicit, from truly speaking what was on his mind. I wondered if this was the reason Cate had brought me along.

'All in good time,' Cate purred, dismissing his concerns with a smile and a wave of her hand. 'You shall achieve your desires, and I, mine. Do not fear.'

'I do not fear.' Eldric gritted his teeth as he said the words, then caught himself. His face once more became a blank unemotional mask. 'The Kin have been draining the leys of their magic long enough. I demand an end to this practice before...'

'I have given you my assurances.' She cut him off with a snap of her fingers and her voice thundered across the tiles expanse. 'What more do you require apart from my word?'

Cate seemed to grow several inches as she drew herself up in anger at his words. They continued their stare down for several moments more.

He set his mouth in a grim line, and then he bowed cordially to her. 'Till that time, then.'

From where I stood slightly behind her, I could see her shoulders relax, just a fraction.

'Till then, my friend,' she replied with the slightest bow of her own head in return.

And Eldric and his bitches disappeared from sight. Their haste was possibly rude.

I had questions for Cate, of course I did, about the events which had just unfolded, but she refused to answer them. Instead, her face took on a drawn, haggard look.

'In politics,' she advised. 'We sometimes find ourselves playing both sides of the net. It is a juggling act, but a necessary one, if one is to achieve one's goals.'

CHAPTER 25

C ate looked exhausted after this meeting with the Dark Elf king, and distracted, so I took my leave. I had a lot to think about. The older witch had not only answered some of my questions, but she had opened my eyes to many things, especially about myself. It was with pride that I coasted down the hills of the old city on my bike, the wind in my hair and my back held straight.

And I had reason to feel so good. I was fitter than I'd ever been, physically, and this one evening with Cate had taught me so much.

Dad was sitting in the dining room at home. He'd set it up temporarily as a home office, with a small lamp lighting the papers before him and an old sheet used as a tablecloth to protect the polished surface. Not that we were so short of rooms in that house, but the renovations had started on the library. Once the walls were redone and the windows replaced and the massive bookshelves polished up, that room would be his study.

'Hey,' he said, peering over his half-glasses when I paused in the doorway. 'Had a good night?'

I was still feeling flushed with all that had happened that evening, and couldn't contain my smile.

Seeing that, he pushed himself back in the captain's chair, and mirrored my smile. 'How is Brin?'

Oh, right. He needed a report. I hemmed a little, hawed a little, until he removed his glasses and gave me the Dad look. 'How is Brin?' he asked again, this time without the smile.

If I'd been smart, I would have prepared a story on my long ride home instead of spending the whole time dreaming of what could be in my life. I would have to wing it. I quickly gauged how much to tell him.

Brin was worried about some kind of bomb in the Temple, but Cate had dismissed the possibility of anything too serious, pointing out that elves had no access to the Kin's place, guarded with wards and everything as it was. She didn't seem to think it was a threat.

And on the other hand, while I had first suspected that Cate was involved in this movement to bring down the Veil, that she was working hand in hand with Eldric, what I had seen that evening had proved this theory wrong. She was another double agent in the field between Kin and elves, and she was far more effective at it than I could ever be. I felt assured she had the whole thing in hand.

And Eldric had claimed the Kin were drinking from the leys in their cleansing ceremonies.

I took a seat across the wide table from him and smoothed the thin cotton underneath my hands. 'I couldn't get a lot out of him, because Alice was there,' I said to him truthfully. 'But there's whispers of a bomb.'

He became very still. 'What kind of bomb?' he asked. His forehead wrinkled, the angle of the light exaggerating the shadows of his face's lines.

I shook my head and shrugged. 'What sort of bombs do elves have access to?'

I watched him carefully as he thought about it, then the lines disappeared as his mind found ease. 'They don't,' he said. 'That's not an elven thing at all, far too unsubtle.'

He gave a small laugh. 'A bomb,' he repeated himself, chuckling. 'That's sounds more like a dwarven tactic, not that the dwarves would ever act outside the law.'

The dwarf community was largely responsible for hammering out all the legalese of the Convention and were hard-ass sticklers for rules and tradition so, no, normally dwarves would not act outside their own law. There had been one dwarf, though, last fall, one dwarf who'd been willing to illicitly work with me in order to grab the fairy gold.

'What is it?' Dad must have seen the expression change on my face.

'It's just that, Alice also told me that Brin has been hanging around in Alt, visiting the vampires down the road from her...'

'This is the first I've heard of this,' he said. His voice was stern.

I hastily covered my tracks. 'Oh, she just said that very recently, I didn't have a chance yet to put it into a report or anything.'

He nodded slowly and raised his eyebrows, indicating that I should continue with my line of thought. I told him about Dirk, the young dwarf. The one with his hair caught up in a dwarf-bun instead of the traditional intricate old fashioned braids. I'd met him last year when I stumbled into the dwarves den, looking for their help against the fairies, and Dirk had sought me out, hungry for a chance to steal the fae gold. There was a rebel dwarf if ever I'd met one. 'So maybe it's not elves that we have to worry about?'

'That's possible,' he conceded, then was overtaken by a huge yawn. He stretched his arms back and winced. 'At any rate, doesn't sound too serious. Nothing to lose sleep over, especially with a big night ahead of me tomorrow.'

'Is that... the cleansing of the lines?'

He nodded.

'I suppose I can't...'

'No.'

'Even to...'

'Absolutely not.'

He waited, poised tensely, for further arguments from me, but I gracefully gave up on that line. I changed my angle of offence. Eldric had insinuated that the Kin were siphoning off the power of the lines in order to keep the Veil in place, and I needed to know more about that. If it was true, it was very wrong, and I had a hard time believing that my father would be involved in such a thing.

'What does it involve, this cleansing of the lines?' I asked. 'How? And why do you need to do it?'

This caught him by surprise. I waited as he searched for an answer simple enough for me to comprehend.

'You don't need to dumb it down for me.'

He lifted his eyes and stared at me across the table. 'Very well then,' he said. 'The cleansing ceremony is performed by a coven of witches, twelve of them. We stand in the Circle, you remember the Drawing service at the Solstice?'

I nodded.

'The Temple was built so that circle is located directly over the convergence of the lines. By meeting with our minds, we enter the lines.'

'You touch the lines?' Cate had said that was dangerous.

Dad shrugged. 'Not physically of course, but mentally. We massage them. To help clear any debris which might have accumulated over the past fifty years.'

'How can debris get into the ley lines? Aren't they powerful magic seams? Wouldn't they knock anything out of the way just by their natural force?' I had so many questions for him, questions that Cate couldn't answer as she wasn't a part of this ceremony. 'What's actually going on in that ceremony? You open the lines, you say. But how? How do you touch them with your minds?'

He harrumphed. I'd read about that in old English novels, but had never heard someone actually do it. My father was starting to bluster under fire of my probing questions. I watched in fascination as Jon de Teilhard, head of the Avalon Kin, squirmed in discomfort.

'It's not so simplistic.' His face was reddening even as he spoke. 'You wouldn't understand.'

But there's where he was wrong. I would understand, I would comprehend. If he told me the truth, that is. In that moment a faint niggle of realization squirmed inside me, one that I didn't want to acknowledge. Perhaps Eldric was right. Perhaps the Kin were siphoning off the magic of lines in order to keep the Veil between Alt and Normal.

He might have seen my eyes widen, but he could have no idea what was going on inside my head.

'No, of course we don't touch the ley lines. That would be suicidal, no one can survive a surge of magic that strong. It's more, we allow them to...' He was searching for the words. 'We open the lines and they flow more freely. We flush them, basically. You can actually watch it, but from afar. You and Hugh should. It's quite the sight, seeing them brighten.'

'How can you flush them? How do you open the lines?'

'Through the dozen Kin minds working together,' he said. 'It's like a water pipe. You see the city letting the water run out of the fire hydrants sometimes? It's done to flush the lines and keep the pressure up. So, the ceremony is much like that.'

I'd seen that, of course, the fire hydrants spouting precious fresh lake water for hours at a time, even in the dry summers, all the excess water running down the hills, into the gutters and sewers and then into the harbor. It had always seemed like such a terrific waste of a valuable resource.

'Where does the magical energy go? The excess flushed from the system?' My voice was barely a whisper. I cleared my throat and tried to speak normally. 'You're diverting the energy from the lines. Where does it go?'

He stared at me across the table, the desk light highlighting every crag and furrow on his face. I could tell he didn't want to answer the questions I was posing, because he knew what my reaction would be.

'The excess energy is directed toward the Veil, to keep it in place,' he confessed finally, bluntly, not finding the appropriate sugar coating for the concept. 'It takes an enormous amount of energy to keep it there, and would tax individual Kin if we had to be constantly powering it ourselves. But think of it like tapping the sugar maples in spring. Our action helps the lines clear anything built up, and that helps the lines flow more cleanly.' My father sat back in his chair the better to judge my reaction.

'The Kin are siphoning off energy to keep the Veil in place.' I had to clarify, just to be absolutely sure. So Eldric was right, in part.

He shook his head. Dark storm clouds were gathering on his face. 'We'd have to do it even if the Veil was no longer in place,' he insisted. 'Like, with the seal hunt in the spring for example. Mankind had made themselves part of the natural ecosystem for centuries, and when they stopped the annual hunt, the seal population burgeoned and all these numbers impacted the amount of cod in the oceans, necessitating a purposeful cull in the seal herds. Likewise, even if we stopped diverting the excess energy to the Veil, we'd still have to cleanse the lines.'

I didn't totally buy this explanation, it sounded suspiciously like an excuse. My father was a party to this Kin-sanctioned action to consume the actual magic of the ley lines, and for what purpose? To keep the super naturals in their prison of Alt. I was already shaking my head. 'This is wrong, on so many levels.'

'You mean about the Veil. You think we're not aware of this?' His voice was rough, as if worn out by expressing this fact too many times without anyone listening.

'You're using the energy of the earth to do this? Do you know the consequences?' I wasn't sure, but Eldric seemed to know all about it. About the irreplaceable magic running through the earth that was siphoned away, never to be regained.

'Of course we know the consequences,' he snapped. 'And that's why we're trying to get the Veil taken down. We can't keep this up indefinitely. We have to change our ways, and we are in the process of this.'

'Why don't we just stop it? Stop diverting energy to keeping the Veil up?' I was almost yelling by now. 'It's easy enough to do, just don't do that ceremony, let the Veil disintegrate on its own.'

'It's hardly that simple!' He roared back and thumped his fist on the wooden table. 'You don't know the intricacies involved, the logistics. Planning for an inundation of super naturals into the Normal world, we're totally unprepared for this.'

'But it's their world too! Why not just let the worlds come back together? It doesn't take a Parliamentary vote or a ton of bureaucratic red tape to do this.'

It *was* that simple. Stop diverting power from the ley lines and allow the world to heal. Let nature take its course.

He stared at me wearily, unwilling to keep up this argument which neither side would ever win. 'We're working on it, okay? It will happen, maybe not in my lifetime, but in yours. And not before time.'

'Maybe now is the time to begin it.'

....

It was so unfair, I fumed to myself as I got ready for bed. I'd walked out on Jon because there was no settling that argument. Only action would make a difference. And we were at the crossroads, a decision had to be made, for the ceremony only happened every fifty years. Now was the time to act. But how could I stop the ceremony?

And who was I to think I could? A half-blood who had stumbled on to greater powers through an accident, and despite my new status I had no pull in the Kin. I couldn't stop the ceremony any more than I could lift the Veil. But I could help, if only the Kin would allow it.

The Kin didn't know what a treasure they had hiding in their midst. I'd seen the hunger in Cate's eyes when she told me that few witches had the power of flight like I did.

Surely Cate must be aware of what happened at the ceremony, how the excess energy was being siphoned off to hold the Veil in place. She was on the side of loosening the grip of the Veil, like the elves, but she didn't condone their violence.

Despite my assurances and slight subterfuge with Dad, I wondered what the elves were truly playing at. Before I'd gotten to know her, when I'd first found out she was responsible for my being posted back home, I had suspected that Cate was working with the Dark Elves in whatever evil deeds they'd been planning against the Kin. Yet, what had puzzled me was that Cate herself was Kin through and through, and how could she work against her own family?

It wasn't the case, as I had seen tonight. Cate had positioned herself to be working against the elves, while pretending to be on their side. Even I could see that. She was playing Eldric, and she'd been exhausted by keeping up this pretense.

But still, I comforted myself as I got under the faded patchwork quilts of my childhood bed, my evening had been unexpectedly well-spent. I still couldn't believe that in that short hour, the older witch had been able to pass on more practical knowledge than I'd learned in the months with Nachtan and Hugh combined. My father's wife had long been my sworn enemy, yet almost overnight had become my hero, my true mentor. Being of this time and place, she understood the issues I faced like no other witch could.

The last thought I remember having, the one that finally rocked me into my dreams, was the memory of Cate's voice. *I have no one to pass this mantle on to... Only you, Jon's daughter... There might be a way yet...*

Could such a thing be possible? Not that I would want to inherit from Cate, I had much greater things planned for my life, a life that wouldn't be worth much if Sasha found out she'd been passed over for the inheritance. No, I wouldn't want to take on Cate's mantle of responsibility for the Huxor. Still, her words comforted me and gave me confidence in the acceptance implied.

And I had to trust she knew what she was doing and would win at the game she played. I vowed I would help her anyway I could.

CHAPTER 26

The next day, being a sunny Saturday in late June, meant that the house was silent and our own again. The workers weren't there with their endless machinery and banging and loud radio and the inevitable shouted conversations to be heard over all that. I slowly walked down the grand staircase, breathing in the serenity of this peace. The sun streamed through the stained glass over the front door, and the bevelled windows cast prisms of color through the dust still in the air. The dust which, Mom had assured me, would be with us for a long time after the crew had left.

I was looking for her, to let her know I was back from the gym. She'd wanted to take me shopping for summer dresses. Yes, I rolled my eyes over that, but if it made her happy, then I could spare the few hours for a stroll downtown and lunch at a fancy spot.

She wasn't in the kitchen, or upstairs, and I hadn't spotted her in any of the gardens, hence the reason I was descending into the main hallway instead of down the cozy back stairs which we mostly used. Her car was still in the driveway, so she had to be here somewhere.

I heard a scraping sound behind the closed door of the library, the room that was to become Dad's home office. I opened the door silently, noting that someone had already oiled and polished the ancient hinges.

The drapes had all been removed, allowing the sun to shine unobstructed through the leaves on the trees in the garden. The dust motes whirled and danced in those beams, indicating that someone was definitely present in the room, although at first glance I could see no one.

The large furniture, the pieces that were too heavy to move, they'd all been draped in cotton drop sheets to prevent the worst of the dust from settling into the corners and edges. The bookshelves were bare, the books having been boxed up and stored in the parlor for safe keeping. Even the oak panelling had been removed from the walls in places in order to save it from the careless drills of the electricians as they rewired the house.

I couldn't see anyone at first, but then I heard again the sound that had drawn me in there, the scraping of wood on wood. I stepped further into the space and looked to my left, over by the fireplace. In the nook to the right of it, Mom stood on a small stepladder, a hammer in her hand as she poked and pulled at a tiny door.

I watched her a moment before I spoke. Like tiny wheels and gears, things were clicking together in my mind.

'It's not in there anymore,' I said softly. 'Dad removed it after you left. After I found it.'

She whirled around, almost losing her balance. Her hair was done up in a Rosy Riveter kerchief, and her cheek was smudged with dust. She caught her balance and carefully shut the door, banging it into place with the flat end of the hammer before she gracefully stepped down.

'What's that?' she asked as if she didn't know what I was referring to.

'The book,' I replied patiently. 'The Grimoire. I found it after you... after you left all those years ago. I had been gone crazy searching for some sort of clue, and it called to me.'

She flashed a guilty look up at the surface of the nook. You could hardly see the outlines of the panel which had hidden the secret crevice by the fireplace chimney. The lock had been dismembered ten years ago and the small cupboard nailed firmly into place.

My mind flashed back through the years, to the last time it had been opened. Dad in his rage, with the hammer in his hand just like Mom, only he had been closing the small nook up, hoping it was forever.

'I didn't know you had put it there,' I said softly. 'I guess he didn't tell you.'

Her shoulders slumped and she lay the hammer on the mantelpiece. The dust rose again in little eddies, magnifying the movement.

'Were you planning to use it?' I thought for a moment. 'Again?' I added.

Mom shook her head. 'No,' she answered in a quiet voice. 'I wanted to burn it.'

'I think it's time you told me. The whole story, of how you managed to get yourself stuck in the Ice Kingdom. And how you got the Book. And how the hell you were able to do anything with it.'

Despite my words, I wasn't angry. No, I was filled with wonder that my mother, who I'd always believed was Normal, had somehow tapped into the magic in that ancient book.

She looked up at me and nodded, a rueful smile on her face. 'You're right,' she said. 'It's time you found out your true heritage. On the Martin side.'

Mom drew her dusty arm around me into a hug, then reached up and removed the kerchief from around her head. 'Come on,' she said. 'This requires good coffee, none of that drip stuff, and fresh croissants. Fortunately, I'm prepared.'

I made a couple of cappuccinos from the shiny new machine Dad had temporarily installed in the butler's pantry, pending the kitchen renos, then made to sit at the table but she shook her head.

'Let's go out somewhere, into the fresh air and away from the house. I don't want us to be interrupted.'

She loaded up a wooden tray with our oversize cups and matching plates for the croissants and led me past the formal garden outside the front and down the hill a bit. We sat on the grass with our backs against the low stone wall which was sun warmed in this sheltered spot. The barely budded branches of the chestnuts created a dappled light. We couldn't see Topsail Road below us, the shrubs of the property shielded us from view of anyone.

Mom sighed as she looked ahead of us, gazing off into the past. 'Not sure where to begin,' she said with her cup held close to her mouth with both hands.

I knew what she meant, I myself had so many questions that begged to be answered that I could hardly pick out which was the most pressing.

'The Book,' I said finally. 'I don't understand how it could have been of any use to you.'

She laughed then, and drank a swallow of coffee. She lay the cup back down on the tray and wiped the foam from her mouth, then idly picked up a pastry.

'This whole story about me being Normal?' She glanced over at me. 'Not quite true.'

I sat up straight. 'What? But you're not Kin, I mean, surely to God I would have heard if you were,' I said. 'Even if you were half-blood, someone would have brought this up before!'

She shook her head. 'No, not Kin at all,' she replied. 'But, and this was kept very quiet, we do have witch blood running through our veins.'

I shook my head to clear it. Yeah, that information had been kept hidden alright. It was a huge secret. 'But why? What's the big deal? And ...'

'Your great-grandmother Martin,' she said, cutting through all the new questions she had now raised. 'She came from Bonavista Bay.'

I nodded. I'd heard the story, about how Elsie White, the wife of Mom's grandfather, had been a fisherman's daughter and had come to the city to find work. She'd been hired as a seamstress in the Martin clothing facto-ry, had met the owner, the two had fallen crazy in love and, defying all the class conventions of the time, had married and lived happily ever after.

She glanced over at me. 'You know us Martins,' she said wryly. 'We act from the heart, not the brain. Things haven't changed much through the generations.

'Their marriage was scandalous enough in itself,' Mom continued with a smile. 'All the St. John's society ladies were horrified, and would have cut the whole family off except that Grand-dad was rich and didn't care a hoot what they thought. He wasn't Kin, but her half-blood witch status though... even Art Martin couldn't have carried off that one. Not back then.

'Those were very different times, remember,' she cau-tioned before I could lay judgement.

I sat and thought a while, trying to adjust to this new definition of myself. Mom was part witch? But how could this have happened?

Mom shrugged. 'The story that's whispered is that two or three hundred years ago, during one of the Scourges, the witch hunts in the old country, a group of Irish half-bloods fled on a fishing vessel, and jumped ship in a tiny cove out in the Bonavista Bay area. They settled there illegally, built homes and farms. I say illegally, because they were officially Catholic in their persuasion and Irish to boot, and back then neither were allowed to become permanent residents of the island, which was an English and Protestant colony.'

I'd never heard this aspect of my maternal grandmother's history, that had been a well-kept secret indeed.

'They kept quiet about the witch blood in their line, but eventually the White's became known for being healers and midwives, even wart charmers,' Mom continued. 'Hedge witches, sort of.'

'Are you saying there are a lot of people out that way with witch blood in them?'

She shrugged again. 'The magic tends to skip around, and pop up unexpectedly,' she said. 'Sort of like red hair, it must be a recessive gene. Depends if both parents have it.'

'Of course, no one talked about it, mostly through fear and shame because after all, people were being killed for being half-bloods. But yes, that was the story my grandmother whispered to me.'

'Wait a moment,' I said as the thought occurred to me. 'Is this why you were able to use the Grimoire? Because of some line of magic coming from her?'

Mom nodded. 'Yeah. It's a different strain of magic, of course, than the Kin's, and those with the power have never been formally trained in any way, but it's powerful just the same.'

'So there's an Irish version of the Kin?'

She laughed. 'Not officially. They don't make the same distinctions. Everyone's equal in their society, some have more magic than others, just as some have brown eyes versus blue. They're not like the Kin at all.'

'So that makes me, what? A double half-blood? A three-quarter blood?'

'Yeah, something like that,' she said, nodding slowly. 'You are.'

'How absolutely cool.' I turned to her. 'And no wonder all the Kin were surprised I had so much power, when they thought the magic should have been more diluted. Do the Kin know about the Bonavista Bay witch line?'

'They've never acknowledged it, snobs that they are.'

We munched on the fresh croissants and sipped our cappuccinos in silence for another while. A single fresh crunchy pastry was a wondrous thing. To eat two of the concoctions at a single setting was just plain greed, but I managed it anyway.

'This is all very interesting,' I said as I picked the large flaky crumbs off my t-shirt and popped them into my mouth. 'But the Book. Where'd it come from?'

'Yeah.' Mom dragged the word out then heaved a sigh. 'The Book. Well, what I'm going to tell you doesn't paint me in a good light, okay?'

And thus began the story of love and jealousy. 'Your Dad and I, we fell in love. I knew right from the start that he was married and there was little chance he'd leave his wife, but I got stupid. After you were getting older and started going to school and asking why your Dad didn't live with us, I began to resent his ties to Cate, and well, she kept on having kids, so I knew full well what that meant about their relationship.'

She gave a laugh that was still bitter through the dust of the intervening years. 'Looking back, I can't believe I was so jealous of Cate. Sure, she had the marriage, the estate, Christmas Day, yet I had the most important thing, his heart.

'It didn't help that I became 'friends' with Cate,' she said, as her fingers made air quotes. 'And Jon encouraged that, thinking this would keep things on a civilised keel. He's always been such a dreamer.'

Mom munched on the last of her pastry, licking her fingers before she continued. 'That woman is insidious,' she remarked. 'She really screwed with my mind. She found out about my magic, which was actually latent, and she encouraged me to dabble.'

I shifted uncomfortably. Despite the warmth of the day, the grass was damp under my shorts and soaking through. 'Is that where the Book came from?' It hadn't been an ancient Irish text, that was for certain. It had been written in a mixture of old English which was closer to modern German, and Latin.

She nodded, still looking off into the distant past. 'Hind sight is everything, they say. And I've had plenty of time to look back on the events of that summer. I had the one thing that witch wanted and would never get, but I never realized my good fortune, and I thought I wanted more, and that *I* could use *her*.'

I felt the deep sigh come from her. 'She tutored me, taught me enough to give me confidence in magic, all of course without telling Jon. Cate convinced me not to say a word, that it would be a secret between us girls, because it would upset his masculinity or some such nonsense. And I fell for it.'

'I don't remember Cate ever being here,' I said.

'No, she would wait till all you kids were at school, or summer camp. You remember the summer you went to the day camp?' I nodded slowly. Yes, I did. The one year I'd ever attended such a thing, we had swimming and camping and all sorts of outside activities, every day had been filled. The best summer of my life, right up until the day Mom had disappeared.

'Cate left the grimoire behind one day, now I know she did it on purpose. She knew full well that I wouldn't be able to hold back and start reading it,' Mom continued. 'It fell open on a page to banish your enemy.'

'But weren't you two friends by then?'

She shook her head. 'On the surface, perhaps, but I still wanted her out of his life.' She took a deep breath. 'So I tried the spell, just to see if it worked. Took some of her hair cuttings, some of my own, did everything it said to do. I even used the medallion she'd given me...

Such a huge mistake. She had hexed it, so that any spell worked would reverse, would backfire onto the caster.'

I caught my breath. The medallion, the one that had screamed my mother's name when I held it in Zeta's witch store, was it only last year? It had marked the start of my journey, my search for that piece of magicked metal had led me into the clutches of Willem and to the Crystal Charm Stone. Where was it now? The last time I'd seen it was when the Elder in Scarp, Johanna, had removed it from me. She must have recognized the evil intent inside it. I hoped she'd destroyed the wretched object.

'I always believed Cate was behind your disappearance,' I said softly. 'Did Dad not understand?'

She turned to me, her blue eyes flashing in the sun and her mouth set grimly. 'Oh, we have discussed this matter, believe me.

'He suspected it too, but he couldn't do anything,' she said. 'He didn't know where I'd gone, and if he pissed her off anymore, he would lose all hope of finding me, ever. He had to suck it up, and act like everything was normal all those years while he was secretly searching for me.'

She became very still. 'So while I was stuck in my prison, he was in a prison of his own, despite the appearance of freedom. I guess... I guess when he found you with the Book, he must have known then that Cate was behind it all. He didn't tell me about that.'

Possibly because he was embarrassed at his own actions that day, but I kept that thought to myself. There was a special little hole inside me that I crawled into whenever I remembered, an afternoon much like this when he had come upon me and the grimoire and he'd screamed at me and torn it from my hands, forbidding me ever to practice magic again.

All those years I'd thought he hated me, blamed me somehow for Mom's disappearance, when in actuality he had understood right away what had happened. And blamed himself.

Mom stood up, brushing the crumbs from her jeans. 'Well, I guess we don't need lunch anymore. But how about we stroll downtown and look for those summer dresses?' Her tone was as light and airy as that summer's day.

I looked up, disbelieving. No. She'd just dropped this bombshell in my lap and thought everything was all okay? Thought we could go out and frivolously shop for fun sundresses and cute sandals? I opened my mouth to express my feelings, but immediately shut it again, once I realized what was really bothering me.

'Maybe tomorrow, Mom?' I said. 'I need a little time to digest all this.'

'Oh, sure,' she said, her big eyes contrite with understanding. 'I sort of dumped all this on you, didn't I?'

She reached out her hand to help me up. 'Well, how about I make a nice blueberry pie for dessert tonight? We have all those berries Alice's mom gave you last year, we need to make room in the freezer.'

'Sure,' I agreed, still dazed, as if blueberry pie would help sort out the mess in my head. 'Blueberry pie.'

CHAPTER 27

I went on a long walk that afternoon. It was too warm for the bike, so instead I found the old railway track trail, the one that went straight on across the whole island if I chose to walk the thousand kilometers to Port aux Basques. I didn't of course, Mount Pearl was about my limit before I turned around and retraced my steps.

The whole trailway, I didn't really pay attention to the pleasantness of walking in the dappled shade of the trees as the path meandered along the river's bank. I didn't notice any of it because my mind was working too furiously.

Mom's story had blown me away. All of it, from the Irish half witch blood flowing in my veins to her so-called friendship with Cate and her belief that Cate had set her up to fail in order to remove the competition for Jon's affections. Yes, I'd had my differences with Dad's wife, and I'd also suspected for a long time that she was responsible for Mom's disappearance, but things were different now. Now that I'd gotten to know Cate personally.

And now Cate had taken me under her wing. I couldn't deal with that line of thinking, not just yet, for I had an uncomfortable feeling right in the back of my mind that I could end up betraying my mother.

Instead, I forcibly brought my thoughts toward the ley lines and the Veil. Dad said the cleansing ceremony was necessary in order to flush the system, and if they didn't use the excess energy, it would just dissipate like the water let loose from the fire hydrants by the city crews. He claimed the Veil had to be brought down slowly or else society wouldn't be able to handle the change, that neither Normals nor the super natural element would be able to adjust without major upset and possibly blood-shed on both sides.

Yet Eldric claimed, rightly, that the Kin were siphon-ing off the excess to further their own agenda. He had hinted that individuals were actually drinking from the lines to empower themselves, a thing which Dad had vehemently denied. But Eldric also wanted to work to remove the Veil entirely, and he was planning to bring this about. Somehow.

What would the outcome be if the division between Alt and Normal disappeared? Would it be such a terrible thing? I thought about the super naturals I had known, the local ones here in town and the surrounding areas, and the poverty and wretchedness I'd seen lurking in the corners and the dark alleyways. And then I remembered walking through the streets of Edinburgh, where they had no Veil separating the worlds. They lived in peace, both Normals and super naturals going about their daily businesses without impinging on the others. No blood-shed, no violence, no confusion.

Who was right? Eldric or my father? Or both?

On the home stretch of my walk, cutting up under the canopy of trees in the ancient Protestant Cemetery, my thoughts inevitably returned to Cate. Straddling both camps, playing the game against the Dark Elf king while working for the Kin. I could only trust her, and it wasn't just because she was giving me what I'd craved all these years. No...

My phone let loose with its old-fashioned ring tone and I was glad for the distraction.

'Hey there.' He could probably hear the smile in my voice, and would have thought it was for him. 'Where've you been all day?'

'I have the bike fired up,' Hugh said. The enthusiasm in his voice was catching. 'Ready to share the first ride of the summer? I thought perhaps a drive, a burger and then go watch the sunset over the ocean.'

He'd put the barfing incident behind him by the sounds of it, which was a relief.

Mindless driving around, protected from the wind by his strong back, the roar of the motor as it outpaced the racing thoughts in my head? Yes, I was definitely up for that. 'Got an extra helmet?'

'Packed and ready.'

'I'll meet you at the house in five minutes.'

I sprinted up the last bit of hill to our home and quickly exchanged my shorts and t-shirt for jeans and a hoody and the leather jacket of Mom's which I had claimed for myself a couple of years ago.

'That looks familiar,' she was saying to me right when Hugh walked in.

I shoved my arms into it and flashed her a grin. 'You weren't using it.'

She rolled her eyes and flicked me with the dish cloth. 'Go on, get out of here. And have fun, you two!'

I was to remember her last words later, many hours later once the dust had cleared. The events that followed that evening were many things, but definitely not what I would call fun.

....

It started off very innocently. We drove down the Southern Shore on his Harley, stopping to eat burgers, fries and milkshakes at a little place right on the water's edge in one of the many tiny communities dotted along the coastline. I was starving. The fresh air always had that effect on me. Not to mention my long walk and the fact that I'd only eaten a couple of croissants for lunch.

'So, what's the deal with the bike, anyway?' I was determined to keep up the chatter, to keep the thoughts in my head down to a dull roar.

'It's mine,' he said.

'Yeah, but you don't live here.'

'I bought it once when I was visiting. Couldn't pass up the deal. It's registered in Jon's name, I keep it at his garage,' Hugh said, then caught himself. 'In his former garage, I should say.'

'At Cate's,' I confirmed. I stuffed some fries into my mouth and chewed them thoughtfully, then washed them down with the chocolate milkshake. 'So even though Dad moved out, you're still friendly with her?'

I hadn't mentioned my own connection with her to him. No reason, really, except that she thought it might be best to keep it quiet from our Kin connections.

He shrugged. 'Why ever not? The separation is amicable on both sides, very civilised of them, as to be expected. It's much easier this way. I work with them both, we're all part of the larger Kin organization, they don't bring their personal issues into the working relationship. And that's how it should be.'

So he wasn't aware of the reasons Jon had stayed with his wife all those years. Or at least, the reason according to Mom. Interesting. Perhaps Dad and my boyfriend weren't as good friends as they claimed to be. Or perhaps no one had true friends among the Kin.

'I heard that the cleansing ceremony is tonight,' I said, switching tracks. 'I wouldn't mind seeing it.'

His eyes fired up again with enthusiasm. 'Absolutely. We can't miss it.'

'What exactly happens?' Dad had said they didn't touch the lines, just opened them up to clear out the excess. I couldn't imagine it was actually much to see, and I said as much.

'It's... it's a wonderful experience, to watch the lines being cleared,' Hugh said earnestly. 'There's nothing like it in this world. You'll see.'

He sat back with a smile. 'There's so much I want to show you in this world.'

And there was so much I wanted to see, and with Hugh by my side. But I was beginning to realize that I didn't necessarily want him showing me, I wanted us to explore and discover. Together, as equals.

More and more, I was coming to understand that I wanted to be an active partner, not just a 'plus-one'.

We wandered back out to the motorcycle, but before we put our helmets on, I stopped and inspected the bike. It wasn't a ginormous one, not like some of the Japanese and American ones I saw around town. It was old-school, bare bones really, and didn't offer a very comfortable ride for the passenger.

Who would want to be a passenger all their lives? This wasn't going to be my future, I decided right there and then.

'Teach me to drive.' I turned to look up at him.

'Sure,' he answered me, surprise in his voice. 'Your aunt's car would be the best to learn with. We can start anytime.'

'No. Not a car. The bike,' I said. 'Your bike.'

'*My Harley?*'

'Do you have another bike?'

His mouth was set, and I could see a battle going on inside him. 'I don't, that is, I mean...'

'Teach me to drive it,' I said again. 'What's wrong, you don't want to give up control?'

'It's not that,' he brushed aside my words. 'But you need a learner's permit. Once that's in place, you can get proper lessons. It's very important, you know, for safety reasons.'

'I can get a permit,' I said. 'But I want you to teach me right now. Just the basics. Right here in this parking lot.' I didn't know why I was challenging him, taunting him really. He loved his Harley. Maybe I was testing to see if he loved me enough to let me drive it. If he trusted me with it. I kept my eyes on his the whole time.

'Mmmm,' he finally said after wriggling a bit, but finding no way out. 'Okay, just around here. But I can't be on the back with you, you have to learn how to balance it first.'

And to give Hugh his due, he taught me the bare basics of driving his precious Harley, watching me jealously the whole time as I made my slow way around the empty parking lot. There was a lot of stopping and starting and dangerous overbalancing on my part, but I did it. I picked up the change of gears and the brakes and even how to lean into the curves.

Satisfied, I kicked the stand and stood up. I wasn't sure what I had just proven or gotten out of my system, but I felt a lot better about me and him and our future.

'Thank you,' I told him as I stood back to let him take charge of his bike again. 'This means a lot to me.'

'You know it wasn't easy for me.'

I laughed. 'Yeah, I know. I think that's why I wanted it.'

He took me in a big embrace, squeezing me in his arms. 'Sorry I haven't been around much since I got back into town,' he murmured against my helmet. 'But you know. Work.'

'Hey, I've been busy too, with my own work,' I reminded him, speaking into his leather jacket.

'Yes,' he said. I heard the smile in his voice. 'Your little
assignment.'

I stiffened, pushing against the arms that held me
close. Did he even realize how patronizing he'd just
sounded? I stepped out of his reach. But he didn't notice
anything amiss, and busied himself fitting his helmet on,
brushing his lustrous dark waves of hair away from his
face.

'And have you given any thought about what we were
discussing the other night?' He turned to me.

Oh right. He'd reminded me about our marriage, right
before I upchucked all over him.

Marriage. I didn't say a word in response, pretending
to be busy putting on my own helmet. Would marriage
to Hugh be like this all the time? Being his passenger as
he brought me places, showed me things? In between
my Duchess duties of course, providing the heir and a
spare for his dukedom.

Both Cate and Margaret had strongly advised me not
to agree to it, that it would tie me down for twenty years
or more, that I wouldn't be able to develop my own
career or explore my own desires. I would be weighed
down by the extremely ugly heavy ring which his mother
couldn't wait to pass on to me.

I stopped and stared at his bike before I got on behind
him. He was revving it up, raring to go, while I, I was
preparing to be his passenger. On the bike that he owned
and steered and controlled.

Maybe, maybe what I really wanted from life was a
motorcycle of my own. Not literally, of course. But I
knew I wanted to steer my own way through life.

CHAPTER 28

I n the dusk of the evening, Hugh steered the Harley up the steep road to the tower at the top of Signal Hill. It was the best place to be if you want to take in the whole city at once, well the old parts of it anyway. The stone building sat on top of more than five hundred feet of sedimentary rock which rose straight up out of the ocean. A powerful place in itself, it was always the perfect spot to sit and ponder. Tonight we were going to watch the light show of the ley line cleansing ceremony. He promised me it would be worth it.

'Will we be able to see it from here?' I asked him, my voice raised above the wind which, although it was blowing steady from the east and we were sitting comfortably in our little nook on the opposite side of the hill, was still managing to lift our hair and cut through our leather.

'The best viewing point is directly over the Temple,' he said. 'We need to fly.'

He didn't mean we would *fly* fly, of course, not the way I'd been practicing whenever I could. Hugh was referring to the mind flight which was very easily done. I settled my back against the solid rock behind us and prepared to relax my body enough to loosen my thoughts. My phone buzzed inside my jean jacket pocket, but this was not the time to be checking it.

'I've got something special to tell you,' he whispered, close to my ear. He took my hand in his and squeezed it. I looked up at him. Those green eyes were gleaming with excitement.

My stomach gave a small lurch. I hoped it wasn't about the ring, that his mother had insisted he give it to me. We had different views on that clunky piece of metal, valuable though the gem stones might be, for it was heavily laden with meaning. I prayed he wasn't going to take it out right there and then and force me to refuse it.

'Oh yeah?'

'They've asked me to prepare to take part in the next cleansing ceremony.'

My whole body relaxed and breath could enter my lungs again. My phone buzzed again, I continued to ignore it.

'Dude, I hate to rain on your parade,' I said in a dead-pan voice. 'But don't hold your breath waiting. You're going to be like, in your mid-seventies the next time this is done.'

'Stop your teasing,' he said, poking me with his elbow. 'You know I don't mean here. It'll be in Africa, or if that doesn't work out because of politics, in Spain.'

I thought about what he said for a moment.

'Aren't you awfully young for this... this honor?' Dad had told me it was only the highly regarded Elders, those who had proved they were trustworthy over many years.

His chest rose under the leather jacket. 'Young in age, perhaps, but not in maturity. This is what happens when you follow the prescribed path, do everything right. The influential witches get to know you, and that smooths the path.'

Hugh was right to be proud, for in the world of the Kin, reputation was everything. Yet the more I learned about the Kin and their ways, the less I was drawn to being a part of this structure. Even just a few days ago, I'd wanted the same for myself. But now, knowing what I did about the ley lines and the tapping of them during the cleansing ceremony, I was beginning to have my doubts.

'I don't think I'll ever be asked to be a part of the ceremony.'

He thought a moment, then shook his head in agreement. 'No. You're too much of an unknown still. With your history... But still, you have many years ahead of you. And having children calms the female hormones, they say. So...'

My eyes widened. Shit, really? He said those words like they were a good thing. To cover my reaction I took my phone out and checked to see who was so desperately trying to get in touch.

Brin. He'd phoned five times. I flicked to the texts, although he really didn't like sending messages so I wasn't expecting much. But he had texted finally, as I hadn't picked up his calls.

Y rnt u anser phon? Brin wasn't great at spelling. It wasn't because he was stupid, he just didn't respect the history of the printed English language, and he was right as a lot of it didn't make sense. *Hav packge from T must giv u. Bad.*

What was he trying to say? And who was T? Whatever. My friend was really going off the deep end, I feared. His contact with Eldric must have him spooked, but it could wait till the morning. I put the phone away and prepared to straighten Hugh out about the hormone thing. And the whole ring thing.

'With time, and my guidance, of course, you'll be able to go far.' Hugh squeezed my hand reassuringly.

I took a deep breath. I couldn't do this any longer, and it was only right to tell him. Marriage between us was looking less and less likely every time he opened his mouth. I prepared to let loose but he was already looking at his wrist watch.

'It's time,' he said. 'Let's go.'

I admit it was easier not to begin that difficult conversation right then, to wait for a more auspicious moment. He kept hold of my hand and I felt him relax beside me. I used that deep breath I'd just taken to also force my own body to relax and move into astral projection mode. There would be time enough later to discuss our futures.

And we floated over the city of St. John's, unmindful of the strong easterly breeze coming from the North Atlantic Ocean. The sun had fully gone from the sky by now, and being above the city lights, I could look up and see the stars in their glorious path across the sky. The town below us was quiet, yet something felt off. It was undefinable and unseen, like the faintest whiff of a forest fire a hundred miles away, so faint the conscious mind doesn't register the presence of smoke. I looked all around, and everything seemed normal, yet something about the movement of the shadows in the old alleyways below was almost catching my eyes.

I need to do this in Alt.

No, we don't have to. We'll see things fine from this perspective. He was urging me north to where the Temple lay hidden in its valley.

But I refused to budge. *I'm going back, in order to do this in Alt. Something is off down below. I can feel it.*

We had to return to our bodies in order to do the switch. I sensed his impatience, but he reluctantly trailed me back to the hill.

When we were both present again in the physical, I opened my eyes to find him staring at me, his brows drawn and his mouth turned down.

'It's starting soon,' he warned. 'We don't have much time.'

'Humor me,' I said. 'You coming with?'

He nodded, slowly. And so we flipped through the Veil to Alt. Immediately the lights below us dimmed and the city shrunk, the gaslight of the streetlamps soft and yellow, kerosene lamps in the windows of the larger homes, tallow candles in those of the poor. The shadows were darker and more pervasive here.

'Ready?'

He opened his mouth as if he was going to object but then he shrugged. And we relaxed our bodies again to let our minds out over Alt. While we hovered past the ancient winding streets, I searched with my mind's eye and also with my other senses for whatever had alerted me. And then I saw it.

At first, it was just a subtle movement deep within the shadows of the tall buildings on Water Street. Then, another one on Duckworth Street which ran parallel but up the hill that was the old town. As my mental eyes adjusted to the dimness, I saw the shadows of the super naturals emerge. There were many of them, vampires, dwarves, trolls and the unnameable ones who lived in the old sewer systems deep underground. Further up the hill, there were Fae and nymphs flitting along the trees of the old burial grounds, long disappeared in real time.

They were swarming like bees, congregating in groups, silent, this mass of bodies and their faces were set with worry. Yet beneath these drawn faces, I could also sense a buzz of excitement running through the crowds of super naturals. They stood in the darkened doorways and beneath the trees, their tenseness permeated the air.

Look below, I said to Hugh. *Something's happening.*

He paused in midair, the better to let his eyes adjust to the dimness, and he searched the crowds.

It's the cleansing ceremony that has them excited, he assured me after a moment.

But they look worried, some of them. Others are...ex pectant. I don't have a good feeling about this.

Some of the super naturals don't like the ceremony, he admitted. *They wrongly feel that... well, it's no matter. We don't have much time.*

You don't suppose...

What? I could feel Hugh's impatience to be gone and over to the Temple.

Could this be the rumblings of rebellion the Kin were worrying about? Do you think they have something planned for tonight?

I think we would have heard about it, he said with not a doubt in his voice. *We have a very good intelligence network.*

This isn't normal behavior, I insisted. *Look at them!*

And he did. He slowed down his flight to really examine the groups far below us. *But the rebellion, that's the elves*, he pointed out finally. *There's no elves in this group.*

I looked down and searched the crowds, what I could see of them below the tree branches. He was right. The only Kith missing were the elves.

Come on, he urged me. *To the Temple! Time's running out.*

We flew on north, past the ponds that fed the farms and the cattle and sheep and we crested the final hill. I looked back a couple of times, and searched amongst the trees below us, but could see no more evidence of the inhabitants of Alt. I had to let my bad feelings go and concentrate on the show that was about to happen.

He positioned us over to the side of the Temple. I knew if we moved over a tad closer we could look down through the moon window and see the Elders, my father included, in their circle preparing to perform their ceremony.

Can you see the lines? Hugh was pointing off to the west.

I adjusted my mental eyes to allow the light from the seams to surface, and yes, there they were, the bright green, pulsing with the delicious force of life. They felt so close I thought I could swoop down and touch them. How could these wondrous lines of life energy need any assistance?

Wait for it.

They glowed, and suddenly, all the ley lines leading to the Temple, their point of convergence, they all grew even brighter if that was possible. The lights seared into the darkness, burning molten gold and red and neon blue like they were going to burst out of the earth and rain into the sky. It was like watching the Aurora Borealis, but coming up from the ground.

I took a deep breath.

Yet then just as suddenly the light of the lines calmed down again, back to the delicious green shining only, no hint of gold within the seams again.

I waited for a moment longer, but nothing else happened. *Is that it? Is that all there is?*

Hugh nodded beside me. *I know, it only takes a moment. There's more to it, I'm told, but we can't see it because the ceremony is inside the Temple. And no, we can't peek through the moon window.*

I felt cheated, and not a little disappointed. *A bit of a let-down, actually. It should have been more exciting after all that pre-ceremony hype.*

He shrugged. We turned away from the lines to head back to our bodies far across town, and that's when I saw them. Beneath the trees in this boreal forest of Alt, not too far away from the Temple itself, there was the slightest of movements that wasn't the wind in the leaves. When I focused my eyes past the mass of foliage, I saw the pale faces glowing eerily in the shadows, and over by the entrance driveway to the Temple, there was Brin. He was accompanied by one of Eldric's Bitches. No, he was being held by him and struggling to escape the iron grip the other had on him, his eyes wild and terrified.

Brin glanced up at the sky and I know he couldn't see me, but perhaps he sensed my presence far above. 'Dara!'

Hugh! I screamed out in my mind. *Look down below. What's going on?*

Shit. The Elves! Are they going to attack the Temple during the ceremony? Hugh sounded outraged.

I made to swoop down closer to my friend, not that I would be able to help him, being out of my body as I was, but before I could move at all came the fireworks I'd been missing.

An explosion rocked the night, the lights came first, followed a millisecond later by the deep rumbling crack of magic unloosed, like the sound of ten thunderstorms all simultaneously below us. The lights, oh the beauty of the magic exploding from the veins of the ley lines, it was a sight never to be forgotten, like the mushroom cloud of an atomic explosion, but in technicolor with a rainbow of hues shooting off in all directions and billowing out amongst itself. And the cloud of magic rose and rose like a volcano let loose, the magic sparks flying off and raining on the surrounding area like ash, burning everything it touched.

What the unholy fuck...

The ley lines. They bombed a ley seam, I told him.

It's impossible! They can't... they wouldn't...

Eldric did.

And then we saw what looked like a flock of birds taking flight away from the spot. But they were large birds, and the bodies moved in a straight line, not floating on the wind, and they weren't flapping their wings.

They were going far too fast for birds, I only saw them for a split second out of the corner of my eye. The Dark Elf warriors, fleeing the scene of their destruction. I paused for that moment, instinctually wanting to chase them down, hunt them, make them pay for what they'd wreaked. But I stopped myself, for what good would that be? Time to deal with it later, after I'd help to mend the ley. If I could.

I gave them one final glare, and in that moment I saw that one of the elves carried with him another figure. A small, goblin shaped body. Trevor! I gasped. Was that the 'T' Brin was referring to in his text? But I had no time to lose.

I could sense Hugh staring at me. *What do you know of this?*

And then he began searching in my mind. I felt the familiar warm fingers of his touch at the forefront of my consciousness, slipping in with a lover's caress, and it was my turn to be outraged. My mental barriers clanged shut and I glared at him.

What did I know, indeed. I'd known Eldric had been planning this, or something like it anyway. And I hadn't passed this knowledge on to the Kin via my Dad. But Cate had known it too, I screamed in my head in self-defence. So what did this mean? Had Cate lost the game she was playing with the Dark Elf, or was she a party to this attack? And why?

But there was no time right then to figure out the blame or to argue with Hugh about what he'd just attempted to do. Action needed to be taken. Hugh was urging me forward toward the Temple.

What's the good of that? I asked him. *We aren't in our bodies!*

Being projected as we were, we would be able to do no more than watch, watch as the ley lines burned and melted and scarred and ruined the countryside and lives of all for miles around. Everything Cate had told me came back in a rush, and she had been explicit in her detail. Life as we knew it in this old harbor port would never be the same.

Unless... There was the slightest chance that the track of this devastation could be stopped. Of course, it would require three witches. I glanced over at Hugh. He would do, in a pinch, and surely to Goddess I'd be able to find another Kin at the site. There wasn't a moment to lose. If I was going to attempt this, it had to be started before the damage spread.

Where are you going? I felt him tug against me.

Back. We need to go to the Temple in person.

But...

I didn't wait for him to figure it out. He gave up his argument and followed behind me. Once the decision was made, we almost immediately returned to our bodies still sitting in the sheltered nook on Signal Hill.

'There's a chance that we can undo the damage,' I told him breathlessly. 'But we need to get there fast.'

'The Kin will be working on it,' he said, a worried frown on his face. 'The Elders will know what to do.'

'Do they have the power to hold back the wards?'

'That's what the ceremony is all about, a momentary holding back. Of course they can.'

'And are they able to weave the lines together again?'

He stopped, and looked at me dumbfounded. 'That's impossible.'

Was it? Had Cate lied? 'We need to try. And we have to act fast.'

'Come on, then,' he said jumping up immediately. 'The bike!'

I hesitated, remembering the winding roads leading north to the Temple, figuring out the fastest route, and I shook my head. Even with Hugh's ability to set the traffic lights in his favor, it would take too long, doing things the manual way. The route would be much faster if we took a direct line. Flying as the crow does.

'No,' I said. 'We need to fly.'

Hugh had been about to jump over the low stone wall leading to the walkway around the tower, but he paused at my words, and looked at the distance. There was, of course, no evidence of the explosion here in real time, just perhaps the merest shimmering of the air over Pippy

Park, a darker darkness in the sky but it wouldn't be long before the effects were felt.

'Oh, no,' he said, shaking his head vigorously. 'I can't do that.'

'I can. You know I can. I'll... I'll carry you. I've been working on my flight.'

'What, and have you drop me half way?' He shuddered. 'You aren't that strong, I don't think you'll make it. The bike will get us there, not that there's much we can do to help with the situation.'

He really didn't know that the damage could be healed if we started it soon enough, that time was of the essence. He didn't know things that I knew, thanks to Cate's instructions. He didn't know that I needed three witches.

'Trust me,' I said through gritted teeth. 'I've been working out and practicing the flight. I need you to do this with me.'

'No,' he said, just as firmly. 'We're not risking our necks. Get on the bike!' He disappeared into the dark without another word, expecting me to follow.

I stared after him, shaking my head. 'Sorry, dude,' I said softly. 'So sorry.'

Yes, I was sorry that he didn't trust me to carry him. Sorry that he expected me to jump at his orders, and sorry that he had actually tried to get inside my mind back then, without my explicit permission. Sorry that I might never have to wear that ugly old family ring of his? Not so much, I realized right then and there.

I stepped onto the low stone wall and prepared to jump. He might not trust that I could do it, but I knew I could.

CHAPTER 29

'I *can* do this,' I said firmly as I hovered over the rocks, even as I knew I shouldn't waste my energy needlessly. I set my face toward Pippy Park across the wide valley of the city. The distance appeared multiplied tenfold now that I was actually in the air and moving away from the safety net that was my perch.

I swallowed hard and pushed myself to move. Far below me I heard the squeal of tires and out of the corner of my eye I saw the Harley rip through the night, down the curving hill toward the city.

And I was moving through the air. I set my sights on the multi-colored mists that now covered the Temple's location and I pushed at the top speed I could, leaving him far behind to navigate the city's one-way streets and narrow roads that had been designed to avoid natural hazards. It was no longer a race, for there was no way Hugh could catch up with me.

One to guard, one to weave and one to… What was the third? And was that even the right order?

As I flicked myself ever onwards, I realized that it was just me now, not the three witches I needed in order to weave the broken seams to health. Bloody hell. Not that

I could have counted on Hugh to help, not without an argument and his need to take control of the situation and mansplain when he didn't really know what he was talking about.

I pushed myself, but could feel my energy flagging. Thank Goddess I'd been working out my physical body, I wasn't totally breathless with this extreme effort, but why hadn't I practiced flight more?

I couldn't do this all by myself, and Hugh would never make it in time. Perhaps Cate and one of the Elders? But I couldn't deal with perhaps, I needed a certainty. I reached inside Mom's leather jacket for Margaret's brooch. It was still there, I hadn't removed it, and I breathed a sigh of relief even as I rubbed it.

Margaret, I called out into the ether. *I need you.*

I pushed myself further, passing over the university now, with Long Pond glinting darkly right up ahead. Where was that witch? Was she still nursing a grudge because I'd refused to throw in my lot with her and give up my dreams of the Kin?

My body was faltering and I felt myself losing altitude. If I wasn't careful, I could end up with a dunking into the reeds of the water directly below me. I looked up at the steep hill ahead of me that I still had to climb. The tops of the fir trees loomed treacherously pointy.

Come on Margaret, I can't do this by myself!

But still no sign of her. I pulled all my energy into the upward flight to avoid the firs, following the line of the landscape below me. I was breathing heavily now with the effort. What, was she waiting for an apology? Well she wasn't going to get one.

It's time to bury the fucking hatchet! Get your ass over here. Please? I yelled this with my last remaining strength as I crested the hill. What difference did it make? I wasn't going to get there. I could feel myself dropping, I couldn't hold myself up anymore in the air. We were so close, I could see the valley of the Temple dead ahead, although the actual structure was still covered in the mysterious mist.

And then I slowly became aware of her by my side, the scent of an exquisite cologne custom made for her, the swish of her silken robes, the heat of her sun kissed body below me as she swooped in and carried me, bringing me back up into the air.

'About frigging time,' I muttered.

'You weigh a ton,' she said through gritted teeth. 'Have you been eating cake for lunch again?'

'This is pure muscle, thank you very much.'

'What happened here?'

As we approached the Temple, I gave her the highlights.

'Damn, the elves blew up the lines?'

'Yes,' I said. 'Are you familiar with the process for weaving them back together?'

'I've heard of it,' she said, and she paused us in a tree top. The mist was all around us now, thick as London fog, only an eerie glow showed the direction of the Temple. 'I'm familiar with the process, but only theoretically.'

'We need to do it.'

She hesitated. 'We need another witch.'

'Hugh will be here shortly,' I said desperately.

She barked a short laugh. 'As if.'

'Well, surely there's another witch down there somewhere who can help.' I waved one hand down below our precarious perch as I held on tight with my other. The mist was beginning to clear, we could see the outlines of the building in the space between the treetops. Fortunately, it looked like it hadn't been damaged in the explosion. 'There's a whole coven of Elders here for the cleansing ceremony.'

'I don't work with Elders,' she sniffed. 'Especially not the ones siphoning the lines.'

I shot daggers at her with my eyes. 'You could at least try to be helpful.'

'Besides,' she continued as if I hadn't spoken. 'I make it a matter of policy never to interfere with Kin business.'

'But Margaret,' I said, in disbelief. 'This is my *home* we're talking about. My loved ones live here. Are you willing to let it all be destroyed because you have a gripe with the Kin? Allow this beautiful land to turn to desert? We have to heal the lines. For my sake?'

She had the grace to look a tad uncomfortable at that. 'We can't do it without a trustworthy third,' she muttered. 'Not a Kin Elder. Neither of us has ever performed this before. We need someone who understands the process, we don't have time to explain it.'

She looked across the tree top at me. 'This is uncharted territory! It's very dangerous for all. One slip and we're burned. If we can't find an acceptable third, it's not on.'

In the space after this speech, I knew the truth of what she said. I nodded slowly. Numbly.

And then a voice wafted up through the mists and the branches.

'Dara? Is that you? Come quickly, we need to begin.'

A smile slowly spread across my face, and I looked back over at Margaret. 'There's our third.'

Margaret and I flew down to the ground to meet our third witch. Behind us in the Temple grounds, we could hear the Elders and other Kin squawking and panicking. Under the awning of branches in this small glade, the two sized each other up, both standing firmly with their arms.

They were almost mirror images, with their similar height and stance and attitude, but in all other ways were as different as night from day. Cate was a vision of black velvet, her raven locks flowed gleaming down her back, and her black eyes flashed in the starlight. Her legs went on forever in the space between her short dress and those exquisite high heels, and she was pure deadly muscle.

I had dragged Margaret from her beach hideaway on the other side of the world where the sun was still beating down warmly, and she wore a simple kaftan, silk and brightly colored like an exotic butterfly. Her red curls were laced with the crystals of a friendlier ocean in their crispness. I could smell the beach off her, the salt and the lazy heat and the lemon margarita. She was the first to speak.

'Kin, through and through,' she said with a tinge of disgust. 'The Huxor, I'd say. And no more power than any of them. How is *she* going to be able to help us?'

I didn't need to defend Cate, for she was more than capable of holding her own.

'Well, well, well,' she replied. 'If it isn't Margaret Forsythe, in the flesh. I must say, I'm quite impressed, Dara. You hobnob only with the best.' She flicked her hair to indicate that she included herself in that description.

They were like two cats meeting on the border, each determined to defend their territory, sniffing and growling and generally trying to scare the other with their display of arched backs and hissing.

'We need to get started,' I interrupted the pair with words as I didn't have a pail of water to throw between them. 'Three witches, right Cate? Here we are.'

'How much do you know of this process?' Cate's dark eyes were boring into Margaret's green ones.

The Scottish witch shrugged one shoulder. 'Was it an adamantite bomb?'

'Looks like it.'

'And I wonder where they got that from?' Margaret murmured cattily under her breath.

Cate's cheeks stained slightly but she held her level stare. 'Not from my mines, at any rate.'

'Does it matter where it came from?' I looked from one to the other. It was only then that I noticed a very un-Catelike smear of dirt down the side of her face but before I could ask about it the Scottish witch continued as if I hadn't even spoken.

'Healing the seams after an adamantite attack,' Margaret said, shaking her head. 'It won't be easy. I doubt if either of us has done this before? I know the basics, I suppose we'll have to wing it under my direction.'

'It's a rare thing,' Cate remarked coolly. 'A purposeful attack on the ley lines using the adamantite. But not unheard of. Being the Huxor, as you pointed out, I've studied all things adamantite in depth, it's my duty. I'll take the lead, and you two will follow.'

Margaret opened her mouth to object, but Cate remained inflexible. 'I haven't the power needed to hold the wards or knit the seams. I will watch over and be prepared to step in as necessary. Shall we go?'

I pushed at Margaret to force her to move, and Cate led the way to the site of the explosion. We threaded through the trees, circling the Temple until we reached the other side, and I could feel us pushing through as we left the warded grounds to enter the deep boreal forest.

The elves hadn't detonated the bomb on the convergence of the lines, of course, having no access to the interior of the Temple, and besides, to do that would have annihilated everything in the surrounding land. That was not the point of this attack.

I didn't think to ask how Cate knew precisely where to go, where the explosion had been laid. And perhaps Margaret wondered, but it didn't matter. Nothing else mattered, not the 'whys' or the 'hows'. We had to fix the damage before it curdled through the lines and devastated my home land.

The bomb site itself was deserted, and there was surprisingly little to show for the explosion which had rocked our world so recently, only a five foot circle of dug up land. It had been a magicked bomb on the ley lines, and the colorful display and thunderous sounds had been pure ley reacting at the enforced contact with the adamantite. The surrounding trees and grasses and hillsides had not been physically damaged, but already the grass beneath our feet was crispy and dry, and crunchy as we walked on it like the first fall frost. The life would soon be receding. We needed to act fast.

'Are we going to be interrupted?' I asked, getting nervous now the moment was upon us. And by interrupted I really meant saved from having to do this dangerous work ourselves. I removed the heavy leather jacket and tossed it onto the grass.

'The Kin are too busy conferencing,' Cate said. 'No doubt. Trying to figure out what happened and who to blame and how, and looking for consensus on the best way to deal with the situation without stepping on anyone's toes.'

'Hugh knows,' I said. 'We watched the explosion happen.'

Margaret snorted as we took our places in the circle and linked hands under Cate's direction. 'Then why isn't he here? Why did you feel the need to rip me from my beachside bar?'

Her hand was cool in mine. 'He wouldn't fly with me,' I said quietly. 'He didn't trust that I could do it.'

The older witches were silent as they looked at me and said nothing. They didn't need to.

'Let us begin,' Cate said quietly. 'We need to be in the Alt, with no Veil hampering our efforts. Then we will slip into the ground below us, mindfully. One will hold the wards.' She turned her head towards Margaret.

'One will weave the seams.' And looked at me.

I felt Margaret's hand jump in mine. Cate would have felt it too. 'What nonsense is this? You can't have her do such dangerous work. She's untried, she doesn't have the confidence, she...'

'This is her home,' Cate said crisply. 'She has the need to do this. She has the youth and stamina of mind to perform it. I need your greater will to hold back the curtain so it's safe for her. I will be the watcher. There is no other way to do this.'

Even Margaret couldn't argue with her logic, so she shut her mouth again and we began. I only knew what Cate had told me about the process, so I listened carefully and followed the other's lead.

She began a soft hum, like we had at the drawing of the moon. The sound filled my head, and I took her up on her note, as did Margaret. We allowed ourselves to slip down into the earth as one, conjoined in our minds. I searched the ground until I found the answering note coming from the leys themselves, and that lent strength to our sound.

Once we had found it and were reverberating with its music, Cate changed her pitch, taking a lower note in harmony and Margaret a higher one. As instructed, I stayed on my note that echoed the ley line itself, the better to attune myself for entering.

I could feel the strain in Margaret's mind as she lifted the barriers aside, like heavy satin curtains protecting the line, and with sheer force of will she kept the space for me to slip in while Cate remained at my back.

At the last moment I hesitated, my note faltered, and the other two sensed it.

I am with you always, Cate said, her cool voice lending me strength.

Just get in there and do it, Margaret scolded me. *I can't hold this gate open forever. And whatever you do, don't touch the strands. Use your mind power only.*

And I slipped into the folds and felt the power of the ley before me. I had no need to keep up my note any more, although Cate and Margaret did theirs. I searched for the broken ends of the magical seams, using every sense I had at my disposal.

How to describe the sight I beheld, here in the heart of the ley? The picture could only be described in three dimensions, but it was so much more, spanning four or five or even six. The magic was overwhelming and warm, so warm. The seam was a living being like a hive of bees, the colors singing the notes of the harmony, the music rising and falling with every pulse beat.

Yet the closer I drew, the more I could hear the disharmony, the cry of pain, and then I saw it.

The wounded seam. Not all the threads were damaged, but enough were severed to cause the screaming. The broken lines bled blue and purple and black like fresh bruises and the damaged ends burned like daggers in my mind.

CHAPTER 30

I winced and couldn't go any further for surely I would become that torn edge myself. And there was too much to do, there were too many loose ends, how could one witch mend them all? Especially an untried witch like myself. An ignorant, arrogant and errant witch like me. I hesitated, faltered and turned away. I couldn't do it, this was too important a job for me to mess up. I had to give this role to Margaret, I could never accomplish this, not me.

'Just do it,' I heard the voice of one of the others sound flatly through the agony. 'This is not the time to indulge your insecurities.'

Bloody hell! I reared back in anger. I wasn't like the other two witches, I didn't have a lifetime of confidence and training behind me. Didn't they realize it wasn't childish doubt that caused my hesitation? The entire future of my home was at stake here, in my weak and shaking hands. How could they ask this of me?

'You have the most at stake.' The voice came from behind me.

And she was right. I swallowed hard and stepped up to the task, gritting my teeth and ignoring the tears which flowed down my face. I didn't need my physical eyes for this work. With my mind, I stared at the tangle of pain that was the broken ley seam.

Fine to say, 'just do it', but how? Cate hadn't expressly told me *how* this was to be accomplished. Despite the proximity of the other two witches, I was on my own. I studied those broken edges, the disharmony grating through the very fiber of my being, disrupting any conscious thought I might have, like nails on an old-fashioned blackboard but multiplied ten thousand fold. I thought the atoms of my whole being might echo with these chords and disarrange themselves.

I couldn't use my hands for fear of being burned by the terrible force, this would be a purely mental effort. And I would find a way to do it, even if it killed me.

I took a deep mental breath and reached out with my mind to the nearest damaged thread, using the only thing I had. Love, or something like it, compassion and sorrow all mixed in with it. I told it I knew its pain, and that I would help if I could but like a wounded animal the thread flinched away from my approach. But steadily, steadily I pushed on, having only room for love in this crying hurricane of magic loosened and bleeding. And I drew it to me, and with my other mind I drew its mate, the other end of the thread and held them almost touching together, praying they would find each other and meld together. I didn't know what else to do.

And it worked. The first was done. I had accomplished the undoable, me, Dara Martin de Teilhard. I almost laughed with joy, but then I looked up and my sense of victory was soon squashed, for there were many more left undone. Tens, hundreds, uncountable. How could this Herculean task be accomplished?

But the more threads I drew together, the more the ley understood what I was trying to do, and it assisted me, bringing its damaged parts to me for healing as if the wounded animal understood I only wanted to help.

You're doing it. I felt Cate breathing down my neck.

Yes, I was, but I had no time or energy now for self-congratulations, there was too much left undone.

I don't know how long it went on, this process, for I was outside of time by now, concentrating only on the colored strands before me. As each one drew together, a small victory, but always another took its place, demanding to be healed. I was tiring, but surely I must be reaching the end?

Watch out for that shred of adamantite, Cate told me. *It's there, in the middle of the tangle. If you can draw that out, your path will be much easier.*

Adamantite? She hadn't told me how to work with that. That was unknown magic. The only thing I knew about that precious metal was that it was extremely unstable under certain conditions, that one touch could burn the mind. I looked into the muddle that was left, and I saw it there, a black hole in the midst of the glowing seam, sucking any light and hope into its ebony dullness. I panicked. How could this metal be caught there, the ley and the adamantite were opposing forces. If I loosened the magic threads around the metal, what would happen? Another explosion, with me positioned to take the brunt of it?

Just work around it, Cate said. *You got this. I'm right here with you.*

I drew another deep metaphorical breath to steady myself and dove in. I cautiously picked out strands all around it, like a deadly version of Jenga, that kids' game we used to play where we picked out the blocks, but the tower that would come crashing down in this awful game was my home, my family, my world. Barely breathing with my physical body, I wove and sung those ends back to together, but then I was left with the final snarl. I looked, and I searched, but I couldn't undo this final knot. Not without brushing against the metal.

I can't ... I was exhausted and helpless by this point, unable to garner the strength to push past.

Let me help.

Stop right there! Margaret finally spoke out. *Dara don't let her...!*

But it was too late. Cate had deftly worked around me and, with a tweak her long fingernails expertly plucked the offending shard of adamantite out of the gnarly mess. She flicked it far out of reach but even as she did so her hand slipped into the seam as if pulled by the magnetic force right into the heart of the knot. It was only for the barest split second yet I could see the magic leap the span and flow, the fine veins and arteries glowing green as the pure force of the ley leapt into her flesh. She screamed with pain even as she gathered the strongest of will to pull herself free from the flow of pure unadulterated magic power.

Dear God! How could anyone survive that force? Margaret and I had both carried the Crystal Charm Stone, inadvertently soaking up its power and changing our very genetic structures. But that rock, revered and powerful as it was, was a pale shade of the magical force in the original ley lines themselves. I hesitated, faltered, worrying for Cate but she urged me to continue with my work.

Finish the job! Her mental voice was strained as if she struggled with pain, and so I pushed on. There was nothing I could do to help her right there and then.

Her action had freed the last remaining strands and like a master weaver I was able to hold the ends together and let them melt into the correct strands. And it was done.

I looked once more at the seam with my new eyes, and I could see that it was good. It flowed and pulsed like a living being, a carrier of the life force of our planet. The green of the power lived as if it had never been broken and the individual strands – I knew each of them intimately now and could trace their unbroken lines and couldn't tell where they had been healed. No scars remained.

It was over. I blinked, seeing with my physical eyes again, back in the small glade in the huddle of trees, the stars overhead lending little light but enough to show my companion witches.

I did it. Yes, I couldn't have done it without the help of the other two, but it was me. This was an accomplishment of a lifetime, and I, Dara Martin de Teilhard, had done it. I almost collapsed with relief. But Margaret didn't allow me to rest on my laurels.

'Brilliant. Just fucking brilliant,' she spit. 'How the hell are you going to clean up this mess now?'

CHAPTER 31

I turned to Margaret, stunned at the vicious outrage in her voice. 'What are you talking about? You saw the seam! It's all healed. I... *We* did it!'

The anger came off her in waves, causing me to quail, and I looked back uncertainly at my handiwork, unseen now deep within the ground.

'Yes, you certainly did it, you've single-handedly created a monster,' she flashed back at me. 'I suppose you'll tell me now that you had no idea of her plans? Please, don't bother. I don't want to hear about your willful ignorance.'

What the hell was she on about now? This was my moment to shine! Couldn't she at least let me have this victory?

I tried to move toward her, to reach her, to shake that terrible anger from her face, to stop her accusation, but I couldn't lift my feet. They were encased ankle deep in the dirt of the explosion site; the knees of my jeans, too, were filthy and caked with mud. I lifted a hand to clear my hair from my face and felt the smear left behind, for my hands were covered in that mud too, right up to my elbows. I picked at my nails with the fingers of one hand, but it was ground in well and good, so I just wiped my palms against my thighs to take the worst off.

Margaret was still pristine, she hadn't even broken out a physical sweat during the whole process, but her face was dark. I followed her glittering eyes toward Cate.

Cate's knees, too, were muddied, and the velvet toes of her shoes were still buried in the muck. As if in a daze, she lifted one foot, but the heel remained firmly in the ground. She stared at it for a moment then bent down and with one hand wrenched it out of the dirt, and then stepped out of the other and likewise removed it from the encasing mud.

Her right hand was also filthy, like mine, mud up to the elbow. She shifted her shoes to her other, then turned her face and body toward me and smiled weakly, and I saw the worst of it.

Cate glowed. Her pale face was a luminous green like radiation, and against it her teeth gleamed whitely, all framed by the black hair which hung straight down on either side. She wiped her mouth with the back of her left wrist, and sparkles of magic fell away with the movement.

'Oh, Christ, you're...' I breathed. She was damaged, how could she not be after having her hand immersed into the depths of the very ley line itself? Even if it had only been for the tiniest fraction of a second. 'Cate, you've been... hurt.'

It was worse than I'd feared. When her hand slipped into the knot the pure magic had burned her, ran through her entire system, even her legs were taking on a bright green beneath the caked mud on her bare skin. I had glowed, yes, that night on Scarp, but not to this extent. Cate's body was now neon bright like the Vegas strip at midnight.

'I'm fine,' she replied and I watched, uncomprehending, as her watery smile strengthened. I'd never noticed her canines were the slightest millimetre longer than the rest of her perfect teeth as she threw back her head and laughed.

I looked at her in helpless horror, unable to move, unwilling to touch her for fear of being burned myself. Didn't she realize what had happened?

'You need help.' The words had hardly left my mouth when the sounds of thrashing came through the under-brush, a distance off. It was the Kin, having finally agreed upon the necessary line of action, come to save the day and not a moment too soon. I needed someone else to take charge. 'The Elders are coming, they'll know what to do.'

I moved to take her arm, to help her sit down.

'Don't touch her!' Margaret barked, but her warning was unnecessary as Cate twitched out of my reach.

'We have to do something.' I met Margaret's granite gaze with my own. 'We can't just leave her like this.'

'I'm fine,' Cate repeated, her voice stronger now, but she too had heard the crashing in the trees, and her eyes darted all around. She moved back onto the hard undisturbed ground and bent to replace her shoes. 'I need to go, need to withdraw from company for a while until this calms down,' she said breathlessly. 'But I'll be checking my emails.'

'You've already helped her enough,' Margaret said to me with disgust. 'She has everything she wanted. Look at her.'

'What are you talking about?' My voice was edged with panic, and I tried to calm down, to reason with the Scottish witch. 'Cate accidentally touched the lines when she plucked out the metal shard, and now look at her. We can't let her go off like this, she's been burned. What can we do?'

Margaret's head fell back and she let out an exasper-ated huff as she stared at the heavens.

'But the power's too much for her!' I cried. I lunged toward Cate again, but she hopped out of my grasp, still bent over as she placed the other shoe on her foot.

'Leave her alone, Dara,' Margaret said, her voice tired now. 'Don't you see what happened? She played you. I can't believe you, of all witches, didn't see that coming.'

Cate finally straightened up and had no hesitation meeting me square on. Even the whites of her eyes were glowing greenly now. 'Thank you,' she said, with a heartfelt sigh. 'I appreciate your assistance in this matter. I really couldn't have done it without you.'

Her shoulders shook, then a bubble of laughter forced its way through her mouth and she gave in to the pleasure of it. 'And to think it was Marion's own daughter who gave me this gift! Oh, the utter delicious irony of it all, yet I somehow doubt that Jon will see the humor.'

She made to go into the forest but before she left, she turned back to me. 'Oh, and this?' She indicated the glow of her body. 'In case you haven't realized yet, you don't want to spread the word, for your magic prints are all over it. You can be the hero of the night, and Margaret and I helped you. But if you breathe a word about my 'accidental' slip into the ley... Well, you really don't want me to have to tell the Kin how, after years of hating me and jealousy of my family, you threw me into the lines as I was assisting, hoping I would burn in the power of the leys.'

She couldn't contain another small titter, bubbling over with her new power and her delight at the success of her plan.

My mouth fell open. What the hell was happening here? Cate had been on my side, the new hero I needed to negotiate my way through the ranks of the Kin, my mentor.

I was slow to come to this dawning realization, my body felt heavy like lead. Had it all been an act? Did she betray me, use me, to attain her own selfish goals? She'd promised me so much, and she had delivered on those promises, teaching me. Big things. Things I needed to know. It couldn't be true that she had betrayed me to reach her own goals.

Could it?

She smiled, a hint of her kindness deep within the eerie glow of her face. 'Think what I've just done for you in return. You've just increased your standing within the Kin tenfold, and there's no mention of your visits with Eldric at all. You saved the day, you mended the lines after the Elven treachery. I told you I would help you get everything you wanted, the private jet, the luxurious lifestyle. It's all yours now, like I promised. After this evening's heroics, you'll find you've earned a special place in the Kin, and never forget who got you there.'

The Kin were almost upon us. I could only stand there, helpless, still unable to move. My position in the Kin was nothing to me. Not when they had proven how false even they could be. I opened my mouth to denounce her and the rest of them, to disavow that I would ever take any place in their ranks. From Hugh who only wanted me to lend my magic genes to his offspring that they might further add glory to his line; to Jon de Teilhard who was weighed down with the burden of operating honestly in a dishonest system; to Cate, the greatest betrayal of all.

The betrayal which had wrenched open my eyes. The truth was that right then and there I had no desire for the false riches and fakeness that life within the Kin offered. Margaret Forsythe had been right all along, and I could now see exactly what she meant. Hugh might never accept that I was his equal, and any future together would be full of small jealousies and compromises. I needed to get away, to renounce the Kin, to live a life free of them.

I turned to Margaret, my mouth full of apologies, ready to grovel and ask her to take me with her to her endless beaches and life of freedom.

'It's time for me to say good-bye, too.' Margaret glanced in the direction of the noise, then her face drew back in an aristocratic sneer. She reached over and with a flash of her elegantly manicured hand snatched the jewelled dragonfly brooch from my jean jacket.

I gasped at the action, the loss, and clutched at the empty space where it had been. More than ever before, I needed the company of this witch, this role model. 'Margaret, no,' I cried. 'You can't... I need you...'

'I hope you enjoy this life of yours that you've built, Dara. You made your choices, and I'll thank you not to call on me again.'

With that, she disappeared from the glade. From my life. Back to her beach side hut and margaritas and Kin-free life. Leaving me ankle deep in the muck of the hole I'd dug of my life.

Cate smiled at me again, a genuine one this time. 'They'll be arresting your elf friend right about now. I may have the evidence to prove it wasn't him who set off the explosion of the line, but then again... maybe I don't. That will all depend on how you handle the coming days.

'And I really do want to thank you again for all you've done,' she said sincerely. 'You've given me the gift of almost immortal youth, and my power will rival your own. And the best of it is, I know you won't say a word. It's our little secret.' She tapped the side of her nose with her clean hand as she said it, then looked with disgust at her other one.

She met my eyes and shrugged. 'Oh, well, sometimes you have to get a little dirty to get the job done, right?'

Then she too, was gone, her glowing form receding into the trees as she silently made her exit, leaving me

standing alone in the small forest glade, my body muddied and my soul irrevocably stained.

CHAPTER 32

H ad Cate had set me up, right from the beginning, before I'd even gotten on the plane to come home from Scotland? I tried to comprehend this fact, to wrap my head around the extent of this deceit. Had the whole thing, the explosion of the ley lines, the rebellion of the elves, the consequent saving of the seams by me been engineered by the wife of my father? All of it?

And why?

I allowed Hugh and Dad to hug me and exclaim and make a big fuss over me as they led me back the twisty path to the Temple, a haven of light and bodies after the horror I'd just experienced. I let them comfort me and allowed Hugh to place Mom's heavy leather jacket over my shoulders again.

'I can't believe you did that,' Dad said as he embraced me again. His face was white with strain and relief. 'Do you know the danger you put yourself through?'

'And who helped you?' Hugh had distanced himself a little, allowing Dad his turn to claim me. 'You didn't wait for me.'

Was that jealousy creeping back into his voice? I sighed and turned to him. As Cate said, I was going to claim much of the glory for this night's work, and I realized this might be hard for Hugh. 'Cate,' I told them. 'We did it.'

'Where is Cate?' Dad interrupted. He sounded worried still. 'Is she okay?'

I nodded, then forced myself to say the words she'd told me to say. Brin's future was at stake. 'She had to... had to leave, she was overcome.'

'Was she harmed?'

'No, no, not at all.' I summoned up the energy to press this home. Cate may have been changed forever by what she'd done, but she didn't consider herself injured. Far from it. 'She's good, she'll be fine.'

The drama of the night still continued in the parking lot of the Temple. Elders stood all around in a loose circle, speaking grimly in their official dark robes, shaking their heads. One figure stood out a whole head above the others. They surrounded him, had shackled his hands and feet to prevent him from fleeing on those long elven legs of his. He looked up from his terror and cried to me.

'Dara?' Brin said. 'What's happening?'

I came to life as I mustered the energy to spring towards my friend, but Dad kept me firmly in his grasp. I struggled against him but to no avail.

'What's going on?' I screamed as I saw Brin being led away to the back of a huge black SUV. 'Let him go!'

'No, Dara,' Jon said sadly. 'I'm afraid, I'm afraid we've all been betrayed by him. He had us fooled.'

'Brin didn't do anything, he couldn't have!' There was no way Brin, silly Brin could have laid the adamantite bomb. He didn't have the magical strength, he didn't even want to be a part of Eldric's plan anymore. He would have refused, even on pain of death.

'Kin should never trust an elf,' Dad said, shaking his head. 'I truly thought this one was different. Yet he had the evidence on him.'

But Brin *was* different. I saw the uncomprehending terror in his eyes before they stuffed his head down into the vehicle and slammed the door. This elf couldn't have done the deed. And I remembered the presence of Trevor, my erstwhile goblin companion, as he flew off with the Elven brigade and I caught a sharp breath. My body sagged with this new realization, and I was held up only by Dad's arms.

'What evidence?'

My father's mouth was set in a grim line. 'A box of adamantite,' he said. 'All packaged up.'

The package Brin needed to give to me. Bad, he'd said. It hadn't made sense. Nothing about this evening made sense.

Until the little wheels began to whir in my mind, the gears began grinding and suddenly, click by click, I connected the dots and everything made terrible, awful sense, in a horrible way. I flinched away from that vision, but the dawning light in my mind was too bright. I helplessly followed the whole trail to the bitter end.

Trevor gave Brin a package, and told him it was for me. Brin tried his best to deliver like it was a hot potato, but I'd ignored his attempts to contact me. Trevor had somehow known I would, and that Brin would be left holding the bag, literally. My friend wouldn't have told anyone it was mine, and so he'd been arrested for having the magical metal on him at the site of the explosion.

Even if he tried to explain to the Kin, they wouldn't believe him, for he was an elf and a known political activist. Whereas I... I had just saved the day, I was the hero.

And Trevor was safely out of harm's way, for I'd seen him being flown back to the Wilderness right after the bomb had been set off.

It was Trevor who had planted the bomb, it had to be. He would have had the assistance of Cate in overcoming the wards of the leys. Yet the goblin was never a major player in this drama, he was merely a foot soldier of the powers behind the scheme, Cate and Eldric together.

She'd been false with the Dark Elf kin too, I realized, playing both sides and pretending to be sympathetic to his cause to remove the Veil in order to increase her own personal power. To drink from the lines. I still couldn't believe she'd done such a terrible thing.

Even more since with her actions, she risked the life of her very home land, and mine. If I hadn't been able to call on Margaret's help and save the day, the island as we knew it would have withered, the greenery would have died and shrivelled, the plentiful waters would have dried and become salt. Her own home, her children's heritage, all gone because of her greed.

A month ago, I would have had no problem believing in the depths of her treachery. But she had reached out to me, nurtured me and used my own pride against me. Yes, because of Cate I now had everything I'd dreamed of achieving. That only made my devastation all the worse.

I reached out toward Brin, but Hugh blocked my way. 'Don't worry,' he said. 'We have it all under control now.'

'It wasn't him,' I called out weakly as the SUV drove away, red tails lights glowing in the mist which still clung to the Temple environs, before I collapsed in a heap at Dad's feet.

My last conscious thought was that through it all, through all her machinations and schemes, Cate had had the ultimate trust that I would be able to pull off the impossible, the mending of the lines, to heal the damage she'd purposefully wrought. It was almost a compliment.

Almost.

··········

Mom told me later that Hugh had picked me up off the ground and carried me to Dad's SUV, and followed us back to the house on his Harley. It was all a little fuzzy to me, but I did remember coming to as he brought me inside the kitchen, and sitting at the table while Mom's voice rushed all around me with worry.

Dad and Hugh spoke tersely, and then I heard them leave again, and I hadn't seen either of them since. They were busy with the Kin business of investigations and reports into this unprecedented occurrence.

More than twenty-four hours passed, during which I kept silent about Cate's machinations concerning the events that night. Hugh and Dad were nowhere to be found, they were tied up with the inevitable crises management conferences in the aftermath of the Elven treachery, and I had no way to reach them, to tell them about Brin's innocence. The whole time my friend remained in the ancient Penitentiary by the lake. He was heavily guarded, I learned when I tried to get in to see him, being accused of terrorist action and all the authorities took that threat seriously. I wandered the perimeter of the old stone and concrete walls topped with barbed wire rolls, trying to peer into windows far above my head, but I couldn't even reach him through my thoughts. I recognized the imprint of Kin wards all around the building.

Yet my silence wasn't enough, it turned out, not enough for Cate to free my friend. Cate had lied to me. Was I surprised? She had no intentions of setting Brin free. I should have known better than to believe her in that last promise, and time was running out.

I was a hero now, to the Kin. I ignored all the invitations that poured in. Summer barbeques, hang outs with

Sasha and her crowd, Tiki parties with people I didn't even know, people who had never previously acknowledged my existence.

'What happened the other night?' Mom finally had enough. She sat me down at the kitchen table, brandishing a slice of her signature chocolate cake, made especially for me even though it wasn't a special occasion. 'All the Kin suddenly love you, I've been fielding calls for you all day. But you're not happy. Speak to me!'

I cut off a tiny corner of my piece of cake, and stared at it. Not even the cream icing was appealing. I couldn't tell her, even though I now knew she had her own magic running through her veins, because there was still a smidgeon of hope flaring inside, hope that Cate would do the right thing for Brin. I mushed the soft cake back onto the plate, mixing it with the icing.

Seeing that I wasn't going to answer her, Mom changed tack and attempted to insert some normality by carrying on a conversation, I guess in the hope that she could put me at ease.

'I also had a call from Lady Sabiston,' she continued. 'Hugh's mother. She told me of your plans – I can't believe you never mentioned a word to me! This is so exciting. When is the wedding? And where? She's pushing for Scarp, of course, and I have to admit that would be fun, seeing my one and only getting married in a castle.'

Mom bustled around the kitchen, acting as though I was participating in the discussion. 'So romantic, isn't it? That's the Martin blood in you, all or nothing when it comes to love, eh?'

Yes. Love, if you could call it that. I had wanted the future Hugh was offering, and part of me still yearned for it, the comfort to be found in his strong arms and the security of knowing that he was my partner for life. Yet...

Yet I wanted to practice magic, it was what I was born to do, either within the Kin or without.

My heart ached for the loss of Margaret from my life. Now she had removed herself, I could see her value to me, how I could have learned so much with her. But - to renounce everything for the kind of freedom she offered?

No. I stood firm on that decision. I wanted, I needed, to make my own way. Be my own version of a powerful witch, perhaps be a role model and a beacon of hope for all the scorned half blood girls who came behind me.

I couldn't stand being in this limbo anymore. I needed Brin freed from his prison for he was innocent, blatantly framed by Cate's greed, and I needed to know what more she wanted from me, if my silence wasn't enough.

'I have to talk with Cate,' I said, interrupting Mom's flow. I'd made my decision and had to act now, before I could convince myself to back down.

Mom started back, as if I'd lashed out at her.

I knew the witch couldn't be too far away, for with the infusion of magic still fresh in her veins, she wouldn't chance getting on a plane or helicopter. Not yet. The most likely place for Cate to be hiding was at the summer home, the large estate built out around Conception Bay back in the time before the trains and highways. It had once been a half day's carriage ride away from the town over a rough gravelled road, but nowadays the old beach house found itself surrounded by suburbia on all sides. With the new highways in place and at the right time of day, it could take a fast car less than half an hour to reach the gates.

But I didn't have a car, or a license. I glanced out the window. Hugh had left his precious Harley here the night I'd been brought back after the whole bomb episode, and I could see his keys neatly hung up on the key rack by the back door, waiting for him to reclaim them.

A motorcycle driven by an inexpert driver would take longer, but it was doable. Wasn't it?

Today was bright and sunny and the pavements were dry, and I had confidence that if I drove over the old highway, I could make it out to the summer house. Mom didn't realize what I was doing until she heard the Harley's throaty roar in the driveway, and I saw her in the side mirror as she watched me going up the hill, leaving only blue exhaust in my wake.

My thoughts whirled again around the events of that fateful night, trying to make sense of them. Yes, Cate had gotten her darkest desire fulfilled, but what of Eldric? How had he profited from the bomb?

I stayed to the old road which hugged the bays, too nervous to go at the great speed demanded by the newer Autobahn-like scar which ripped across the high lands. It took me a full hour this way, around the twisty old roads and through each community which over the years had grown and spread to become one mass of urbanity, until I reached the oasis of ancient trees and stone walls which signified their summer estate. I stopped the bike outside the iron gates. They were firmly closed and locked against visitors.

My butt was stiff and sore and numb at the same time, and I had to stretch largely before I entered through the pedestrian gate that led into the summer garden. It was a whole different mini-biosphere here, with the heritage roses already in bloom, the garden in a riot of color that would rival a Monet painting. Clematis covered the archways, even a mimosa tree was in full flower. I took a deep nourishing breath of the spicy and green smells. Such a beautiful spot that harbored the viper Cate.

I reached into my pocket and took out my phone, setting it to record before I casually placed it back.

The heavy front door was firmly locked. I peered through the prisms of bevelled glass, but could see no movement within, so I quietly stepped along the covered wooden porch that wrapped around the ground floor. Around the corner, the ocean gleamed blue and glittery, so close I could almost touch it. And there she was.

She sat in the shade at a delicate wrought iron table painted white, a tray with fine china in front of her. Cate looked up when I approached, though I knew I hadn't made a sound. She was dressed in a long white cotton sundress.

'Welcome, Dara,' she said, her eyes hidden by the large sunglasses, discreetly branded with a designer logo. 'I've been waiting. What took you so long?'

CHAPTER 33

I took a seat opposite her and merely looked at the witch. In these shadows, I could tell her skin still held the glow of the magic she had deliberately infused into her body. Even through the expertly applied layer of makeup, the sickly green hue of her face shimmered.

'You haven't kept up your side of the bargain,' I began. My voice was harsh and whispery after the long ride on the Harley.

She inclined her head as if in thought. 'Bargain?'

'Brin.'

She laughed, tinkling and puzzled and light all at the same time. 'Your so-called friend who betrayed you and Jon? I believe that elf is safely locked away under the care of Her Majesty's Penitentiary. Treason and terrorism, oh my.'

'You know what I mean.' I was beginning to sweat in the afternoon heat. The weight of Mom's thick leather jacket wasn't helping.

Cate's smile was saccharin as she calmly lowered her sunglasses. The cool depths of her black eyes were empty voids. How had I ever thought this witch was on my side?

'Phone on the table.' She tapped the iron table top before her. 'I know you only have the one on you.'

Reluctantly, I drew it out of my pocket and placed it before me. With a single tap of her red nail I heard it fizzle and saw a small spark leap from it.

'Oops,' she said as her mouth formed a perfect moue of surprise and she placed her hand over her red lips. 'You're right, the electronics don't stand a chance around me. I'm still trying to get a handle on all this glorious new power you helped me achieve. Never mind. You do go through your phones quickly, don't you?'

'Brin.'

'Hmmm. Now that we can speak honestly without fear of recording, I think you still have to prove to me that you're trustworthy.'

'What? What more do you want me to do? I haven't said a word about what you did, how you endangered all of us by your scheming. How you ... you drank from the line behind my back.'

'Drank the line, how dramatic,' she chided. 'Speaking of drinks, I've been remiss as a host. Let me pour you a cup of my special lavender tea. It's surprising how refreshing a hot drink can be on a warm day.'

The fine china teacups were so delicate I could see the liquid rise in them as she poured. The sickly smell of lavender permeated the windless space.

She set the teapot back onto the tray, then continued in a dangerously calm voice. 'And I believe you when you claim you won't say a word. At least for the moment, until I get your little friend out of jail. But then...'

She leaned closer. 'But then I have a problem. I need to ensure your continued silence.'

I could only stare at her blankly, but my mind was running through possible scenarios. How could I save Brin and still get revenge on this false witch? I made sure that my mental shields were good and solidly in place.

'How can I do that?' she asked, her eyes wide and darkly innocent. 'How can I ensure you won't run to the Kin with your grudging stories? After all, when a certain amount of time passes, they will wonder that I didn't speak out right away, about how you pushed me into the ley and tried to burn me. It will look odd, won't it?'

I said nothing. I would just let her have her fun, for I had a feeling that nothing I said would make any difference anyway.

'I've pondered this problem over the past couple of days while I've been waiting for you,' she continued, staring off to the depths of the sea. 'Until it came to me. This solution will bring much joy into many lives.'

She turned back to me, and noticed my small china plate was empty and I hadn't drunk my tea. 'Have a macaroon or two,' she said, pushing the platter towards me. 'I had them made especially for you.'

I didn't touch them.

'They're not poisoned,' she said acerbically. She took a blue one from the top and bit into it. Small crumbs broke away, then with a sigh she swallowed the whole thing. 'Delicious. See? Perfectly safe.'

The sun had passed its midpoint and was creeping under the cover of her sheltered verandah. I shifted my chair a little to escape its burning rays.

'Eldric is grateful to you, by the way,' she observed as she spread a delicate Oriental fan and languidly wafted air toward her neck. 'And having the Dark Elf in your debt is no small feat.'

'I don't see what he gained by this whole debacle. Why bother with the bomb?'

She paused her fanning, her eyebrows lifted as if surprised, but I knew by then this whole visit was an act, a charade.

'It interrupted the siphoning ceremony. Yes, you saw the initial clearing of the lines, but the real action happens right after. The bomb was timed perfectly.' She smiled. 'Everyone wins, you'll see. The Veil is weakening already. Not that I care about that. Veil or no Veil, there's always a market for adamantite.'

'Everybody wins except Brin,' I reminded her heavily.

Her eyes narrowed confidently like a cat about to pounce on its prey. 'Yes, your elf friend.' She sighed, enjoying the tension between us. 'Quite the dilemma, isn't it? Tell me. What would *you* do in my place? How would *you* solve my problem?'

Cate sounded interested, as if she really wanted to hear my take on it.

I took a deep, steadying breath, then shrugged the leather jacket off my back. I could feel the sweat greasing my armpits and I wiped my forehead with the back of my hand. 'I would trust,' I replied. 'Trust that Dara Martin would be as good as her word. What choice do I have, as you've so clearly pointed out?'

She laughed, that tinkling sound of broken glass. 'Yes, that's good.' She nodded. 'But not quite enough for my security.'

Cate cut off her merriment abruptly. She stared at me. 'I want more.'

I shrugged my shoulders. 'So tell me. Enough of this foolish play. Just tell me what it is I have to do to get Brin freed from your trumped-up charges.'

She took a delicate sip of her tea and savored the steam rising from the cup. 'You have everything you ever wanted, now, don't you agree?'

'My new-found recognition from the Kin, you mean?' My voice was bitter. That fame was meaningless, now I knew how it had come about. That it had been a set-up right from the start.

'I gave you that,' she continued in her calm voice. 'And I would still like us to join forces. If you're by my side, I can give you everything you want, even more, a fast-track to glory.'

I was lost for words. She'd blindsided me with this unexpected, ridiculous suggestion.

'What the fuck, Cate? How does that.... What does that...' I could only sputter out my incomprehension at this strange request. 'How could you even *think* I would want to align myself with you now?'

And I certainly didn't want what she was offering. I'd given the matter a lot of thought as I'd driven over the old highway. A life away from the Kin with Margaret learning to use my power was no longer an option – I'd screwed that up entirely.

So what did I want? After this past two weeks, I wanted nothing more than a nice tidy life, a safe one, removed from treachery. A Normal life was out of the question for me now with all I'd been through, I accepted, so my future had to lie with the Kin. I could still work my way up through the Kin ranks on my own merit, with Hugh at my side as my equal. I wanted to prove myself and earn my way. Then perhaps, probably, we would marry, but only when I was ready, at some distant time in the future. Only then would we have the family he desired.

She was shaking her head. 'I know what you believe you want, but I'm afraid life doesn't work that way. You see,' she continued, her rueful tone matching the sad smile on her face. 'Despite this newfound glory, it hasn't really changed how the Kin view you. They don't truly trust you, and they never will. Not without my championship behind you. Not even as Hugh's partner.'

Cate sat back and took a thoughtful sip of tea. 'Quite frankly, they *can't* trust you. You're too powerful, and that still scares them. You're a loose cannon in their eyes. Even though you saved the ley line, did the impossible, you didn't follow the correct steps, didn't go in the prescribed pathway to take such a big decision. Do you see what I'm saying?'

But I would have Hugh by my side. He believed in me. I opened my mouth to say this, but she carried on as if she were reading my mind.

'Hugh is not going to help you in this matter. You must know he doesn't actually have your best interests at heart.' She shook her head decisively. 'Yes, I don't doubt that he loves you. But is that really why he's so anxious to tie you down in marriage? Pressure from his parents is the force behind that. They want to ensure the line of succession, an heir and preferably a spare. And they're positively drooling at the fresh magic your blood will add to their line, absolutely quivering with delight. Once you get that horrible Sabiston ring on your finger, your life will not be your own, not for a long time.

'In time,' she continued. 'Yes, in time, you'll be freed to do your own thing, but right now? What about your dreams right now?'

'No,' I cut in firmly. 'Brin doesn't need me to sacrifice myself to you in order to get justice. Besides there's no proof, except for the adamantite which was planted on him.'

Then I remembered the text he'd sent, the text which stated Trevor had given him a package for me. Why hadn't I thought of that before? 'In fact, I have the proof that it wasn't his.'

'Your phone's dead now,' she quickly reminded me. 'If that's what you're relying on. Any texts he sent you have disappeared. Besides, that's not evidence at all, it only ties you in deeper with him. It could be used to prove that you were working with him. In the right hands.'

She continued to smile as I could only stare at her, desperately searching for a way, a reason, for her to be wrong.

'Join up with me. It's the only way. I'll make sure Brin is freed,' she continued, her voice very kind and reasonable. 'By the way, the Kin? They don't treat terrorists kindly, you know. Death will come, but not soon enough, your poor little elf will find.'

'My father would not be a party to such cruelty.' That much I could be certain of, no matter how betrayed he felt at Brin's supposed treachery.

She shrugged. 'Too bad Jon's not in charge of the judicial system here.' She blinked slowly. 'My cousin runs that branch of the local Kin.' Her face took on a grotesque mask of sickly sweet sympathy.

'I just don't understand,' I said, my voice cracking. Defeat was looming. She controlled Brin's future. I thought of Alice's absolute heartbreak if her soulmate was locked away, even put to death, all because of the choice's I had made.

And Cate's words about the Kin and my future within them, I knew she spoke the truth. Sure, right now they were all happy and celebrating me, but when they got off that high of relief, they would realize I had greater power than any of them, and they would shut me down, keep me down, like they'd kept Margaret in the dungeon for all those years. It wouldn't be as obvious a prison – I wouldn't be kept behind bars or cursed - but I also wouldn't be moving up through the ranks of the Kin. They would never trust me, not without a sponsor by my side. A sponsor of Cate's stature.

A sponsor which should have been Hugh, but our love was already tarnished with his all too human jealousy. I was no longer the ignorant disregarded halfling who crushed on him, who looked up to him as a shining example of what I could achieve in life. I had matured, grown in my own power, and besides, he'd spoke with far too much enthusiasm about our life in that secluded castle on the Scottish island, where I would be busy making babies and living a life of quiet domesticity.

And Margaret. Margaret had abandoned me. I'd had the chance to go off with her and live a life of learning and utter freedom from responsibilities, but that portal was forever closed to me now.

I thought back to the days when I faced the threat of Trade School and a Normal life, and a future with a Normal guy. That picture of what could have been was looking pretty rosy from where I stood here.

'Why? Why this? Why do you want me?' My shoulders sagged, and Cate's face was lit with triumph.

'Because,' she said. 'Because together we can reach heights undreamt of. A partnership, of sorts.'

I was numb by this time, and I just let her talk.

'When the dust clears, there will certainly be questions about your actions with the elves. I can explain that your investigation found out, at the last possible moment, about the adamantite bomb. And that you called me in a panic, knowing I was the most likely expert on this precious metal. I made the executive decision to act quickly to undo the damage, without conferring with the Kin, for I knew we had little time.'

'And Margaret? How about her role in this?'

She laughed again. 'Oh, I wouldn't bring her name into this. You wouldn't want to jeopardize your newly won reputation, would you? No, best if we say it was just the two of us acting.'

And I had no doubt the Kin would believe her when she told them this. After all, she was the expert on adamantite. 'What exactly do you want from me?'

'What I want from you is simply what you yourself desire,' she said. 'I want you to climb the heights of the international Kin, to become the darling of the whole Kin world. Your future is shining brightly, and I'm going to pave the way for this rise.'

'And I'll be a puppet for you.'

'Hah! I wouldn't put it that way, but if you insist...'

My excuse in accepting her offer was that I didn't have a lot of other options ahead of me, not if I wanted to save

Brin, and not if I wanted to have the kind of life I had set my heart on. I nodded, slowly. Reluctantly.

'But,' I said. 'I need Brin freed right now. Prove that your word is good.'

She gave me a level stare as if debating, then she drew out her phone and tapped it a couple of times.

'Jon,' she spoke into it, all the while keeping her gaze on me. 'Yes, I'm recovering quite nicely, thank you. I've remembered something about that night.' And she told Dad about Trevor, how she'd seen the goblin lurking suspiciously around the Temple grounds. How Trevor had stolen adamantite from her private stash and, working with the Dark Elf king had engineered the whole thing.

'I'm devastated with the goblin's betrayal,' she told him, her voice filled with false sorrow as she winked at me. 'And Eldric, I never thought he'd go so far. But the elf Brin? He wasn't a player. He's far too insignificant.' She gave an intimate laugh at something he said, a laugh that spoke of years of marriage, and I bristled for my mother's sake.

She put her phone away. 'It's done. I've proved my part. Now, how about you?'

'I'm in. What more do you need from me?' Yes, I sounded sullen. I certainly felt that way, entering into this reluctant partnership.

She reached into the pocket of her white lawn dress, then held out a tiny object, a small stud of the blackest metal.

'This. A tiny earring for you to wear,' she said. 'Don't worry, it's adamantite, but it's not magicked or anything. Well, not much. It will be unnoticeable behind that lovely mass of hair.'

'What's the purpose of it?' I asked dully. The black stud didn't glitter or reflect the light in any way. It lay on her palm dully, not even casting a shadow as it sucked up the light all around it.

'It's only purpose is to show your fealty.'

'You have my word already, what more do you want?'

'I want proof that your word is good,' she replied in a mocking echo of my own demand. 'Don't worry, this won't hurt.'

I started to undo my own earring, one of the silver hoops I always wore, but she stopped me.

'No need to do that,' she said as she got up from the table and moved towards me. Cate lay one hand on my shoulder, and with the other took the top of my ear.

I jumped as I felt a sharp pinch, which just as quickly disappeared.

She was right, it didn't hurt at all. And in time, I wouldn't even feel the heaviness of that metal, although it would ache from time to time, deep in the darkest nights. But that was in the future. Cate brushed my hair back over my ear, hiding the black stud from view.

'Your future is set now,' she said, her voice low and triumphant. 'Be free little bird, fly up to your new heights.'

To the outside world my life might have the appearance of freedom perhaps, but nobody would be able to see the confines of my invisible golden cage.

CHAPTER 34

I had never felt so alone as on that long ride back into town. I had never missed the weight of that dragonfly brooch more, my only line of communication to Margaret.

The Harley ate up the miles too quickly. There'd be hell to pay with Hugh for borrowing his precious bike, no doubt, but that was the least of my worries.

A small delegation awaited me when the motorcycle finally pulled into the driveway of Richmond Cottage. I approached Brin first, and he allowed me to give him a hug.

'Thank God,' I said as I removed my helmet, then stepped back to examine him. He didn't have any marks of suffering on him. 'I'm so sorry.'

The elf shook his head. 'For what?' His face wore that selfless, generous smile still. He had no idea of my role in his incarceration. 'Just please,' He glanced nervously over at Hugh, and lowered his voice to a whisper. 'Just don't tell Alice, okay? She doesn't need to know about any of this, don't you agree? Not that I want to keep secrets from her, but she'd only worry.'

I nodded. I was getting good at keeping quiet about things.

'You have my solemn word I won't be getting mixed up in politics anymore,' he continued earnestly. His eyes darted over at Hugh and he spoke in a whisper again. 'Heads up - he's been pretty quiet. He may be a little annoyed about his bike.'

I nodded again. 'I can handle it.'

Brin gave me one last uncertain smile, then quickly disappeared into my house where, judging by the smell, Mom was cooking lasagne. That left me alone with Hugh.

'The bike,' I began. 'I know. But I had no choice...'

He didn't say anything.

'Look, no damage.' I pointed to the Harley. It had a fine layer of dust on it by then, but no dents and scratches or cracked fenders. 'As good as when I took it.' I tossed the keys to him, almost as a challenge.

He caught them in mid-air with one flick of his wrist. 'I don't care about the bike.' He took a step closer to me, then another one, till we were almost touching.

'I care about *you*.' His eyes searched mine. 'You've changed, there's something... You weren't hurt, the other night?'

'No,' I denied. Not physically touched by the lines, at any rate. 'Look at me, you can see.'

He nodded slowly. 'But something's not right.' He took a deep breath and placed his arms around my shoulders. The weight was almost tender. 'Tell me what's going on.'

I leaned my head against his shoulder, the white cotton of his t-shirt clean and fresh. I could stay here in the safety of his arms, unburden myself. Tell him about Cate, and... What would he do?

I shook my head almost imperceptibly. Hugh would feel the need to protect me, like a knight in shining armor. He would take charge. And no matter how well-meaning his deeds, he would somehow put his foot in it. And who knew what would be the repercussions from that devious witch Cate? There was no way I could tell him. But I had to give him something, he was far too perceptive to let it go.

Lifting my face, I sought his eyes, the pure green with the hidden flashes of gold deep within, and I braced myself.

'Our marriage,' I began, and I could feel his arms tighten around me. I took another deep breath and forced myself to continue. 'I'm not ready to settle down yet.'

He abruptly relaxed his hold as he stepped away from me. 'Well, thank God for that.'

'What?' I admit I felt outrage for a short second, his reaction was so natural and relieved. 'I thought you wanted to tie me down and start producing babies and wear that stupid ring.'

'Doesn't sound very enticing when you put it that way.' His laughter escaped from him as if the weight holding it down had been suddenly lifted, but on seeing my face he cut it short and gathered me into his embrace again.

'I do want to marry you,' he murmured into my hair. 'I want to spend the rest of my life with you, and have the family, but... not yet. We have way too much to do first.'

'So why were you always going on about it?' My voice was muffled in his chest and I pushed against him, struggling in vain to get out from his arms, to see his face.

He relented and loosened his grasp. 'I thought *you* wanted it. You seemed so happy talking about it in Edinburgh, and of course anything you want for us, I want.' He threw back his head and laughed again. 'And Mum grabbed the idea and ran with it. I must admit, I was feeling cornered.'

'Why didn't you say something?'

'Why didn't *you*?'

'Because...' I faltered. Because I'd allowed the words and the prejudices, of both Cate and Margaret to cloud my vision. Perhaps I'd wanted to hear it come from their mouths, because I didn't have the courage to give voice to my own feelings. 'Shit.'

'Well, I'm glad we've cleared that up,' he said decisively, rolling past my hesitation, mirth still dancing in his eyes. 'Christ, we could have both been miserable for years and blamed the other. Imagine what hell we would have put ourselves through. Ensign Martin, we're a team. And we are going places.'

It wasn't really cleared up, though, was it? So much was still not spoken between us. But it would have to do for now.

'And Cate's praise for you has been glowing,' he hastened to add. 'You've positioned yourself to move up the ladder very quickly. You won't be an Ensign for too much longer, I suspect. We have so much to thank her for.'

Yes, on the surface, everything was fine, yet as I lay in Hugh's hotel bed much later that night I knew things weren't fine, not at all. From this vantage I could see out the window down to Water Street below. In the dark corners and forgotten alleys shadows moved, met, conferred, then moved on again. Cate was right, without the additional energy from the ley lines, the Veil was thinning already.

I watched as Hugh slept the deep untroubled sleep of the innocent and I couldn't help but dread what the years to come might hold.

I had the brightest of futures to look forward to with Hugh on one side of me and Cate as my sponsor, yet my eyes were now opened to the realities of life within the Kin world. A world of mind-numbing bureaucracy, a web of politics and rules and intrigue that must be navigated with care. But I was learning from the best. I was learning from Cate Huxor.

As I fingered the tiny stud in my ear, a deep chill settled in my gut. I'd play her game, but I'd play my own too. The path twisting before me gave me no pleasure, for I was treading it with a new mantle hardening my heart. I was on the road to becoming an embittered witch, perhaps, but I would win.

The end

···•·••····

The story of Dara, Hugh and yes, Cate, continues in the last book of the Witch Kin Chronicles, *An Embittered Witch*, available from LizGraham.caor your favorite retailer.

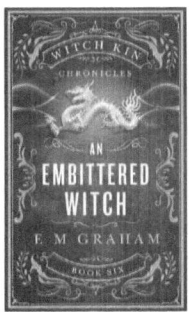

Dragon magic. An unholy alliance.
The ultimate choice.

In this final book of the series, Dara is rising to
great heights within the Witch Kin, with Cate on one
side and Hugh on the other in an uneasy alliance.
Yet the price of this unholy partnership is greater
than she could have imagined.

She holds the fate of the supernatural world in her
hands when she reaches a fork in the road of her
life. She can continue on the path to glory and the
realization of all her material desires while she
saves the world as she knows it, or she can give it
all up to rescue the vestiges of herself from the
flames of the dragon.

ACKNOWLEDGMENTS

The life of a writer can be lonely, but I'm really fortunate to be surrounded by a great online team. The many FaceBooks groups – I couldn't do it without all of you. I've learned so much, and there's always more inspiration to be had! Thanks to Bob Serrine who casts his eye over the final book (but all errors in this book now are totally mine). James at Go-On-Write, he's a wonderful creative artist, writer, musician, editor ... the list of his abilities goes on and he's a very nice bloke too. I'm so thankful that we connected. And a heartfelt 'Thank You' to fellow paranormal writer Shelley Dorey for reaching out, for her encouragement and also for being my ideal Beta reader. I am truly blessed!

And of course, dear reader, I'm not forgetting you. If you weren't right there, then I wouldn't be here, would I? Thank you for your support. And you know, you already have the magic in you.

ABOUT THE AUTHOR

E M Graham is the Fantasy pen name for Liz Graham. Sheis an author and artist working from her home in St. John's, Newfoundland and has a weird affinity for feral cats.

www.ingramcontent.com/pod-product-compliance
Lightning Source LLC
Chambersburg PA
CBHW031155050726
47495CB00019B/1867

* 9 7 8 1 9 9 0 6 6 7 0 6 0 *